PRAISE FOR

Ali Novak

"When I wasn't reading this book, it was all I wanted to be doing. Adorably romantic and fun! I loved it."

—Kasie West, author of *The Distance Between Us*, for *The Heartbreakers*

"With lots of eye candy, this is the best kind of beach read—just enough bitter to make it extra sweet."

—*RT Book Reviews* for *The Heartbreakers*

"A fun summer romance that doesn't shy away from the deeper issues of family, illness, and self-discovery."

—*School Library Journal* for *The Heartbreakers*

"Fans of boy bands will be on this like tattoos on Harry Styles's chest."

—*Kirkus Reviews* for *The Heartbreakers*

Also by Ali Novak

My Life with the Walter Boys

THE HEARTBREAK CHRONICLES

The Heartbreakers

Paper Hearts

My Return

TO THE
WALTER BOYS

My Return to the Walter Boys

ALI NOVAK

sourcebooks
fire

Copyright © 2025 by Ali Novak
Cover and internal design © 2025 by Sourcebooks
Cover design by Brittany Vibbert/Sourcebooks
Cover and internal image © CACTUS Creative Studio/Stocksy

Published by Sourcebooks Fire, an imprint of Sourcebooks
P.O. Box 4410, Naperville, Illinois 60567–4410
(630) 961-3900
sourcebooks.com

Cataloging-in-Publication Data is on file with the Library of Congress.

Printed and bound in the United States of America.
PAH 10 9 8 7 6

For Jackie, the world's best brother.

Sorry for stealing your name when we were kids,
but thanks for being a good sport about it.

prologue

Thur, Jun 6 at 1:32 p.m.

JACKIE HOWARD

I'm mad at you.

COLE WALTER

For what?

JACKIE HOWARD

Kissing me!

COLE WALTER

Weird...

You seemed pretty happy about it two hours ago

JACKIE HOWARD

Yeah, but now I can't stop thinking about you which sucks because we won't see each other for months!

COLE WALTER

That was kind of the point

JACKIE HOWARD

You're the worst.

I'm boarding now. We'll continue this conversation later.

COLE WALTER

I know you have stuff to deal with at home, so why don't we talk about it when you come back in August?

JACKIE HOWARD

Ugh, fine.

COLE WALTER

Have a safe flight

Thur, Jun 6 at 9:37 p.m.

JACKIE HOWARD

Home sweet home

COLE WALTER

Glad you made it back safe.
Do me a favor tho?

JACKIE HOWARD

Knowing you, that depends…

COLE WALTER

Don't show Danny too good of a time.
I'm afraid he'll never want to leave NYC

JACKIE HOWARD

Sorry, but I can't make any promises.

We created a list of our plans for
the summer on the plane.

COLE WALTER

We? I find that hard to believe

JACKIE HOWARD

Okay, fine. I made the list.

COLE WALTER

That's what I thought

JACKIE HOWARD

For your information, Danny was
the one who started talking about
all the things he wanted to do.

I just wrote them down.

COLE WALTER

Like what?

JACKIE HOWARD

Tell you about it tomorrow? I'm exhausted and my bed is calling.

COLE WALTER

Dream of me

JACKIE HOWARD

Good night, Cole.

Mon, Jun 10 at 8:12 a.m.

COLE WALTER

Forget about me already?

JACKIE HOWARD

What?

COLE WALTER

You were supposed to tell me about the plans you and Danny made

JACKIE HOWARD

Crap, I'm sorry. It's been an off few days for me.

COLE WALTER

No worries

Off how?

JACKIE HOWARD

I don't know. It's strange being back here.

COLE WALTER

Want to talk about it?

JACKIE HOWARD

I can't right now. I'm starting an internship today.

COLE WALTER

Shocker! You know, if your college application gets any longer it will take admissions months to read it.

JACKIE HOWARD

I'm being thorough, okay? I don't need to hear this today.

COLE WALTER

I'm teasing Jackie. Congrats

Where are you interning at?

JACKIE HOWARD

My dad's company. I'll fill you in later.

COLE WALTER

Good luck

Mon, Jun 10 at 7:28 p.m.

COLE WALTER

So how did your first day go?

Fri, Jun 14 at 3:52 p.m.

COLE WALTER

Guess what? The manager at Tony's quit. I've been promoted.

Sat, Jun 15 at 10:11 a.m.

JACKIE HOWARD

That's awesome, Cole! Congratulations!

COLE WALTER

Thanks! It means less time working on cars, but I need the money for school.

Anyway I went home for dinner last night and it felt weird without you and Danny there.

Sun, Jun 23 at 4:34 p.m.

COLE WALTER

Conspiring against me, huh?

JACKIE HOWARD

I don't know what you mean.

COLE WALTER

Liar. You took Danny to a Broadway show

JACKIE HOWARD

Is that a crime

COLE WALTER

It is when he says it was the best live performance he's ever seen.

I won't be able to convince him to move back to Colorado if he falls in love with New York.

JACKIE HOWARD

Should I lock him up and never let him out?

COLE WALTER

Yeah that would be preferable. Anyway, how are you? You never told me about your internship.

Wed, Jun 26 at 11:02 p.m.

COLE WALTER

Did I do something to piss you off?

JACKIE HOWARD

No, why?

COLE WALTER

Because you've barely spoken to me since you left.

Fri, Jun 28 at 5:16 p.m.

JACKIE HOWARD

Hey Cole. I'm sorry for going AWOL. It's been more difficult than I thought to be home again. I need some time to figure things out. Can we talk when I get back in August?

one

THE FIRST TIME I ARRIVED in Colorado, I was a nervous wreck. It made sense, given the circumstances. Not only was I forced to leave the only home I'd ever known, but I had to move across the country to live with a stranger, one who conveniently forgot to mention her *twelve* children until we were settled on the plane.

This time was different, though.

When my flight touched down at Denver International Airport, I couldn't blame those past things for the uncomfortable fluttering inside my chest; New York was no longer the only place I'd ever lived, Katherine had become a mother figure to me, and her twelve kids? They had taught me that I didn't always need to be perfect.

There was a singular reason for my current apprehension— sooner rather than later, I would have to face Cole Walter, and God only knew what kind of reception I'd receive. As I waited for the baggage carousel to deliver my suitcase, I almost texted him. Thankfully, I only typed out three words before realizing what I was doing and deleting the message. Maybe that made me a coward, but what could I possibly say after not talking to him for nearly two months? Besides, if he didn't already know I was back, he'd find out soon enough. News and gossip spread like wildfire in the Walter household.

Hopefully by then, I could find the words I needed to apologize.

I don't consider myself a violent person. But when Isaac Walter pulled up to the curb over an hour later with a shit-eating grin plastered across his face like he wasn't inexcusably late, I couldn't help but picture my hands wrapped around his throat. After stowing my suitcase in the bed of the truck, I yanked open the passenger door and threw him the chilliest glare I could muster.

"Where *were* you? I've been waiting for—"

"Hey, Jackie. *So* good to see you," he said, flipping down the sun visor to inspect his reflection. "Before you give me whatever dressing-down I'm sure you rehearsed, I have a question for you." He raked his fingers through his jet-black hair before glancing over at me as I climbed inside. "Do you have your driver's license?"

"No," I said through gritted teeth. Growing up in the city, I never expected to need one. "Why does that matter?"

"Because if looks could kill, you'd have a body to hide and a very long walk home. Shouldn't you be thanking me for picking you up?"

"Not when you were supposed to be here ages ago!"

"It's not my fault your flight was delayed," he replied, which I grudgingly had to admit was true. Katherine was originally meant to collect me from the airport, but then my morning departure was pushed back to the point where my arrival conflicted with Jordan's soccer game.

"No, but your aunt promised me you'd be—"

"It doesn't matter what she promised, because she did it without asking me first," Isaac exclaimed, a muscle in his jaw twitching. He took a breath, then added in a calmer tone, "I had plans."

"Okay, fine," I grumbled as I buckled my seat belt, "but would it have killed you to let me know?"

"Sorry, but you called at a bad time. Well, bad for you. Amazing for me. Let's just say I was…at the *climax* of things."

I narrowed my eyes at his turn of phrase. Judging by the smug tone of Isaac's voice, ignorance was bliss, but if my suspicion about his tardiness was true, then I'd be willing to reconsider my stance on nonviolence. The lacy blue bra abandoned on the floorboard was suspicious but not concrete proof. While finding underwear in the boys' shared vehicle wasn't a frequent occurrence, it wasn't out of the ordinary either. What caught my attention, however, was the number of cigarettes in the empty Glacier Gulp cup Isaac was using as an ashtray, enough to make me think another person had been smoking in the truck with him. Besides, the cab smelled like tobacco and—my face flushed.

Sex. The truck smelled like sex. I didn't notice it initially since the eau de lung cancer masked the odor, but the distinctive scent of musk and sweat lingered in the cab.

"Oh my God!" I rolled down the window to let in some fresh air. "Were you screwing someone in here?"

"*Moi*?" He splayed a hand against his sternum, brows knit together in exaggerated offense. "That's a serious accusation. What makes you think that?"

"Because it reeks of sex!"

"Okay, you caught me," Isaac said, flashing me another violence-inducing grin. "But tell me—how do *you* know what sex smells like?"

The flush on my face deepened to the point of burning. While I had zero experience with *that*, this wasn't the first time the truck had been used for something other than transportation. I would never forget the mortification of getting inside one day after school, wrinkling my nose, and asking what the foul smell was. Danny, Lee, and Nathan had laughed the entire drive home.

"Let me get this straight," I said, ignoring his question. "You made me wait for more than an hour because you were hooking up with someone?"

Isaac didn't even attempt to look contrite as he put the truck in drive and carefully navigated back into the hectic *Tetris* that was the arrivals pickup area. "Like I said, I had plans."

Taking a deep breath, I willed myself to remain calm. Spending the summer in New York helped me come to a startling realization—I liked living with the Walters. As a whole, they were fun-loving, supportive, and always made me laugh. But while absence did make my heart grow fonder, it also made me forget how irritating some of them could be.

"You're unbelievable."

His lips quirked. "So I've heard. Repeatedly."

Even though I wanted to throttle Isaac, it had been a long day of travel, and I didn't have the energy to put up with more of his typical nauseating innuendos, so I put in my earbuds. Maybe I would bribe one of his younger cousins to help me get revenge once I had a good night's sleep.

"Aw, come on, Jackie," he pouted. "Don't be like that. We haven't seen each other all summer."

"Which clearly wasn't long enough."

Turning up my music, I pointedly focused my attention out the window and settled in for the drive. I only had to ignore Isaac for two minutes before he gave up trying to talk to me, and without the distraction, my thoughts wandered back to Cole. How could they not when the last time I took this road, albeit in the opposite direction, I'd been on cloud nine even though I was soaked to the skin? My heart stuttered as I recalled our goodbye kiss, but I quickly shoved my feelings down; they'd only make my reunion with Cole more difficult.

By the time we reached Copper Valley, the small mountain town near the Walters' ranch, my mouth tasted faintly of blood from chewing on my lip. My nerves were quickly forgotten when we drove down Main Street.

"What's going on?" I asked, looking out the window as workers unloaded barricades on the corners surrounding the town square.

"Oh, are you speaking to me now?"

"That's subject to further review." Like whether he continued to be an ass.

"They're setting up for the block party tomorrow," he explained. "There's gonna be cotton candy and face painting and a water balloon toss. Exactly the kind of wholesome bullshit you're into. I'm sure you'll have a blast."

I raised an eyebrow. "And you wonder why I don't want to talk to you?"

Ten minutes later, Isaac pulled onto a familiar gravel drive. When we crested the hill and the ranch came into view, a slow smile spread across my face. Everything looked exactly the same. Backdropped by endless blue sky and green fields was the large farmhouse with welcoming yellow shutters, multiple additions, and a wraparound porch that still needed a paint job.

Katherine was out the front door before my feet hit the ground. "Jackie, you're here!" she said, pulling me into a tight hug. "Oh honey, I missed you so much. When Isaac told me your flight was delayed again, I felt awful. You must be so exhausted."

Delayed *again*? I narrowed my eyes at Isaac over Katherine's shoulder, and he smirked.

Ugh, what a lying little shit!

I pulled away from the hug but didn't bother correcting Katherine.

Snitching was a cardinal sin among the Walter siblings, a lesson I learned the hard way, so no matter how much his dishonesty irked me, I refused to make the same mistake twice.

"Thanks, Katherine," I said as she guided me into the house. "It's good to be back."

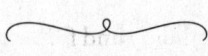

My sister, Lucy, used to love making fun of my obsession with lists.

Blame my type A personality, but making them soothed my soul: daily to-do lists I completed with regimental proficiency, whimsical bucket lists I never looked at again, birthday and Christmas gift ideas lists organized by price, best-of lists used to rank my favorite books and movies. I even had one to rule them all—a master index list of all my important lists.

A few weeks into summer, when Danny mentioned how homesick he was, I made a list of everything I missed about Colorado so he wouldn't feel so alone. At the very top of that list was Nathan's music. I loved hearing him play, whether he was in the middle of composing a new song and the notes were clumsy or it was a piece he long ago perfected, because it helped me slow down; no matter what I was doing or how many thoughts were rushing through my head, I always stopped to listen.

So now, when I reached the upstairs landing and was met with a soft guitar melody coming from his room, the stress of the travel day immediately melted. Eager for our reunion, I left my suitcase by the stairs and stepped inside without bothering to knock.

It was a mindless mistake.

Nathan's bed was empty, but movement on the opposite side of the room captured my attention.

Three whole seconds passed before I processed the scene in front of me, and when I finally did, I drew a sharp breath. Alex was settled against the headboard, his hands grasping a girl's slender waist. It took me another second to recognize her long, sleek hair and realize said girl was *Kim*, Alex's childhood bestie and one of the few friends I'd made after moving here. She was straddling his lap, her mouth attached to his neck, and both of them were shirtless.

"Oh my God!" I bumped into Nathan's desk as I scrambled backward and accidentally knocked a guitar capo to the floor.

Kim's head jerked up. She squeaked at the sight of me, then rolled off Alex to cover herself.

"Crap, I'm sorry," I said, squeezing my eye shut to avoid seeing anything else. Without waiting for a response, I fled the room.

"Jackie?" The bed squeaked, and a pair of feet slapped against the hardwood. "Jackie, wait!"

Which was, quite honestly, the last thing I wanted to do. Hightailing it down the hallway, I abandoned my suitcase in an effort to escape. I'd almost reached the safety of Katherine's old art studio when a hand circled my wrist.

"Hey," Alex said, gently tugging me away from the door. "Where are you off to in such a hurry?"

Since I caught him dry humping Kim, I thought the answer to his question was obvious: anywhere that *wasn't* his bedroom. But when I looked up at Alex for the first time since leaving, all I could do was open and close my mouth like an idiot.

Summer had been good to Alex Walter. He was sporting golden, sun-kissed skin, and his blond curls were lighter than normal, like he had spent every moment of the past few months outside. He'd hit a growth spurt too, because he now stood a full head taller than me. His lips curved into a smile as I took in each change. It wasn't cocky, like a certain older brother's, but it was decidedly knowing.

"Um, hi." I offered him a hesitant smile and pretended there wasn't a blush creeping up my neck. "This isn't awkward at all."

Alex slipped his hands into the pockets of his gym shorts and leaned a shoulder against the wall. "Well, I'm not the one who barged in without knocking."

"Right," I said with a grimace. "I can't say this enough, but I'm *so* sorry. I heard the music and thought it was Nathan."

"I'm sorry too," he replied. "This wasn't how I planned for you to find out about us, but all is forgiven as long as you promise not to be mad at Kim? She's worried you won't want to be friends anymore." Judging by the expression on Alex's face, Kim wasn't the only one who was worried.

His concern was sweet but unnecessary. Spending the summer in New York only confirmed that our decision to split was the right one, because I'd hardly thought about him at all.

"She has nothing to worry about. We broke up, remember?"

"Yeah, I was there." His tone was light and teasing, but I could hear relief as well. "So we're good?"

"Better than. Honestly, I'm happy for you both," I told him, "but... um...I really did want to see Nathan. Any idea where he's at?"

"Oh, I see how it is." Alex was still shirtless, so when he folded his arms and smirked down at me from his recently acquired height, I had to make a conscious effort not to look. Just because we weren't together anymore didn't mean I was blind. "You dump me, and Nathan steals my spot as your favorite Walter? I'm hurt, Jackie."

I almost shot back that he was never my favorite but bit my tongue at the last second. "Don't you have a girlfriend to get back to?"

"Touché." He pushed off the wall and headed back in the direction of his room. "Nathan's been spending a lot of time in the loft, so I'd check there," he told me. "I'll see you at dinner."

"Alex, wait! Do you know if—I mean, will your brother be home tonight?" If so, I needed to brace myself for the encounter.

He paused but didn't turn around. "Which brother? I have a few of those."

"You know who I'm talking about," I said gently.

"And you know we don't talk, so you're asking the wrong person."

"Okay," I said, letting the subject drop. I should've known better than to bring up Cole with him. "I guess I'll see you later."

After retrieving my suitcase and depositing it in my room, I set out in search of Nathan, mind whirling as I chewed over the afternoon's bombshell of a revelation. My ex, who I *lived* with, was dating my friend, neither of whom bothered to tell me about their newfound relationship. Not that they owed me an explanation, but some kind of warning would have been nice.

I didn't lie when I said I was happy for the both of them. Alex and Kim were friends long before I came into the picture. Plus, they shared all the same nerdy hobbies. It had always been a point of contention in our relationship—my disinterest in *GoG* and his inability to understand the importance I placed on doing well in school. That said, this development would take time to get used to. Alex and Kim might fit well together, but it was still a startling change.

I was so lost in my thoughts, I made the five-minute walk to the barn on autopilot. When I cleared the top of the ladder and the loft came into view, I blinked in surprise. Here was another change. A dozen plastic dairy crates were stacked against the back wall to form a makeshift storage unit, and Nathan's collection of vinyl was housed inside. Additionally, the ancient TV was missing from the media cabinet; in its place sat a record player.

Nathan was stretched out across one of the lumpy couches, pencil in one hand and a book in the other. He must have heard my entrance and assumed I was someone else, because he let out a long-suffering sigh without looking up from what he was reading. "Jordan, I know I promised to help curate the soundtrack for your documentary, but you have to give me more than a couple hours. I haven't started yet."

"Not Jordan."

The pencil clattered on the floor as Nathan's head snapped up.

"*Jackie*?" he exclaimed, a grin stretching across his face. He tossed his book aside and scrambled to his feet. "You're back! I've been so— Wait, why do you look angry?"

I propped my hands on my hips. "Because you have some major explaining to do." Since I wasn't actually mad at him, I only waited a moment before dropping my angry act and pulling Nathan into a hug. Like Alex, he'd grown more than a few inches over the summer, and I grumbled to myself as he rested his chin on top of my head.

There was a hesitant look on his face when we broke apart. "About what exactly?"

"Hmm, let's think. Does Alex and Kim ring a bell?"

Nathan blinked at me. "But…you only just got here. How do you even *know* about that?"

"I heard music coming from your room when I went to put my suitcase away." The partial explanation was all it took for Nathan to cringe, and I had a feeling he knew exactly where my story was going. "It's no excuse, but we haven't seen each other in nearly three months, and I *missed* you."

"Oh no," he muttered, flopping onto the couch. "You walked in on them, didn't you?"

Nodding, I took a seat beside him. "They were half-naked and in the middle of a full-blown make-out session. Do you know how awkward that was?"

"Are you so traumatized that you forgot I share a room with Alex?"

Nathan asked. "Why do you think I'm hiding out here? I've basically exiled myself to the loft since they started dating."

Oof, I hadn't considered that.

If the changes to the loft were anything to go by, he spent more than a fair amount of time in the barn. On second glance, I spotted a wicker basket filled with blankets and pillows. The thought of Nathan sleeping out here because Alex and Kim were getting busy frustrated me on his behalf. Unfortunately, a precedent of discourtesy toward one's roommate was already set in the Walter household—Danny once confessed sharing a room with Cole was a contributing factor as to why he was such a night owl—and the dark circles under Nathan's eyes were telling.

Just how long had this been going on for?

When I asked him, he winced. "Er…they got together a couple of days after you left, so pretty much the entire time?"

"Are you *serious*?"

Nathan misconstrued my reaction. He muttered something to himself that sounded suspiciously like "shitshow" before launching into a misplaced apology. "I'm really sorry, Jackie. I knew this would happen. I've been trying all week to think of the best way to break the news to you, but—"

"Nathan," I said sharply, and he pressed himself so deep into the couch, it looked like he was trying to meld with the cushions. "I'm not upset because of what I found out but *when* I found out. We've had, what, half a dozen conversations this summer? Why didn't you tell me?" Even though I was fine with Alex and Kim's relationship, it would have been nice to process the news while in New York instead of being caught flat-footed the moment I returned.

"I know. It's just…you were gone, and it wasn't my place to say anything. Plus, it seemed like you needed a break from the drama. Honest to God, I planned on warning you once you got back. I figured I'd have more than a millisecond to do so, but I guess I should've known better considering my own experience this summer."

"Are they really that bad?" I asked after deciding to let things go. That Nathan had kept this secret from me was still upsetting, but I couldn't blame him for sticking to whatever bro code he had with his brothers.

"Remember when Isaac was hooking up with one of Danny's friends from drama club? You know, the girl with the lip mole who always dressed like someone from a period piece?"

"No. I think that was before my time, and honestly? I don't want to know the gruesome details of your cousin's love life."

"That's fair. You can picture it, though, right? Isaac and the odd but pretty theater geek? They were one of those couples that exemplify why people hate PDA."

"What's your point?"

Nathan sighed. "Alex and Kim are a thousand times worse."

Yikes. No wonder Nathan was practically living in the barn.

"So…" he said when I didn't immediately respond. "Just to be clear—are you sure there's no hard feelings about the Kilex situation?"

"Kilex?"

"I thought it had a better ring to it than Aim. You don't like it?"

I screwed up my face. "It sounds like an off-brand Kleenex for assassins."

"Kilex! The only tissue that will blow you away!" Nathan said like one of those late night infomercials that sold products by shouting at people. He snorted at his own joke. "You're right. That's terrible."

"Obviously," I drawled.

"Hey, it's not like you're throwing out any good suggestions."

"Yeah, because that would be super weird of me." Psychotic even. Who came up with ship names for their ex and his new girlfriend?

"Aha!" He pointed an accusing finger at me. "So you *are* upset."

"What? No!" I whipped a hideous ruffled pillow at his face, which he ducked while laughing at me. "I swear, I'm cool with them dating. I think they make a lot of sense together."

"They do," he agreed. "I'm not sure if it's Kim or because Cole isn't living at home anymore, but Alex is different. Less bitter, more confident."

"Or maybe it's because he gained five inches and some actual muscle? The Walter genes are so unfair. It's ridiculous how attractive you all are."

"That's a common misconception. It's actually in the water, not the baby gravy."

My nose wrinkled. The reason Nathan and I clicked so well was because he was mature for his age, but every once in a while, he'd say something that reminded me he was, in fact, a teenage guy, one who was related to Isaac. "First off, gross. Please don't ever say that again. Second, if that's the case, I'm ready for my glow up."

He laughed. "Sorry, but you have to live here for longer than a few months for the magic to work."

"Well, I don't have plans to leave anytime soon."

"Good. Things haven't been the same without you." Nathan paused, then let his head roll to the side so he could get a good look at me. "Did it help, going home?"

"A bit. Being in our apartment again brought up all sorts of memories, so it was…rough at the beginning. Danny was a lifesaver, though. Having him around really helped." I paused and took a deep lungful of air, not ready yet to get into the details. "Enough about me. How was your summer?"

"As previously mentioned, awkward." Nathan sighed as he fiddled with his necklace, sliding the guitar pick back and forth on its chain. "Other than that, there's not much to tell. It's just been me chilling in the loft."

"That's it?" I asked skeptically. Surely, something exciting happened.

"I got into sudoku." He motioned to a paper book of number puzzles lying nearby. "Does that count?"

Judging by the way Nathan was avoiding eye contact, he clearly didn't want to talk about himself. And now that I thought about it, he'd been light on detail whenever we spoke over the phone, always directing the conversation back to me. The curious part of me wanted to push for a real answer, but my logical side was quick to point out the hypocrisy. After all, hadn't I just changed the subject to dodge his question?

"Of course it does," I told him. "So what's this I hear about a block party?"

This perked Nathan up. "It's Copper Valley's annual end-of-summer bash. Happens on the second to last Saturday before school starts. There are food trucks, live music, and games for kids. Some of us like to act like we're too cool to go, but everyone always does."

"Everyone...including Cole?"

The instant the words left my mouth, Nathan arched an eyebrow. I swallowed and dropped my gaze to my lap. *God*, I thought as I wrung my hands together, *can I be any more pathetic?* Here I was, back for less than a day and already questioning Cole's brothers about him. I couldn't help it, though. The fluttering feeling that unfurled in my chest the moment I landed in Denver was only getting worse the more I anticipated seeing him again.

"Still haven't talked to him, huh?"

Groaning, I collapsed back against the threadbare cushions. "I am *so* not having this conversation with you."

Nathan smirked—*good grief, he looks so much like Cole when he does that!*—but let it drop. "To answer your question, no. I doubt he'll be there. He's too busy working. If he's not at Tony's, he's lifeguarding at the community pool or picking up a shift at the Gas Exchange. We don't see him much, but he always comes home on Friday for dinner. I don't think he'll be here tonight, though. He mentioned something about packing up his apartment."

Although I knew Cole would be starting college, an inevitability that I'd factored in during my many soul-searching sessions over the course of summer, my stomach still clenched when faced with concrete proof that he was leaving. The Walter household would feel *less* without him here. And if he wasn't coming back to the ranch tonight, did that mean I wouldn't see him for an entire week? God, I could kick myself for being too chicken to send him a text. Waiting that long might kill me.

I wanted to press for more details, but a crackly, disembodied voice suddenly spoke from somewhere inside the couch.

"Jack for Nathan. Come in, Nathan."

Nathan sat up and dug around in the pillows until he found a walkie-talkie, which he brought up to his mouth before pressing the talk button. "Go for Jack."

"Dinner will be ready in five."

"Thanks. Ten-four, out," he said, then tossed the device onto the coffee table.

"What's up with the walkie-talkie?" I asked.

"My dad bought a bunch of them for Zack and Benny's Cub Scout group. It was part of earning their radio merit badge. Service out here is crap, so they come in handy when someone up at the house wants to get a hold of me." Nathan heaved himself off the couch before offering me a hand. "Let's head out. If we don't hurry, the little heathens eat everything."

The kitchen was the heart of the Walters' household, so when Nathan and I walked in five minutes later, we were greeted by the usual chaos that occurred anytime the majority of the family gathered inside—laughter and horseplay and coinciding conversations. Dogs weaving underfoot as food was prepared. Music, bickering, and more laughter. It was hectic in a way that bordered on overwhelming while somehow still retaining an air of comfort and warmth.

The pantry door was wide open, and I watched as Benny boosted his twin up so he could reach a pack of Oreos on the top shelf. Will didn't notice the cookie heist taking place right beside him because he was too busy whispering something in his wife Haley's ear. I frowned at the sight of a bucket covering the faucet but then spotted George lying on the floor with his head inside the cabinet and a toolbox at his side.

"Aunt Kathy, we're out of butter," Lee said as he rummaged through the fridge. Tonight must have been his and Isaac's turn to help with dinner, because the latter was slicing up a watermelon.

"No, we're not," she replied as she pulled a casserole out of the oven. "I bought some today. Out of the way, Jack. This is hot." She moved the steaming dish to a waiting trivet, then added, "Did you

check the fruit drawer? Zack and Benny helped me unload the grocer-
ies, and you know how that goes."

Two giggles confirmed her theory.

Katherine was a stickler for serving dinner at the table, so I was
surprised to see her setting it up on the island, buffet style. Then I
spotted the reason for the shift.

"Whoa," I said, eyeing the mess. The entire surface of the ten-foot-
long farmhouse table was covered in stuff—piles of neatly folded
clothes, stacks of books, and tubs filled with old toys and knickknacks.
"What's going on over there?"

Nathan shrugged. "My mom mentioned something about sorting
through old stuff to sell for a fundraiser sometime this fall, but I didn't
catch the details."

"It's a community-wide rummage sale to raise funds for a new
park," came a quiet reply, and when I turned to face the source, I found
Kim watching me with cautious eyes. "Hey, Jackie. It's good to—"

"Jackie!" A small body collided with mine, nearly knocking the
wind out of me. "You're back!"

"Oof. Hello, Parker," I said, returning her hug. "Did you have a
good summer?"

"The best! My dad taught me how to use a slingshot, and I started
tennis lessons. I wanted to sign up for boxing, but Mom says I'm
violent enough as it is."

As she prattled on, I mouthed "Talk later?" to Kim, and she nodded
in agreement. Then I spent the next two minutes listening to Parker as

she filled me in on everything I missed while I was gone. Considering the rocky start to our relationship, I was surprised but touched by her excitement. It reminded me of my younger self and how I always lit up whenever Lucy made time for me.

"All right, everyone," Katherine called over the ruckus, clapping her hands together to get the room's attention. "Dinner's ready. Come get a plate, and help yourselves. We're eating outside tonight."

Having witnessed past Walter feeding frenzies, I decided to hang back for my own safety. It was the right call. While Isaac and Lee jostled each other for first dibs on the drumsticks, Zack and Benny whacked anyone within reach with their paper plates. Sweet Baby Ray's splattered everywhere when Jack unscrewed the cap and, without thinking, shook the bottle, and Alex nearly sent his plate of food flying when he tripped over his father who was still under the sink working on the plumbing.

"Hey, that's enough! Save some for the rest of us," Parker exclaimed as she and Jordan stood over a steaming casserole dish. She tried to snatch the serving spoon from Jordan's hand, but he batted her away with ease, took what looked like his third heaping scoop, and added it to a plate filled with one thing—cheesy potatoes. When he went for another helping, Parker punched him in the ribs.

"Ow!" Jordan dropped the serving spoon, and it clattered back into the casserole dish. "Mom, Parker hit me!"

"Yeah, because you're being an asshole and hogging the potatoes!"

"Language!" came a muffled reprimand from under the sink.

Katherine pinched the bridge of her nose. "Parker, what have I told you about hitting people?"

She huffed but hung her head. "That it's only acceptable in certain contact sports and if someone is trying to kidnap me."

"That's your second warning. If it happens again, you'll be grounded. And, Jordan? You need to eat more than potatoes for dinner. Put something healthy on your plate."

Once everyone else had food, I served myself and spent a few minutes talking with Will and Haley, who I hadn't seen since the wedding. The newlyweds had purchased their first home two weeks ago—a fixer-upper ranch on the outskirts of town—and they had all sorts of plans for how to renovate it. When the conversation turned into a debate on granite verses quartz countertops, I made my excuses and escaped outside.

It was late enough in the evening that the setting sun had chased away the heat of the day, leaving behind a comfortable coolness and a streak of purple clouds across the sky. The air here smelled how I always imagined summer should—a mix of barbecue and chlorine and freshly cut grass. It was a vast improvement over New York's standard bouquet of piss on hot pavement and rotting garbage. For a moment, I stood in place and took everything in, and it was only the sound of someone calling my name that finally broke me from my reverie.

"Hellooo, earth to Jackie."

Across the deck, Isaac, Lee, Alex, Kim, and Nathan were sitting at the patio table. Something about the scene looked wrong, like someone had photoshopped out a part of the picture. That was when I realized it was because the eldest set of Walter twins was missing. My ribs grew tight as I thought of Danny. We'd spent the entire summer together, so his absence was disquieting, but he'd decided to stay behind in New York to pursue acting, and I couldn't begrudge him chasing his dreams.

Alex raised a brow at me, then pushed out the empty chair at his side. "Plan on standing there all night, or are you going to join us?"

A hand wrapped around my wrist.

"No, come sit with me," Parker said and tugged me toward the lawn. "I haven't finished telling you about my summer."

Her smile was too innocent to be trustworthy, but I couldn't face Alex and Kim yet, not when what happened this afternoon was fresh in my mind. After sending an apologetic smile in Alex's direction, I let Parker lead me over to a picnic table where the younger kids were eating, and Zack and Benny watched with rapt attention as she directed me to a specific spot on the bench. Jack was intently focused on his food, but it was obvious something was up since his twin was missing. Knowing Jordan, he was probably lurking nearby with their camera, hoping to catch whatever action arose. Following a cursory look under the table (I'd play along provided their plan didn't involve another encounter with Rumple, Jordan's corn snake), I sat down and braced myself for whatever was coming.

I didn't have to wait long.

Parker tried to distract me with outrageous stories about her week at summer camp, but the Walters didn't do subtle, and I noticed Jack nod out of the corner of my eye. His signal triggered a strange sputtering noise, and a split second later, a stream of water blasted me in the back. I screamed, more because of the cold temperature than the surprise of the attack, and the kids shrieked with laughter. Hidden in the bushes behind me was a sprinkler, and it sprayed me once more before I could scramble away from the table and out of range.

"What's going on?" Nathan stood at the edge of the deck, a frown marring his face. Nobody responded, but it only took him a second to survey the scene and figure out what had happened. He snatched a towel off one of the pool chairs and rushed down the steps. "Jackie, are you all right?"

"I'm good," I said, taking the proffered towel and wrapping it around my shoulders.

My answer must not have appeased Nathan, because he rounded on his siblings with a scowl. "What the hell is wrong with you guys?"

"Lighten up, Nate. It was just a welcome-back joke," Jordan explained as he emerged from the bushes, camera in hand. His accomplices snickered. "I caught the whole thing. Who wants to see?"

The expression on Nathan's face warned of an imminent explosion, so I placed a hand on his arm in an effort to calm him down. "Hey, it's okay. I promise."

"It's not okay," he snapped, still glaring at his younger brothers and sister, all of whom had crowded around Jordan to watch their ambush play out on screen. "You've been home for less than three hours and they've already—"

"Nathan." I threw him a look, and in a much lower voice, I added, "Nobody did anything I didn't *allow* to happen."

He opened his mouth to argue, then paused as my words sank in. Understanding flickered in his eyes shortly afterward. "Oh! So you let them…"

I nodded. "Yeah, it's not a big deal."

And it truly wasn't.

Old me would have insisted on drying my hair and changing, but I'd come a long way from my first meeting the Walter kids when Zack and Benny tackled me into the pool. Dry clothes were never a guarantee in the Walter household. Sometime between being thrown into a freezing cold swimming hole, getting caught in the rain on multiple occasions, and surprise squirt gun attacks, I'd learned that a little bit of water never hurt.

After all, what was a little bit of H2O in comparison to the smiles on their faces?

two

THE REST OF MY FIRST night back was spent reconnecting with the Walters. After dinner, George built a bonfire in the backyard, and we all sat around it swapping stories about summer. Lee recounted a disastrous family camping trip that made me laugh so hard my sides ached, and I told them all about Danny's first experience on the subway, where he was pelted with gummy bears by a woman in a ball gown for no reason other than New York was weird. It was well past midnight when I finally called it a day and went to bed. I hurried through my nighttime routine—teeth brushed, face scrubbed, hair detangled—before trudging upstairs to my room. Katherine's old art studio was a welcome sight. I'd missed the colorful wall murals and sash windows that gave me several different views of the ranch. Even the creaky floorboards made me smile.

The last thing I did before turning off the light was remove my necklace—a dried lavender stem encased in a pendant—and tuck it into the jewelry case on my dresser. It belonged to my mother originally, a prized possession and signature accessory, and although I'd long admired it, I couldn't bring myself to claim the delicate piece after her death. That changed last month when I finally began the process of cleaning out my parents' room. The moment I came across the necklace on her vanity, I'd fastened the silver chain around my neck. Now, I wore it on occasion to feel closer to her.

By the time I climbed into bed, my exhaustion was so great I thought I'd fall asleep the second my head hit the pillow. After all, I could barely keep my eyes open.

Much to my frustration, sleep eluded me. My brain had a bad habit of whirling to life whenever I was most tired, and tonight it zeroed in on one thing—Cole Walter. I was both relieved and frustrated to learn he'd be at work tomorrow. Knowing I didn't have to face him yet felt like a stay of execution. It would give me a chance to enjoy the block party without worrying about our reunion turning into an angry confrontation. On the other hand, I wanted to rip the Band-Aid off, and there was no way I could wait until next Friday to do so. If he didn't show up at the ranch by the end of the weekend, I'd track him down on Monday even if it meant begging one of the Walters to drive me into town.

The two of us *needed* to talk.

Things had changed for me over the summer.

At the beginning of the year, Uncle Richard sent me away from

New York because he thought I wasn't handling my grief well. Not only did he think it was unhealthy for me to remain in the home my family would never return to, but he suggested I was using homework, school organizations, and volunteer work as a coping mechanism; if I burned the candle at both ends, then I could exhaust myself to the point of apathy. Moving in with the Walters had helped to an extent; I learned important lessons about letting loose and being less of a perfectionist.

But it wasn't until I returned to the city and was forced to face my grief by once more living in a place where my memories were inescapable that I realized Uncle Richard was right—I'd been running from the pain from the moment my family passed. I'd acted no differently in Colorado. Instead of school and clubs, I used Alex and Cole as a diversion. Getting to know both boys made it possible for me to ignore the crushing weight of my loss. With that realization came both guilt and regret. My family was gone, and rather than mourning them, I dove straight into dating and concerned myself with unimportant things like flirting and kissing.

Now, I needed to stop distracting myself. Lucy and my parents deserved better. *I* deserved better, and Cole did too. Alex would obviously be fine; we parted on good terms, and he admitted to using me as much as I had him. I wasn't sure about Cole, though, since nothing was ever simple with him; drama followed in his wake at every turn. We weren't even dating, and our relationship was a labyrinth of land mines and obstacles. On top of that, Cole was leaving, and I needed to refocus on my own education.

As much as I cared about him, I couldn't date Cole Walter.

Life would be less complicated if we just stayed friends.

The next day, I watched the sun rise over the ranch while waiting for Nathan to join me for our morning run. When he failed to appear before I finished stretching, I figured he overslept and decided to go without him. The Walter kids made a sport of sleeping in on Saturdays, so I was unsurprised to find the house still silent when I came back. It wasn't until I neared the kitchen and caught the tail end of an argument that I realized someone else was awake.

"...barely seven and you're just getting home," Katherine was saying. "That's unacceptable."

"I already told you I fell asleep watching a movie at a friend's house," someone replied, but I wasn't sure who. Isaac maybe? "What more do you want me to say? It was an honest mistake, I swear."

"I'd be willing to give you the benefit of the doubt if this was your first offense, but you've been pushing limits and breaking house rules all summer." Based on her tone alone, I could easily picture Katherine's unimpressed expression. "I'm done putting up with this kind of behavior."

The coffee maker beeped, signaling the end of a brew.

"Sorry. I promise it won't happen again." Yes, that definitely sounded like Isaac. I could tell by the lack of regret in his voice.

"Be that as it may, you're still grounded."

"*What?* Aunt Kathy, that's not fair!" he complained. "Everyone is going to the block party."

"Maybe you should've thought about that before staying out past curfew and sneaking in at the crack of dawn," she replied without an ounce of sympathy.

"This is bullshit!"

A sudden, heavy *thunk* made me peek around the corner. My eyes bulged at the sight of a hole in the drywall and Isaac shaking out his fist, knuckles bloody.

Katherine sprang to her feet, toppling over the chair she'd been sitting in. "*Isaac Walter!*"

Not wanting to get caught in the cross fire, I backed away from the kitchen as quietly as possible and went to grab my caddy. If I showered before breakfast, hopefully Katherine and Isaac would be done fighting by the time I returned. While I wasn't surprised that he tried to sneak into the house after missing curfew, I found his violent reaction to a basic grounding baffling. Isaac was many things, but hotheaded wasn't one of them. If I hadn't seen proof with my own eyes, I never would have believed he punched a wall.

As I climbed the stairs, carefully picking my way around stray socks and toys, my chest fluttered. The discomfort passed so quickly I almost disregarded the feeling, but as I reflected on yesterday, I couldn't help but notice something had changed about the Walter household while I was away. Sure, it was still the loud, chaotic home I'd been introduced to at the start of the year, but there were differences too: Danny and Cole's absence, Alex and Kim's new relationship, the dark circles under Nathan's eyes, Isaac's attitude. Each of these things would have been insignificant on its own. Added together, though? They were hard to ignore.

Maybe I was overreacting, but the realization that things were not quite right left me feeling uneasy.

Since Isaac was grounded, only four of us climbed into the truck when it was time to leave for the block party, and the drive into town felt... wrong somehow. While it was infinitely more comfortable considering everyone had their own seat, I missed the dynamic energy that defined our usual trips to and from school. Without Cole's calm confidence behind the wheel, Isaac's endless gossiping, or Danny's ruthless guarding of the aux cord to ensure everyone heard a song of their choosing, the ride was quiet in a way that was jarring. By the time Alex found a parking spot a few blocks away from the town square, I was itching to escape.

"Okay, everyone. Listen up," Alex said as he shifted into park and killed the engine. "I promised to drive Kim home, and she has a curfew, so you all need to be back here by eleven fifteen. If you're not, then I'll assume you've found a different ride and leave without you, so don't be—"

Lee threw open the passenger-side door, dropped his skateboard to the ground, and jumped out in the middle of Alex's speech.

"Hey, are you even listening? If you're late—"

"Yeah, yeah," Lee said, rolling his eyes. "I've heard this speech before, and just so you know, Cole does it better. Catch you losers later."

Alex's mouth fell open, but he quickly rearranged his expression into a scowl. "Always such an asshole," he muttered under his breath.

Nathan and I stifled our laughter as we exited the truck. Once we were both standing on the sidewalk, Alex locked the doors, grumbled a goodbye, and took off to find Kim, leaving the two of us to walk together. The sound of live music steadily grew louder as we approached, and when we reached our destination two minutes later, Nathan was bobbing his head along with a bluesy rock song I didn't recognize.

I knew block parties were common in certain parts of New York City, but it wasn't something one experienced living on the Upper West Side.

This seemed more like a cross between a farmers market and a festival. The four streets comprising downtown were closed off from traffic, and as a result, there were people everywhere: waiting in line at one of the many food trucks; wandering through the merchandise booths set up by local businesses; playing lawn games like cornhole, bocce ball, and ladder toss; and standing around in clusters with drinks in hand. Packs of children roamed the outskirts on bikes while families picnicked in the small park at the center of the square.

"So this is a block party?"

"Not in the traditional sense," Nathan replied, stepping around one of the white-and-orange barricades. "This is much bigger and more commercialized. My dad said the original started in a local neighborhood back in the nineties, but when it grew out of control, the town council voted to sponsor the event and move it here."

"What's your favorite thing to do?" I asked.

Nathan pointed to the white pole tent on the other side of the square. "I like to hang out by the stage and listen to local artists perform. There's going to be a battle of the bands this year, and some of my friends entered."

"Your friends are in a band?" As soon as the question left my mouth, I winced. Had I really been so distracted by his brothers that I never learned anything about Nathan's social life? He was my first friend in the Walter household, so the oversight felt like a major failing, one I would rectify this time around.

"Yeah, they call themselves Miami Bay," he said, guiding us through the mass of people.

"And you're not a part of it?" With his good looks and Walter charm, it wasn't difficult to picture Nathan as a magnetic frontman who could inspire an entire fan base.

He shook his head. "I wrote them a few songs, but I've always seen myself as a solo act. Do you want to meet them? I'm sure they're here by now."

I opened my mouth to respond but was cut off by the sound of my own name. "Jackie, over here!"

The street was so busy, I had to scan the surrounding area twice before spotting Riley, who was waving both arms over her head to get my attention. She, Heather, and Skylar were lounging on a blanket in the grass, a cooler parked beside them. The afternoon sun was scorching, and I wondered how early they arrived in order to snag a spot under the shade of an ancient maple tree. It looked idyllic, and I wanted to join them, but my freshly realized shortcomings in regard to Nathan made me pause.

"Go catch up with your friends," he said when I looked at him, lip caught between my teeth. "I'll introduce you later."

"Are you sure?"

Nathan gently pushed me in their direction. "Positive. You're riding home with us, right?"

"That's the plan," I said, scrutinizing his expression as I slowly walked backward. Thankfully, nothing in his easygoing smile betrayed signs of disappointment.

"Okay. If you don't make it over to the music tent, I'll see you then. Remember—"

"Eleven fifteen or else," I finished, wagging a finger. He laughed and offered me a salute before receding into the crowd. When I turned back to my friends, Riley launched herself into my arms.

"Jackie! You're finally back." She squeezed me so hard I let out a strangulated squeak. "Summer was so lonely without you."

The strength of her hug spoke volumes, and I turned to Skylar and Heather with raised brows. The girls—not including Kim, as she spent equal amounts of time with Alex—were inseparable, and although Skylar tended to be more independent, Riley and Heather were his best friends. Had something *else* changed while I was away?

Skylar waived off my questioning look. "Don't mind her. She's being dramatic," he said before instructing me to grab a drink from the cooler and get comfortable. As I selected a lemonade and kicked off my sandals, he launched into an explanation about how, while Heather was away in California visiting her father and stepmom, he'd been busy working as a summer camp counselor, leaving Riley to languish—her word, not Skylar's—by her lonesome.

"Well, what about Kim?" I asked. "Didn't you see her at all?"

The smile on Riley's face faltered.

When Skylar and Heather exchanged a look, I rolled my eyes and added, "You guys don't need to break the news to me about them. I already know they're dating and don't care."

"Really?" Riley perked up. "You're not upset at all?"

"No, our breakup was..." I trailed off as I searched for the right word.

Skylar arched a brow. "A foregone conclusion?"

"Inevitable?" Heather suggested.

"Fated?" he shot back.

"*Amicable*," I finally settled on as I gave them the side-eye. "We both came to the realization we were dating for the wrong reasons. Alex even admitted he wasn't over Mary, so I guess I'm just confused about how he and Kim got together so quickly? Nathan said it was only a few days after I left."

"Kim has had a crush on Alex since middle school," Riley admitted as she dug around in the cooler for another drink. She settled on a cherry cola, shook off the water, and popped the tab before continuing. "She planned on confessing after the Mary drama blew over, but you arrived out of nowhere, and Alex—well, let's just say he was enamored."

"Obsessed," Skylar said with a fake cough.

Heather, who'd been nodding along with the explanation, was quick to cut in. "When Alex told her you guys broke up, Kim just went for it. She didn't want to miss her chance again."

"Oh my God," I said, gaze darting to each of my friends as I pinched the skin at my throat. "I had no idea. She must hate me."

"No," Riley said tersely. "Kim isn't like that. She's one of those annoyingly good people who just wants everyone to be happy."

"Things worked out better for her anyway," Skylar added. "She'd rather be the forever girl than a rebound."

"I guess that's fair, but are you sure she's okay with me?" I asked. "I want to be friends, but I can't help that I live with her boyfriend. What if she's secretly wishing misfortune on me and all my descendants?"

Riley laughed. "It's hilarious how worried you both are of being hated by each other. Kim's practically given herself an ulcer. She'll be so relieved to hear you don't care about them dating."

Alex had said something similar, but boys could be naive when it came to these kinds of things, so having confirmation took the load off my chest.

"Not relieved, ecstatic," Skylar said. "She wants all of us to be a big happy family so we can run a D and D campaign together, remember?"

"Oh God." Riley groaned and flopped backward onto the blanket. "I completely forgot about that. Please don't remind her."

"I would *never*. Last time I was at her house, I hid her player's handbook and collection of dice sets."

"Hey! Focus, people." Heather snapped her fingers at Skylar and Riley to get their attention, then turned back to me. "I need more details. Was it really that clean of a breakup? Because rumor has it you're heartbroken over Alex and that's the real reason you went back to New York."

Ugh, this was what I hated about small towns. It was so much easier to stay anonymous in the city. "That's ridiculous," I told her. "Katherine offered to let me spend the summer in New York, so I was thinking about going even before we broke up. Alex had nothing to do with my decision. Actually, he was the one who convinced me to leave, now that I think about it, but not by breaking my heart. He helped me realize there was some stuff I needed to deal with at home."

"What about Cole?"

"What about him?" I replied, even though I wasn't ready to have this conversation. Not before I'd spoken with him. Nevertheless, I should have anticipated Heather's question. It was a given that my friends would want to know where I stood with Cole, especially after I explained how things ended between me and his brother.

"You and Alex are over," she said as if this was the only explanation needed. "Has Cole made a move yet?"

Not recently, I thought. No way would I be sharing details about our goodbye kiss, though. They'd never let it go. The four of us would be here until Christmas, dissecting all three seconds of that moment as if there were nothing more newsworthy than kissing one of the Walter boys. Instead, I asked, "Why would you think there's anything going on between us?"

"*Please*," Riley said, rolling her eyes so hard she probably caught a glimpse of her brain. "Just because you were dating Alex doesn't mean everyone and their mother couldn't see how bad Cole had it for you. The sexual tension was suffocating."

"I haven't had a chance to talk to him yet," I said, sidestepping the question as best I could. "He doesn't live at the ranch anymore."

"But what about this summer?" Heather pressed. "Didn't you talk at all?"

I was saved from having to answer when something caught Skylar's attention. He pushed himself into a sitting position and nudged his sunglasses down. "Well, you better figure out what you're going to say," he said, his eyes sparkling with amusement. "Your chance is heading straight this way."

"What?" I followed his gaze and—

My heart lurched in my chest. Cutting through the crowd as if he were on a mission was Cole, his attention already fixed on me. Unlike Alex, he hadn't changed at all while I was away. His eyes were the same startling shade of blue, his skin perfectly tanned. Same tousled golden locks and self-assured confidence. I couldn't forget how devastatingly handsome he was, how it felt when he looked at me, but remembering and experiencing the weight of his gaze were two vastly different things, and my entire body thrummed with awareness. For a moment, all I could do was watch him. He didn't look angry, but there was a determined gleam in his eyes that made me squirm.

"Yeah, definitely *nothing* going on between you two," Riley said, snapping me out of my trance. Heather and Skylar both laughed.

They weren't wrong, but that didn't change my decision.

Not wanting an audience for what would undoubtedly be an awkward conversation, I scrambled to my feet and went to meet him, disregarding both my sandals and my friends' good-natured heckling. The dried-out grass prickled against my bare feet as I crossed the lawn, but I was too focused on Cole to truly notice. We reached the sidewalk at the same time, stopping three feet from each other, but Cole didn't say anything. He just stared down at me, his face blank. The fluttering in my chest quickly turned unpleasant and panicky. Then, right as I convinced myself that he was only here to chew me out, that infuriating smirk of his made an appearance.

"Hey, New York. Miss me?"

The mounting dread melted away, but since our usual repartee operated on his smug attitude and my pretense of irritation, I clamped down on my urge to smile. "What would it take for you to forget that awful nickname?"

"Well, *Jacqueline*"—he looked me up and down—"I might be able to think of a few things."

I huffed. Even though I rarely told anyone my full name, I didn't bother asking how he learned such confidential information. Probably Danny, the traitor. "No one calls me that."

"Yeah, but everybody else uses Jackie." He stepped forward, his gaze dropping to my mother's necklace. Without a word, he lifted the pendant with deft fingers and briefly inspected it before letting the flower settle back against my breastbone. When his eyes found mine again, he hit me with another smile. "I wanna be special."

A big part of me wanted to tell him he already was special, almost everyone thought so, but that was too embarrassing of a confession to make. I opted to change the subject instead. "How was your summer?"

He shrugged. "I spent the majority of it working and not nearly enough time talking to you."

"I'm sorry, Cole. I know—"

"Stop," he said firmly. "I don't need an apology. You had some heavy shit to deal with, and we should probably talk about it at some point. I promised my mom I'd be home for dinner tomorrow since I missed last night, so maybe then? But I just finished a twelve-hour shift at the Gas Exchange. All I wanna do is hang out and have some fun."

I wanted to say yes, to have one nice night together before I blew everything up, but would that be fair? Cole clearly wasn't mad at me, at least not enough to hold a grudge for what happened over the summer, so it was safe to assume he wanted to pick up where we left off. Giving him the impression that I wanted the same thing would be selfish.

When Cole's brow arched at my silence, I realized I was overthinking. While I couldn't give him the relationship he wanted, maybe tonight would be enough? He'd be gone soon, anyway. I glanced back at my friends, who were watching us like they were at the movies. The hesitation must have been clear on my face, because Heather offered me a stern look and made a shooing motion. Skylar chucked my sandals at me.

Well, I guess that settles it, I thought as I turned back to Cole.

"All right," I said in agreement. "Hang out and fun. I think I can handle that."

As soon as I slipped on my sandals, Cole took my hand in his and led me into the teeming street. He must have had a destination in mind, because he wove through the crowd with a steadfast focus. I let him pull me along without saying a word as it kept him from noticing how deeply our woven fingers made me blush.

Once my face cooled down, I cleared my throat. "Where are we going?"

"The block party was my favorite part of summer when I was a kid, so I thought I'd show you the highlights, relive the glory days and all that."

"Another tour, huh?" I said, remembering the one he gave me

when I first arrived in Colorado. He'd been so engaging as he showed me around the ranch, like an unprofessional but charming museum docent who couldn't help but flirt. The thought of him in a blazer leading tourists around the Met made me giggle.

He glanced down at me, lips quirked. "What's so funny?"

"Nothing." My grin implied otherwise, but he let it go, attention already shifting.

"Okay, first stop," he said as we approached a pop-up canopy.

There was a line of children in front of the tent, and I peered over their heads to see inside. A long table held trays of paint, tubs of temporary tattoos and face gems, and little pots of glitter. Three folding chairs had been set up for customers; two were occupied by excited kids, each one trying to sit still for their artists. The one empty chair was positioned in front of a surly-looking girl who was snapping a piece of gum and scrolling on her phone. Even though she appeared to be our age, I didn't recognize her from school, and she emanated such a strong "go away" vibe that I immediately understood why none of the waiting children were willing to sit down with her.

"Face painting?" I said, turning back to Cole. "Really?"

"Hey, I'm not ashamed to admit that it's fun. Six-year-old me thought having a spider on my forehead was the definition of badassery. I'll even get something right now to back up my claim." Cole stepped around the line and plopped himself on the empty chair. "You're not busy, right?"

The scowl the girl aimed at him was so frigid that I flinched, but

Cole's smile didn't falter, and after a momentary stare down, she heaved a sigh. "What do you want?"

"Dealer's choice," he told her.

She must have known who Cole was, because she gestured to the football on the menu board. "How about this?"

"No," I blurted out before he had a chance to look. "Definitely not." Cole leaned forward to see what caused such a sharp reaction from me, but I pushed him back into the seat. "No peeking."

After a moment of consideration, I pointed to one of the only options that didn't include either glitter, flowers, or the color pink. The girl shrugged and grabbed a brush. When she finished a few minutes later, she handed Cole a mirror so he could check out the flame that curved around his eye and up his temple.

"Oh, this is *fire*." When he caught my gaze in the mirror, he waggled his brows and added, "You picked it because I'm hot, right?"

"I was aiming for badass, but after that joke, I regret not choosing the clown face."

A little boy at the front of the line gasped. He tugged on the wrist of the woman standing beside him. "Mooom! She used a bad word," he said, pointing straight at me. His mother eyed me with disapproval. Between her and the grumpy artist, I figured it was time to go.

"Come on," I said, yanking Cole to his feet. "Let's get out of here."

He chuckled and clamped a hand down on my shoulder. "Not so fast. It's your turn."

Knowing he wouldn't take no for an answer, I scanned my options as he steered me into his recently vacated seat. I pointed to the purple butterfly. It was small and hopefully wouldn't take long to paint. "I like that one."

"Let me pick something out for you," he said, brushing a lock of hair out of my face and tucking it behind my ear. His fingers lingered on my neck. "It's only fair."

"I-I suppose that'd be okay," I agreed. "But remember how considerate I was. You better not choose something ridiculous."

"Hmm." Cole titled his head to the side, weighing his options. "Right now, I'm torn between the Batman mask or the full tiger face." Despite his teasing, the design he ended up selecting was cute: a smiling sun painted onto the apple of my cheek and dusted with yellow glitter. He paid and thanked the girl who'd painted both of our faces, but she resumed scrolling without another word.

"Okay, what's next?" I asked when we stepped back into the sun.

A broad, boyish grin lit up Cole's face. "Now that we're in proper block party spirit, it's time for the main event."

"Which is?"

Instead of explaining, he brought me over to a group of kids who were gathered around some type of game. When we got close enough to see what was going on, I frowned. Set up on a long folding table was what seemed to be an eight-foot-long PVC pipe cut in half, creating two troughs filled with water. A boy wearing a SpongeBob T-shirt was leaning over one trough, and a girl in pigtails was at the other, and they appeared to be blowing bubbles with straws.

"What are they doing?" I asked, raising my voice so Cole could hear me over the onlookers' cheers.

Cole leaned down and spoke directly in my ear. "It's a minnow race. See the fish? The point is to get your minnow across the finish line first. The only rule is that you can't touch the minnow, so you blow through a straw, making bubbles to get it to move. Trust me, it sounds way easier than it is."

"*This* is the main event of the block party?" I said skeptically.

"For ten-year-old me, it was," he replied as we watched a tiny silver fish no bigger than my pointer finger dart across the finish line in Pigtail's trough. "My dad always gave each of us twenty bucks to spend however we wanted, and since this only costs a quarter, I could play all day. Whoever has the fastest time at the end of the block party wins the pot, and I'm a three-time champion."

I grinned. "Can't be too hard, then."

"Oho! That's some big talk for someone who didn't even know what a minnow race was until a minute ago."

"So? Bet I could still beat you." I didn't actually care about winning, especially since the race looked like it required more luck than skill, but the affronted look on Cole's face was too cute to ignore. I bit my lip to keep from laughing.

"I'll take that bet," he said, his gaze dropping to my mouth. "What do I get when I win?"

"Eternal bragging rights?" I suggested, ignoring the way my pulse quickened.

"You're on," he said, then briefly stepped away to sign us up.

While we waited for our turn, I watched the ongoing races to see if there were any successful techniques I could utilize, but the fish seemed to have minds of their own. Ten minutes later, Cole and I were each handed a straw and told to get into position. A standard "Ready, set, go!" was announced, and my minnow shot off as soon as he was released. The little guy made it halfway down the trough before I even had to encourage him to keep swimming.

In the end, Cole only won because he resorted to dirty tactics. When my minnow was a foot from the end, he reached over the table and poked me in the side. The attack caught me off guard, I sucked a mouthful of water up through my straw, and while I had a coughing fit, Cole's minnow crossed the finish line.

"No congratulations for the victor?" Cole asked after we moved out of the way so the next race could begin.

"Oh, my bad." I glanced around to make sure no little kids were watching, then flipped him off.

A soft laugh rumbled from his throat. "I'm *so* going to enjoy holding this over your head," he said, "but do you know what would be even better?"

"Winning fair and square?" I suggested dryly.

Cole leaned in, and his lips brushed my ear. "A kiss from you," he said, his voice low in a way that made my stomach swoop.

This close, every breath I took smelled of his cologne. It made me want to grab him by the front of his shirt and—

Goddammit. This was exactly the type of situation I'd wanted to avoid. I never should have agreed to spend time with him before we had an honest conversation, but I always made stupid decisions around Cole. He was my weak spot.

"Not happening," I said, affecting a haughty tone and turning my nose up at him.

"You sure?" he asked but pulled away so that he was no longer in my personal space. "I promise to never mention my superior minnow racing skills again."

"Even if I wanted to, which I don't"—*lies, lies, lies,* my conscience chanted—"my mouth tastes like fish water right now."

Cole threw back his head and laughed. When he finally got himself under control, he joined his hand with mine and pulled me back the way we came. "Let's fix that, shall we? Can't have you walking around with fish breath, and it's time for the next stop on our tour, anyway."

"Hey!" I whacked him on the arm. "I meant that there's a nasty taste in my mouth, not that my breath smells bad."

While we walked, Cole told me bits and pieces about his summer: the management position at Tony's paid well, but he disliked that it meant fewer hours working on cars; he and his best friend, Nick, went on a road trip to Yellowstone and got stuck in a bison jam; and the water aerobics instructor at the pool where he lifeguarded, an almost eighty-year-old woman, slipped him her number on his last day. We reached the food trucks in less than no time, and Cole steered us toward one selling shaved iced.

"It's not a block party unless your mouth is stained blue from a blue raspberry snow cone," he told me.

"I'd rather have cherry," I said to be contrary. Truthfully, I'd be happy with either flavor.

Cole groaned as we joined the end of the line. "That's so *boring*."

"It's a classic."

"Yeah, classically boring."

"Blue raspberry isn't even a real fruit," I pointed out.

"None of this is real fruit," he said. "It's syrup. Why don't you just admit you're too chicken to walk around with a blue mouth for the rest of the night?"

I rolled my eyes. "You're right, Cole. We can't all be as *badass* as you."

It took us another minute to reach the front of the line and order, but once we had our snow cones in hand, I grabbed a wad of napkins and made for one of the empty picnic benches. Cole gently grabbed my elbow and steered me in the opposite direction. When we stepped past the barricades and away from the block party, I gave him a bewildered look.

"We're leaving?" I asked, even though the answer was obvious. There was still so much I hadn't seen, like the music tent and the rows of vendors.

"Yup," he replied, his lips already blue. "We're done with all the kiddy stuff. It's time for some real fun."

We walked to a nearby residential neighborhood lined with established trees so big, their foliage created a canopy that shaded the entire length of sidewalk. The homes were old but well-kept, with covered porches, bay windows that overlooked the street, and tidy front gardens. When we reached a green bungalow where a thumping bass could be heard from behind a wooden privacy fence, Cole ignored the front walk and cut across the lawn toward the gate. He lifted the latch and pushed it open, gesturing for me to go first, and I stepped into the most charming backyard I'd ever seen.

A stepping-stone path cut through lush grass and lead to a pergola-covered patio with lanterns hanging from the rafters. There was a sunken fire-pit lined with cushions and pillows, a stock tank hot tub, and a hammock hanging between two trees. Familiar faces from school were scattered all around, some playing beer darts while others gathered around the bonfire, but most were congregated on the patio, talking and laughing.

Walking into the party with Cole reminded me of all the times I'd been at his side in the hallways between class periods; everywhere he went, Cole drew attention without trying. Heads turned, greetings were called out, and smiles followed in his wake. The difference tonight, however, were all the acknowledgments I received, from head nods to friendly hellos. It was a stark contrast to my first month in Colorado when I was stared at and judged for being the new girl. The sense of acceptance was comforting and hopefully a sign that the upcoming school year wouldn't be as bad as the last.

"Patio or fire?" Cole asked me after saying hi to one of his football buddies.

I caught a glimpse of Kim curled up in Alex's lap on a wicker sectional and hesitated. "Um…"

Cole followed my gaze, clocked his brother, and quickly adjusted our course. "Fire it is," he said, but it didn't matter where we went, because he was friends with everyone.

I recognized most of the people at the fire-pit as the ones who cut class with us last spring. Besides Nick, there was a guy with a lip ring named Joe but who preferred to be called Jet, his older sister Molly, and Molly's friend Kate, whose pink hair streak had been changed to purple. Then there were the two defensive linemen with names I always mixed up. Ryan and Tim? Or maybe it was Bryan and Jim.

"Cole, you made it!" Kate jumped up and threw her arms around him before surprising me with a hug as well. "Hey, Jackie. Back for the school year?"

"Yeah," I said, then shook my head when Nick silently offered me a beer. "I got in yesterday."

"Ugh, I'm so jealous," she said, plopping down on Jim/Tim's lap to make room for me and Cole. "I wish I could jet off to somewhere fun like New York for the summer."

Even with the space she freed up, I doubted the two of us would fit. Cole sat down, and when I hesitated, he rolled his eyes, tucked me into his side, and draped an arm over the back of the bench. Once I was settled (and striving to ignore the way his body was pressed against mine from shoulder to knee), he accepted a beer from Nick and popped the tab one-handed.

"Kate," Molly said with a pointed look. "Don't be annoying. You're leaving for Southern Cal in less than a week while the rest of us will be stuck here attending dinky state colleges."

Nick spoke up. "Actually, I'm going to—"

"UF, we know," Bryan/Ryan said. "We've all heard it a million times. If I have to listen to you suck Florida's dick one more time, I'm going to drown myself in the hot tub."

"Some of us still have to finish high school," Jet grumbled under his breath.

"In what universe is Boulder a dinky state college?" Kate asked. "It's literally the largest university in Colorado. You're just pissed you didn't get into Berkeley."

A guy I didn't recognize with curly brown hair threw his arm over Molly's shoulder, his gaze briefly meeting Cole's before he offered her a sympathetic smile. "Hey, cheer up. The three of us will have a blast."

Molly sighed and leaned her head against his chest. "Yeah, I know." She was quiet for a moment before looking over at Cole. "When are you moving into the dorms?"

Cole took a sip of his beer before responding. "This Thursday. You?"

Even though I wouldn't allow this thing between us to develop into something more, my heart still sank hearing his answer. Cole would be gone in less than a week.

The conversation about college carried on into the night, and even though I couldn't contribute much since I still had two more years of high school, I was content to sit and listen. Cole was unusually reticent as well, only chiming in when someone asked him a question. He spent the night staring at the fire and absentmindedly tracing patterns on the side of my arm.

"Hey," I whispered, gently nudging him in the side. "You okay?"

"I'm sorry. I promised you a fun night, but"—he yawned—"I'm beat."

"That's okay. Why don't you go home and get some rest?"

"But you're finally back," he said, burying his face in my hair with a sleepy smile, "and I wanted to—God, you smell like vanilla and citrus. Is that your shampoo?"

"Perfume," I replied, and he hummed in acknowledgment. I waited for him to continue explaining whatever it was that he wanted, but instead of saying anything, he let out another yawn, then nuzzled closer like he was preparing to nap on my shoulder. "Cole, are you still with me?"

The party was dying down, but over on the patio, someone shrieked with laughter.

"No," he grumbled, "so I suppose going to bed isn't a terrible idea, but how are you getting back to the ranch? Do you need a ride?"

"Alex is taking me." I glanced around in search of him, but he and Kim must have left at some point because I didn't see them anywhere.

That jolted Cole awake. "Nope, definitely not." He untangled himself from me, slammed the rest of his beer, and stood with newfound energy. "Let's go," he said, offering me a hand up. "I'm driving you back."

I opened my mouth to respond, but the gleam in his eyes was steely. He always got like this when it came to his brother, stupidly headstrong and impulsive, so I didn't bother arguing. We said our goodbyes, all Cole's friends promising to meet up a final time before leaving for their colleges, and then we made the short walk to the Gas Exchange where the Buick was parked. By the time we reached the ranch, it was almost ten o'clock.

Cole pulled up next to the shed and put the car in park. "Doesn't look like anyone's back yet," he said, glancing over at the house. All the lights were off, which meant Katherine, George, and the younger kids were either still at the block party or already in bed. "You know where the key is, right?"

"Taped to the underside of the porch swing, but I doubt I'll need it. Knowing your mom, she left the back door unlocked."

"You're probably right." Cole rubbed the back of his neck and sighed. "Look, about tonight. I'm sorry if you thought the block party was dumb and that I basically fell asleep at the party, but I've spent all my time working this summer. I'm running on empty."

"You shared some of your childhood memories with me. Why would I think that's dumb?" I told him in earnest. Cole Walter could be a real asshole sometimes, but he was equally as sweet, especially when he wasn't getting into pissing contests with Alex. "I'm glad I got to spend time with you."

He reached across the console and knotted our fingers together. "You mean that?"

"I promise," I said as he ran his thumb over my knuckles. He'd been incredibly touchy-feely tonight, more so than I remembered him being, and every brush and soft touch made my body feel like a live wire. The air was thick around us, and I knew I needed to get away from him before I did something I'd later regret. "I'm going to head in. See you tomorrow night at dinner?"

"Yeah, I'll be there," he replied, but when I tried to pull away, his grip tightened.

"Um, Cole?" I needed my hand back in order to leave. I glanced down at our entwined fingers, then back to him. The way he was gazing at me made my throat tighten. Even in the dark, his eyes were piercing.

"Can we talk then?" he asked. "About your summer and stuff?"

I cleared my throat, but my voice still came out raspy. "Y-yeah. Get some sleep, okay?"

Cole nodded, and this time, he let me go when I withdrew my hand. I offered him a parting smile and thanked him for driving me home, then unbuckled my seat belt and moved to open the door.

"Jackie, wait," he said, taking hold of my arm.

When I glanced at him over my shoulder, Cole leaned forward and pressed his lips to mine.

three

THE TRUTH WAS, THE SUMMER hadn't been easy. I'd never thought returning to the city I loved would be difficult. When Katherine offered to let me return to New York back in June, I seized the opportunity without consideration.

One of the first things I realized, however, was how many memories I had to face there. Returning to our apartment reminded me I would never again watch the nightly news with Dad or help Mom select a fabric for one of her upcoming designs. I'd never steal one of Lucy's tops again, hear her laugh, or curl up on the couch with her for another *Twilight* marathon. I thought I'd dealt with the worst of my grief, that I was well on my way to healing, only to be hit with the pain of it all over again.

The next thing that occurred to me? I was too overwhelmed to think about my feelings for Cole, let alone talk to him. Not when being back in the apartment felt like living with ghosts every day. By the time I felt less emotional and had my shit together, so much time had passed that doubts crept in. Sure, Cole was gorgeous, and we had good chemistry together. He also knew all the right things to say to make me melt, but he could be cruel and petty when it suited him. Would he want to talk to me after I'd gone radio silent? Was our connection real, or had I fallen for the Cole effect like Riley and Heather warned me I would?

The more I thought about it, the more I second-guessed everything. Because if my feelings weren't as strong as I originally thought, what about Cole's? Could I trust that his were genuine, or was I a shiny new toy, just another in a long line of girls whose proximity was convenient?

Kissing him now, I knew our feelings were genuine.

It started out chaste—a simple brush of his lips against mine to test the waters—but that was all it took to destroy the last strands of my self-control. My hand flew up of its own accord and curled around the back of his neck, which was all the encouragement Cole needed to pull me close and mold his mouth to mine. He must have snuck a breath mint on the way home, because he tasted like sugar and cinnamon instead of the beer he drank at the party. I didn't know whether to be pleased or annoyed by his assumption.

When he drew my bottom lip between his teeth and bit down, electricity zipped through my veins. Desperate for more, I tugged on Cole's hair. He responded by grasping hold of my waist and squeezing.

"Come here," he rasped and gently hauled me over the center console. It took a bit of maneuvering, but once I was straddling his lap, he captured my mouth in another fervent kiss that stole the breath from my lungs. His fingers toyed with the bottom of my shirt, occasionally daring to slip underneath, but it wasn't until Cole's lips left mine and started trailing down the side of my neck that my addled brain kicked into gear.

Oh my God! What the hell am I doing?

"Cole, stop," I said, gasping for breath. "I should go."

He leaned back in his seat, chest heaving, lips swollen and glistening, and chuckled as if I'd said something amusing.

"What's so funny?"

"Nothing," he said, mouth quirking up as he shook his head. "It's just…you're like Cinderella—always running away from me."

I didn't know what to say to that. "Your family might get back soon."

With a sigh, Cole placed a final kiss on my forehead and let go of my hips. "Night, Jackie," he said, opening his door for me. "I'll be back tomorrow for dinner."

"Okay." I slid off his lap and out of the car, gravel crunching beneath my feet. "See you then."

Once he was gone, I crossed the yard and trudged up the porch steps, eyes on my phone as I messaged Alex so he knew I didn't need a ride. Somewhere out in the dark, an owl hooted.

"Well, *that* didn't take long."

Without thinking, I shrieked and hurled my phone in the direction the voice had come from. Someone swore as it thumped against the siding of the house and hit the ground. A phone flashlight turned on two seconds later, revealing Isaac. He was lounging in one of the Adirondack chairs wearing only his boxers and a pair of slides. On the side table next to him was a lighter, a pack of cigarettes, and a sweating ice pack.

"Jesus, Jackie! That was almost a headshot."

"Isaac?" I said, pressing a hand to my heart. My pulse was racing so fast, I could feel a vein throbbing in my neck. "You gave me a heart attack!"

"I don't know why you're complaining." He rubbed his shoulder, then winced. "I'm the one who had a phone chucked at their head!"

"Sorry." Spotting my phone a few feet to his left, I scooped it up and checked for any damage. Thankfully, the case had done its job. "I didn't realize anyone was out here."

He reached for his smokes. "That was obvious from the moment you and Cole decided to put on a show."

If the leer on his face was anything to go by, Isaac wanted to get under my skin, but this knowledge didn't stop my hackles from rising. "So you sat here in the dark and watched us like a creeper?"

"Oh, relax." He lit up and took a deep drag before his gaze flitted to mine with a smirk. "You're cute, but I'm not interested in watching you do my cousin."

"That's not—I mean, we didn't!" I spluttered.

Isaac snorted. "God, that was too easy. You're out of practice, Jackie."

Folding my arms over my chest, I settled onto the porch rail across from him. "Any particular reason you're being a dick?"

"Besides the phone that was chucked at my head? You should be more grateful it was me who witnessed your little moment and not someone else. Can you imagine if my aunt caught you? She'd blow a fuse." Isaac turned his head sideways and exhaled a lungful of smoke. "Fair warning, she's been a raging bitch lately."

I'd spent many sleepless summer nights contemplating a potential relationship with Cole. I considered it from every angle, weighing the pros and cons. Or so I thought. Alex had been a small factor, but I never took the rest of the Walters into account, which felt like a glaring oversight on my part. Somehow, I didn't think Katherine would be pleased to find me straddling her son and kissing the living daylights out of him. She wouldn't be happy if she found Isaac smoking either, though I didn't bother pointing that out. It was a miracle she'd never caught him before since the smell was a dead giveaway, but I suspected Katherine didn't know because George sneaked a cigarette every now and then.

"Has she?" I asked, dismissing the hint of panic unfurling in my stomach. "Or are you just butt-hurt about being grounded and missing out on all the 'wholesome bullshit' you think you're too cool for?"

"There we go." Isaac stuck his cigarette between his lips and gave me a slow clap. "That's more like it. If you keep putting in the work, I'm sure you'll be back to crushing spirits and breaking my cousins' hearts in no time."

A headache was setting in, so I decided to let him take this round. "Whatever, Isaac. I'm too tired to deal with your crap right now. I'm going to bed."

"Sweet dreams," he replied, his tone saccharine and mocking.

"Screw you."

"Isn't that Cole's job?"

I gave Isaac a long, measured look. Something was off. There was tension in the way he was holding himself, his words sharper than usual. "I might be out of practice or whatever, but you seem different. I don't remember you being such a jerk."

"Or maybe you didn't know me all that well?" He stubbed his cigarette out on the table. "I'll tell you what—once you get sick of Cole and decide to make your way through another one of us, let me know. We could spend some time getting *familiar* with each other."

It was almost comical how backward tonight was going. I'd prepared myself to face Cole's ire at some point—he could be so cruel when things didn't go his way—but he met me with understanding and kindness and pulse-racing kisses. Isaac's venom, on the other hand, was unexpected. Deep down, I knew he wasn't mad at me, but I was currently in the wrong place at the right time, a convenient option to take his anger out on.

Headlights cut across the porch, and I glanced over my shoulder to see Katherine's van rolling up the driveway.

"All right, that's my cue," I said, pushing away from the railing. "I'll leave you to brood over whatever crawled up your ass."

Isaac didn't say anything as I moved toward the front door, but I could feel his eyes on me as I stepped inside and let the screen door slam shut. All his little digs may have been unwarranted, but there was one thing he'd been right about—Cole and I were lucky his parents hadn't caught us.

It was the same nightmare I always had, the one about my family's accident.

Mom and Dad were in the front seat, while Lucy and I shared a pair of earbuds so we didn't have to listen to whatever boring conversation our parents were having.

Based on the scenery, we were somewhere in upstate New York, possibly Lake George? The sky was clear, and the trees had a light green dusting of new growth. These were the details I dwelled on every time I woke, because they weren't accurate. My family died in the winter, but here it was spring, and the crash happened in the city, not on a twisting, scenic road. Strange how dreams could distort reality but feel so real at the same time.

When the song ended, I knew what was coming next.

My seat belt slid off like it usually did, but I didn't bother to click it back into place. No matter how many times I tried, it always came undone. Then, between one blink and the next, I was standing on the pavement. The trees withered and died, and the sky turned black and stormy.

Our car would speed by next, and I'd catch one final glimpse of my family before the road gaped open like a canyon and they disappeared over the edge, leaving me behind forever.

But this time it wasn't my dad's shiny BMW rocketing past me. It was an ancient minivan with a peeling Proud Parent of an Honor Roll Student bumper sticker and a dent in the back panel. Panic shot through my chest at the sight of all the familiar faces inside: Katherine and Nathan and Parker and Alex and—

I lurched awake, chest heaving.

What the *hell* was that?

To say the dream freaked me out would be an understatement. I tossed and turned for the rest of the night but I wasn't able to get the image out of my head—Katherine's van loaded with all the Walters, racing toward the same terrifying end as my family. It was a twisted version of the torture my subconscious subjected me to on a regular basis, so when morning arrived, filling my room with the soft, purple light of daybreak, I was thankful. I hopped out of bed as soon as my alarm went off, yanked on my workout clothes, and hurried downstairs with an eagerness usually missing from my morning routine.

Running and I had a love-hate relationship; the first fifteen to twenty minutes were always absolute hell, and I loathe feeling sweaty, but it was my catharsis. What started out as a method to stay in shape transformed into an outlet, a way for me to channel and burn off all my anxious energy. Nothing left me feeling calm and clearheaded like a long, grueling run did.

As I waited for Nathan to join me, I stretched on the porch and watched as more light crept over the horizon and spilled across the ranch. At quarter past our usual start time, I figured Nathan was another no-show and left without him. His absence was concerning, but that was a problem future me could deal with. Instead, I set off down our usual path and focused on putting one foot in front of the other.

I didn't stop until I reached the top of the hill on the far side of the property where I collapsed in the long grass to catch my breath. This spot was where Cole and I watched the sunset on horseback during my trying first weeks with the Walters. The memory made me smile. I shouldn't have let him kiss me last night, but from the moment we met, Cole had a talent for sweeping me off my feet; yesterday was no exception. My plan to apologize for ignoring him all summer, then gently let him down had gone up in smoke the moment he appeared at the block party. Allowing myself to be whisked away and everything that followed was one more mistake I'd have to apologize for.

If the previous night taught me one thing, it was that we both cared for each other. But those feelings were just another reason why it didn't feel right pursuing a relationship with Cole. Anything more than friendship might hurt him. I may have finally opened myself up to the grieving process, but there was so much healing I had yet to do. One summer wasn't near enough.

"That's not possible," Parker exclaimed, shaking her head as she stared at the screen. Her mouth was slack-jawed, and she dropped her gaze to the controller in her hand as if it was somehow responsible for her loss.

I held up a finger gun and blew away the smoke. "Better start believing, P-Walt."

During breakfast, the younger Walters conned me into a pool day since they weren't allowed in the water without an adult or one of their older siblings supervising. Isaac, Alex, and Lee vanished from the kitchen the moment Zack mentioned swimming, but I naively fell for his dimpled smile. What followed was a single enjoyable hour relaxing in the sun as he, Benny, and Parker played Marco Polo, followed by a vexing four more as I tried every trick in the book to get them out of the pool.

At one point, I could hear Isaac laughing as he watched me struggle from his bedroom window. Alex was nice enough to bring me a sandwich in the early afternoon, but the nice gesture was ruined when he asked if I'd learned my lesson. Not even Katherine or George came out to rescue me from their children. Parker finally agreed to convince the terror twins to go play on the swing set, but only if I played *Mario Kart* with her.

I took my revenge by crushing her in five consecutive races.

"I don't understand," she repeated for the third time. "You're terrible at this game."

"I'm a Rainbow Road veteran, Parker. I was never bad." I hoisted myself out of the beanbag chair to put my controller away. "The only reason you beat me before was because I let you win."

This shocked her more than my multiple victories. "But...why?"

Her question was genuine; Parker truly couldn't comprehend why anyone would willingly lose. Based on our past conversations and the interactions I'd witnessed between her and her brothers, I suspected Parker felt like being the only girl in the family meant she needed to prove herself. She couldn't just exist. She had to be the fastest, the toughest, the smartest, and that didn't leave room for losing. As a recovering perfectionist, I understood that logic even though I knew it was flawed. Hadn't I spent years emulating my father in order to make my parents proud? I'd only recently learned that trying to live up to perceived expectations was an impossible task. Hopefully, in time, I could show Parker that the only person she needed to be was herself.

"I wanted us to be friends," I confessed, because lead by example and all that.

"Oookay." Her tone implied that my answer was stupid. "Does that mean you don't care about being friends anymore?"

"Exactly." I let a slow grin spread across my face. "As the elder sister, I've decided it's more important to teach my younger counterpart some much needed humility."

Excitement sparked in her eyes. "Can you teach me how to beat everyone instead?"

Alex, who must have heard part of our conversation, stepped into the room. "Don't you dare." He pointed a finger at me. "There will be no teaching your evil superpowers to my younger siblings. I won't have you ruining my title as best gamer in the house."

Parker stared at me in wonder. "You beat *him* too?"

My grin stretched even wider. "Whooped his ass."

"Hey!" Alex exclaimed. "That's not what—"

"YOU'RE NOT MY FATHER, SO STOP TRYING TO ACT LIKE IT!"

Alex, Parker, and I froze at the sound of Isaac's enraged voice. The house stood silent for a single second, then George shouted something back that was indiscernible. Doors flew open along the hall. Nathan, Lee, Zack, and Benny poured out of their rooms to investigate. We all gathered on the second floor landing where Jack and Jordan were already waiting, their camera rolling even though we couldn't see anything from our spot at the top of the steps.

"What's going on?" I asked as the shouting continued.

"Isaac got a tattoo when everyone was at the block party," Jordan whispered in a stunned sort of reverence.

"What an idiot," Lee said fondly as he shook his head. "What's it of?"

"I didn't get a good look before Dad kicked us out of the kitchen," Jack explained as he adjusted his glasses, "but it's on his shoulder blade. Mom was upset because he wasn't supposed to leave the house, but things didn't get heated until she started lecturing to him about permanently altering his body and making decisions he'd regret later in life. Isaac said, and I quote, 'Chill, Aunt Kathy. You need to pull the stick out of your ass.' Dad was calm up until that point, but then he lost it."

George and Isaac were still screaming at each other when someone appeared at the bottom of the steps. We all jumped back, afraid of being caught eavesdropping, but it was only Cole. Everyone relaxed at the sight of him except for me. I hadn't expected him to arrive until dinner.

"Did you see it?" Benny asked, bouncing from foot to foot as Cole made his way up the stairs. "Did you see the tattoo? Is it cool? Can you tell us what it is?"

"A mermaid riding a narwhal," Cole deadpanned.

"Bullshit," Alex muttered under his breath.

"Yeah," Parker piped up in agreement. "Tell us what it really is!"

"All of you should mind your own business," Cole said as if invasion of privacy wasn't a common occurrence in the Walter household. I'd have called him out on his hypocrisy—how many times had I been spied on or recorded without my permission?—but for the rigid way he held himself. The situation downstairs was more serious than it sounded, then. "Go back to your rooms before Mom comes along. She's not in a forgiving mood right now."

"What's a narwhal?" Zack asked, not picking up on the undercurrent of tension.

Alex laughed and affectionately ruffled his brother's hair. "It's a sea unicorn."

Downstairs, the kitchen fell quiet. If Cole's warning wasn't enough, the sudden silence certainly was. Everyone instinctively knew it was time to make themselves scarce.

"Is Cole telling the truth?" Benny whispered as the group dispersed.

"I doubt it, buddy," Nathan replied, biting back a smile as he ushered him along. "Isaac doesn't seem like the mermaid type."

Conversations receded, doors slammed shut, and suddenly I was alone with Cole on the landing. My heart rate ticked up. This was it—we were finally going to have a much needed talk, but instead of being relieved, I felt like a criminal marching toward the gallows. Thankfully, Cole didn't notice my nerves. He dragged a hand down his face, then silently reached for me. If he didn't hate me by the end of the night, then the two of us would need to set some serious boundaries. For now, though, I allowed myself to be tugged against his chest. He blew out a breath, and the tension melted from his body once he'd wrapped his arms around me.

"You smell like chlorine," he said by way of greeting. "Did the little mischief makers trick you into swimming with them?"

More like the devil's spawns. "Possibly," I grumbled.

Cole chuckled, and a shiver of pleasure shot through me at the feeling of his sculpted torso shaking against mine. "Cheer up, Jackie. We've all been there before."

"Exactly," I said, pulling away from him. "You all have a lifetime of knowledge, but does anybody share it with me? Of course not. It'd be nice if someone gave me a warning for once instead of breaking out the popcorn and laughing at my expense."

"But then how would you learn?" he asked, booping me on the nose. "Come on. Let's go somewhere more private."

I scowled but followed him down the hall. Cole filled the silence by describing Isaac's tattoo in detail. Too nervous to give him my full attention, I only caught bits and pieces of what he said. Something about feathers. Or maybe it was fire?

Once we reached the art studio, Cole made himself comfortable on my bed. He left plenty of space on the mattress for me to join him, but I needed to put some distance between us, so I sat at my desk chair instead. If I didn't, I feared this conversation wouldn't go how I planned…again. What happened in his car last night was more than enough proof that my brain would take a vacation if Cole put his hands on me.

"Aren't you going to join me?" he asked, tucking an arm behind his head.

"I'm good over here, thanks," I replied, fighting to keep my gaze on his face and not the delicious stretch of his bicep.

"I promise I'll behave." The velvety tone of his voice told a different story, so I shook my head. "Suit yourself, but I have exciting news to share, and I doubt you'll be able to keep your hands to yourself once you hear it."

My chest gave a tiny flutter, and I almost groaned in frustration. He was making this difficult without even trying. "There's something I need to say first," I said, holding myself still despite an overwhelming urge to fidget.

"Okay, shoot."

I braced myself, then dove into the speech I'd prepared. "Cole, I want to apologize for how I treated you this summer. I should have let you know how I felt instead of blowing you off, but—"

"*Jackie.*" He sounded equally amused and exasperated. "I already told you—I don't need an explanation."

"I know, but it's important to me that you understand. If you don't, then…" I trailed off, my voice shaky as all the words I'd rehearsed slipped away from me.

His brows dipped into a V. "Understand what exactly?"

"Why I can't be with you," I whispered. A knot of guilt and regret formed in my chest, but I knew this was the right thing to do. Not just for me but for both of us.

Cole barked out a laugh. "You're hilarious," he said, but when I didn't respond, his smile faltered, and he sat up. "Wait, are you serious?"

Unshed tears pricked my eyes, and I nodded. "You know I have feelings for you, Cole. I can't lie about that, but…I'm not okay. I wish I could put my grief behind me and focus on us, but I still have anxiety and awful nightmares, and—God, it hurts to *breathe* sometimes." Cole was watching me with eyes so penetrating that I had to look away. "I–I don't have the emotional capacity to put a relationship first when some days I spiral over the smallest thing. It wouldn't be fair, and I care about you too much to do that."

"I could help you." He launched himself off the bed, took my hands in his, and kneeled at my feet. "On the days that are hard. I want to help, Jackie. You just need to let me."

The sincerity of his offer simultaneously took my breath away and pierced my heart. I could handle a hotheaded Cole. In fact, I'd expected him to make an appearance. But this soft, sweet side of him? It broke me, and the tears I was trying to stifle spilled down my cheeks.

"Maybe you could, but this is something I need to do on my own," I said, tugging my hands away from his. "Besides, you're leaving for college this week, and I have Princeton to worry about. I can't have any more distractions."

He tensed at his words. "You think I'm a distraction?"

"That's not—I mean, no. Not entirely. It's just…" I faltered, not sure how to explain myself in a way that wouldn't hurt him. Me using Cole as a distraction from my grief wasn't the same thing as him *being* a distraction. But he probably wouldn't see it that way no matter how I phrased things, so I pivoted. "Remember what you said at the beginning of summer about how the timing between us was never right?" I sniffed and wiped at my nose. "It still isn't right, Cole."

Cole was an inherently expressive person. If something pissed him off, his nostrils flared or he gritted his teeth. Excitement made his eyes gleam while disappointment dulled them. Typically, he was all confidence and sly smirks, so I loved the way his eyebrows squished together whenever he got confused, giving me a glimpse of the softer, less put-on side of himself that I found endearing. So watching all trace of emotion drain from his face made my throat constrict.

"If that's how you feel, then fine." He stood swiftly and turned away.

"Cole, wait!" I scrambled out of my chair so fast I nearly face-planted on the floor. "Can't we talk about this?"

"About what?" The cold edge to his voice stopped me in my tracks. "There's nothing left to say."

The quiet as everyone sat down to dinner was unsettling.

I slid into my usual seat and pretended not to care when Cole moved to the opposite side of the table. Even from a distance, I could feel the waves of fury rolling off him. With the exception of Nathan, who glanced between us with furrowed brows, nobody noticed that something was wrong. The younger kids were beat from spending their day in the pool, while the rest were focused on Katherine. There was a tightness to her eyes that made all of us wary.

Nobody dared look at Isaac, who was slumped at his usual spot between Lee and Alex with a sour expression.

Conversation slowly picked up as dishes were passed around, but it stayed subdued, never reaching its usual level of clamor. When Cole cleared his throat near the end of the meal, my stomach dropped. I had no clue what he was going to say, but I had a feeling it wouldn't be good.

"The lease on Will's apartment ends this week," he announced once he had everyone's attention.

I remembered when Cole packed up his things and left during his and Danny's graduation party. After the wedding, Will moved in with Haley since she had a nicer apartment and more space. He hadn't wanted the hassle of finding a subtenant for three months, so he offered to let Cole live in his old place for the summer free of charge. It sounded like it had been a perfect arrangement—Cole was closer to his job at the garage, and the lease would run out just in time for his first semester in Boulder.

"Do you need help moving into the dorms?" George asked.

"About that…" Cole replied. "After giving it a lot of thought, I've decided to defer my enrollment. I don't want to take out a student loan and get saddled with debt, but I can't afford tuition at the moment. I'm making okay money now that Tony promoted me to manager, so I'm going to spend a year working to save up for school."

Katherine paused, then set down her water glass and gave him an approving nod. "That's very responsible of you, Cole. Are you planning to renew the apartment lease?"

He shook his head. "Actually, I was hoping I could move home."

I almost choked on my bite of meatloaf. I'd completely forgotten his words from earlier, but now they played through my head in a loop: *I have exciting news to share…doubt you'll be able to keep your hands to yourself…*

"Oh, honey! That would be wonderful," she gushed. "You're always welcome here, and we'd love to have you back. I'll need to figure out what to do about sleeping arrangements, though." There was already a far-off look in Katherine's eyes as she contemplated the dilemma. "Maybe Isaac and Lee can move back in together?"

"What?" Isaac exclaimed, breaking his silence for the first time this evening. "That's bullshit! I *finally* have my own room, but he's allowed to change his mind, swoop in, and steal it from me? How is that fair?"

"There was nothing fair about the way you spoke to me or your aunt this afternoon," George said, his voice laced with steel. "What makes you think you deserve your own room right now?"

Jack and Jordan, who were covertly flicking peas at each other, stopped what they were doing to listen. If Katherine hadn't instated a no-camera-at-the-table rule, I was positive one of the two would have pulled it out and started recording.

"What about me?" Lee said as he stabbed a tater tot with his fork. "I didn't do anything wrong."

The problem-solving expression on Katherine's face softened into a smile. "You're absolutely right, Lee. Cole and Isaac can share instead."

"I don't want to displace Isaac or Lee," Cole said. "Plus, I plan on also keeping my other job at the Gas Exchange, and that's typically second shift. Wouldn't it be better if I had my own space? Otherwise, I'll constantly be waking up whoever I have to share with. I was thinking I could set something up in the basement?"

Katherine hesitated. "I'm not sure I feel comfortable with you sleeping down there. We don't have an egress window."

"Mom, Cole can stay in my and Benny's room!" Zack said, bouncing up and down in his chair.

"That's very kind of you to offer, Zack," she told her youngest, "but I don't think there's space for all three of you in there, and your brother is right. He needs his own space."

The table fell quiet as everyone considered the problem, then Parker lit up. "Oh, I have something!" Her eyes flickered over to me, and she grinned. "Why don't Jackie and I share? Cole can take the art studio, since my room is bigger."

Cole's expression was unreadable when his gaze found mine. It was the first time he'd looked at me since sitting down to dinner, and I made an effort not to squirm in my seat. "Is that really such a good idea?" His tone suggested concern, but I didn't believe it for a second. "Jackie's never had to share a room before. It might be difficult for her. Besides, she's so hardworking and dedicated to her schoolwork. What if Parker is a *distraction*?"

I narrowed my eyes. "I can handle it."

"Hmm…" Katherine tilted her head in consideration. "I suppose that could work. Are you sure you're okay with this, Jackie?"

"Of course!" I smiled at Parker. "The two of us will have a blast. Right, P-Walt?"

She nodded eagerly. "We can play *Mario Kart* every night, and I can show you how to burp the ABCs!"

That prospect alone was enough to make me regret my decision, but Cole was watching me with a smug grin, and I refused to give him the satisfaction of backing out now. Besides, if sharing a room with Parker made the situation easier for Katherine, then I could make that sacrifice. I would miss the art studio, but if I really wanted to be considered one of the Walters, I couldn't allow myself to be treated any differently from the rest of the family.

Dinner wrapped up shortly after that. I had yet to be added back to the cleanup rotation, so after bringing my plate over to the sink, I slipped outside for some much needed fresh air and a quiet place to reconcile with the knowledge that I'd lost my safe haven. As I paced back and forth, my racing thoughts split into warring factions—one stubbornly determined to help Katherine and stick it to Cole, the other screaming, "*OhmyGodohmyGodohmyGod*, what have I done?"

The front door snicked open, and Cole stepped out, a private smile tugging his lips. Instead of making for the steps like I thought he would, he stopped and took a deep breath as if savoring the moment.

"Little bit of advice?" he said, not bothering to look in my direction.

Even though I was the one watching him, I startled, caught off guard that he knew I was here.

"You don't have to be a people pleaser ad nauseam. It's obnoxious."

"I don't know what you're talking about," I said politely, even though I wanted to snap. How dare he call me obnoxious when I gave up my room for him? What he should have done was thank me, but since I'd turned him down, he was throwing a tantrum instead. I refused to sink to his level.

Cole snorted. "Don't play dumb, Jackie. I know you didn't want to give up your room."

My fingers tightened into fists. "Well, of course not! But your mom needed—"

"Exactly," he said with vicious satisfaction. "My parents are stuck with you whether you suck up to them or not, so stop trying so hard." He mockingly bowed his head to me when my jaw dropped, then stepped off the porch and headed for his car. "Enjoy your new digs," he called over his shoulder. "I know I will."

four

BY WEDNESDAY EVENING, THE MOVE was official.

I spent Monday and Tuesday packing and hauling the majority of my belongings from one side of the house to the other, but even though Katherine rearranged the furniture and managed to squeeze an extra dresser into the room, there wasn't enough space for all my clothes. After paring down my wardrobe, I was allowed to keep what didn't make the cut at the back of my old closet along with Lucy's nail polish collection.

Other than losing my privacy, I thought the worst part of the situation was the old bunk bed George pulled out of storage for Parker and me to share. Then Cole arrived with all his boxes. Watching him empty them in what had been my refuge in the Walter household, the thought of him sleeping in my bed, felt wrong somehow.

On top of everything, Cole had spent the past two days pretending

I didn't exist. Whenever we passed each other in the hall, he kept his gaze locked straight ahead as if I was invisible. If I walked into the same room as him, he made a point to leave. And the one time I tried to start a conversation with him? Cole glanced at me with emotionless eyes, then looked away without saying a word.

Trying to fall asleep was impossible. I tried to blame my restlessness on Parker's night-light and the monstrous snoring I could hear through the wall we shared with Lee, but the truth was my mind wouldn't slow down. I kept thinking about Cole. How confusing it was that he was suddenly here instead of leaving for college or the way his expression closed off when I told him the timing still wasn't right. I made the best decision for myself, but my thoughts kept returning to how good it felt when he pulled me into his lap and kissed me in the dark of his car.

After tossing and turning for over an hour, I threw off my covers and decided to make Katherine's favorite remedy for insomnia—a glass of warm milk and honey. I nearly tripped at the bottom of the stairs when I noticed a light on in the living room; for a split second, I thought I would find Danny watching one of his favorite crime shows, but then I remembered he was all the way in New York. A lump lodged itself in my throat. While I was happy he'd taken to city life like a duck to water, I missed his easy companionship and our late-night chats. We grew closer over the summer, and while Nathan would always be my best friend among the Walters, Danny had become my brother.

I poked my head around the corner to see who was awake and

grinned. Nathan was stretched out on the couch, one arm tucked behind his head and a bag of cheese puffs on his stomach. The TV was on to a rerun of *Jeopardy!*. Withdrawing to the kitchen, I quickly made my drink and returned five minutes later with a steaming mug in hand.

"Scoot." I pushed his feet off the end cushion to make room for myself, but once I sat down, he stuck them on my lap. "Is that really necessary?"

He smirked and wiggled his socked toes. "What? I was here first."

"Fine, but if I have to put up with your smelly feet, then you have to pay a cheese tax."

Nathan handed the bag over. "Can't sleep?"

"Not at all." I took a heaping handful of cheese puffs before passing them back. My mom had refused to keep junk food in the house, so when I first arrived in Colorado, I'd gone a little wild, trying all the options Katherine stocked her pantry with. These were by far my favorite. "It's weird being in Parker's room."

"Who is Howard Garns?" Nathan muttered, eyes locked on the TV. Then he glanced over at me and said, "I can't believe you agreed to move in with her."

"You and me both," I told him.

"So why did you?"

"Cole provoked me," I confessed, heat staining my cheeks. On screen, the Daily Double was revealed.

"Into giving up your room?" Nathan asked. "How'd he pull *that* off?"

Instead of answering, I stuck out my tongue and snatched the cheese puffs back.

"If you're gonna eat the entire bag, the least you can do is fill me in. What happened with you two? And don't say nothing," he added before I could protest. "I saw the way he glared at you during dinner Sunday night. He's been avoiding you since."

I stuffed a handful of cheesy goodness into my mouth to avoid answering. To tell him or not? The situation was messy, but if there was one person in the house who would listen without bias, it was Cole's mini look-alike, ironic as that was. "Okay," I said after swallowing, "but only if you tell me what's going on with you."

Nathan stilled. "What are you talking about? I'm fine."

"Really?" I tossed a cheese puff at his face. "That's strange, because you haven't joined me on a single morning run since I got back. What's up with that?"

"Oh crap!" He scrambled into a sitting position, eyes wide and regretful. "I'm so sorry, Jackie. I totally forgot."

"About *running*?" That didn't make any sense. Nathan had cemented his morning exercise routine long before I moved to Colorado.

He shrugged. "It wasn't the same without you, so I decided to take a break." His expression was apologetic, and maybe he truly was, but something about Nathan's words didn't ring true. He was lying, but about what and why, I wasn't sure, so I decided to let him off the hook for now. Hopefully he would open up to me when he was ready.

"Well, your vacation's over." I brushed the cheese dust off my hands, unfurled my legs, and stood. "I'm going back to bed. See you in the morning."

"Wait, weren't you going to tell me about Cole?"

I flashed him a cheeky grin. "I've decided to withhold that story as incentive. If you really want to know what happened, then I better see you on the porch at our usual time tomorrow. Only running buddies get classified information."

"Breakfast?" I asked when Nathan and I crested the final hill of our run. The house came back into view, backlit by the rising sun.

"Yeah, and a gallon of coffee," he grumbled. After three months of lying about and sleeping in, Nathan was out of shape. Not only did he nod off during stretches, but he barely kept pace with me on our run. We had to stop for a break halfway through so he could catch his breath, but I didn't mind. It gave me an opportunity to update him on the Cole situation.

Which was why he backtracked as soon as we reached the kitchen and discovered Cole was the only person up. "On second thought, I need a shower," he muttered, spinning around before I could stop him.

"Coward," I hissed at him quietly, but Nathan had no qualms about abandoning me.

The moment he was gone, I could feel it—the tension building in the room, filling the space between me and Cole. How was I supposed to live with him if this was our new normal? I couldn't stand it, so I took a steadying breath and faced him with a smile.

"Morning, Cole."

He was leaning back against the counter in nothing but gray sweats and sleep-mussed hair, a fresh cup of coffee steaming at his side. When he dragged his gaze away from his phone, the indifferent expression on his face doused the hope flickering in my chest that this time would be different. He surveyed me for a single moment before returning to whatever he was doing without acknowledging my greeting.

I mentally sighed. Cole's attitude was disappointing but not unexpected. I'd hoped we could at least be polite to each other if not friends, but I could handle the silent treatment. Realizing it would be more pleasant to enjoy my breakfast on the porch, I grabbed a muffin and thermos before turning toward the coffee maker, which Cole was still standing in front of.

"Excuse me," I said with more courtesy than he currently deserved.

It was if I hadn't spoken at all, because he didn't budge.

"Cole," I snapped, losing my patience. "Get out of the way."

He continued to ignore me.

So this was how it was going to be? Fine. As I reached around him for the coffee pot, I made a point of elbowing his ribs. Not too hard but enough for him to feel my frustration. He let out a quiet grunt but otherwise remained silent.

Just as I finished stirring milk and sugar into my thermos, Alex stepped into the kitchen.

"Morning, Alex," Cole said cheerfully. "Want some coffee?"

Oh, what a petty bastard.

Alex froze midstride and slowly turned to stare at his brother. It took him a solid three seconds to recover his composure. "No thanks," he replied, opening the fridge. He shuffled some Tupperware out of the way and extracted a can of Kickstart. "I'll stick to this."

Cole shrugged, unbothered by Alex's response. "Hey, you busy on Saturday?"

"Why?"

The response Cole gave was cryptic. "The waterfall."

While I knew what he was talking about—I'd visited the waterfall on the far end of the Walters' property a handful of times before—Cole's response lacked enough context for me to follow *why* he'd mentioned it. What made the situation even more frustrating was the fact that he was doing it on purpose.

Alex understood, though, because he tilted his head in consideration. "Who's all coming?"

"Isaac and Lee are in, and I'm sure most of the little monsters will tag along too."

"So pretty much everyone, then." He cracked the tab of his drink and took a sip as he deliberated.

"No." Cole glanced at me and then quickly away again, his lips pressed into a flat line. "Mom mentioned Nathan has a checkup with his neurologist."

Not Jackie was left unsaid. Being excluded stung, but I refused to rise to the bait, since last time, it resulted in me losing my bedroom.

It took Alex a moment to realize what was happening, but as I squared my shoulders and headed toward the door, his eyes finally lit with understanding. "Yeah, sure," he told Cole. "Sounds fun." Then he turned to me with a smirk. "Hey, Jackie, you want to come with us?"

Two days later, I learned that at the end of every summer, right before school started, the Walters planned a day trip to the waterfall. It represented a final moment of freedom before the onslaught of homework, extracurricular activities, and endless practices began. Though I'd always seen the waterfall as a little slice of paradise, I had a feeling that today it would be nothing less than pure magic. There was something in the air, a giddiness shared between the Walter kids that made me feel weightless as I watched them race up the path toward the clearing.

Sunlight burst through the gaps in the trees overhead, dancing across the surface of the water. I paused for a moment to admire the view and breathed in the fresh Colorado air. Meanwhile, Cole, Lee, Jack, Jordan, and Parker were a flurry of moving limbs as they shrugged out of their clothes and tossed their bags to the ground. Lee was the fastest, letting out a whoop of victory as he dove into the water. The others followed suit, all letting out sighs of appreciation as they surfaced.

It was a cloudless day, blue skies for miles in every direction. The heat of the sun felt like warm silk against my skin. I laid down a towel on the edge of the sand alongside Isaac, who'd begrudgingly admitted he wouldn't be able to swim due to his new tattoo. He pushed his shirt-sleeves up over his shoulders, grumbled something about not being able to perfect his tan, and rolled onto his stomach, phone in hand. Alex had invited Kim, and the two lovebirds set up their towels on the opposite end of the small beach so they could flirt in private.

Reaching into my bag, I fished around for my copy of *Great Expectations*, which was the first book we'd be reading in AP English Lit class this semester. I was determined to get ahead before the school year started, so I'd emailed my teacher last week to request the sylla-bus. Though Isaac said nothing, I could tell he was holding back a teasing comment as I opened to the first page. I'd only managed to read a few sentences when a dramatic shriek drew my attention to the water. Parker was being hefted into the air by Cole, who was laughing like a maniac. I couldn't help but watch as his muscles rippled with the effort of holding up his giggling sister.

My mouth felt suddenly dry. Ending things between Cole and I was the right decision, but it was hard not to admire him from afar. The mischief in his eyes was a stark contrast to the scowls I'd been treated to over the last few days. Even if the warmth of his affection wasn't directed at me, I was happy to see it, and I kept my eyes locked on Cole as he tossed Parker back into the water. Jack and Jordan erupted into loud war cries and surged forward, each clinging to one of his limbs. When Parker resurfaced a moment later, the look on her face spelled trouble; she threw herself at Cole, making the fight three against one. Even as he was overtaken and dragged under the water, Cole's expression was one of pure joy.

Something stirred in my gut at the sight. Cole was so good with his younger siblings—playful, but patient—and I'd be lying if I said I didn't find that hot as hell.

It took me longer than it should have to notice the playing had paused. Cole was watching me from across the water, though there was no trace of the warm smile he'd worn only seconds ago, and heat flooded my cheeks. I tore my gaze away and refocused on the book in my hands. The chaos resumed soon after, but I forced my eyes to remain on the open page.

As the sun moved across the sky, the day growing later, I settled into reading and making small notes in the margins of the text. Things had finally quieted down a bit. While Jack, Jordan, and Parker snacked on Goldfish crackers at the edge of the water, Lee floated lazily on his back, eyes closed with the sun beating down on his face. Next to me, Isaac let out a loud groan and finally moved from his towel, stretching his arms over his head as he stood.

"Gotta piss," he said, ambling off into the woods for privacy.

I laughed softly to myself—Isaac always had a way with words— and shifted from a sitting position onto my back. After being hunched over reading for so long, it was nice to stretch out and relax. I'd just closed my eyes when the sunlight shifted, the backs of my lids growing dark. With a sigh, I cracked a single eye open. Cole stood above me blocking the sunlight, legs planted wide and arms crossed over his chest. Not even his muscles could distract me from the cold expression he was wearing.

"It's a little inappropriate to gawk at me when I'm playing with my siblings. Did you forget you dumped me, like, a second ago, or are you just desperate for attention?"

We weren't dating, I wanted to say, but I kept my mouth shut.

His words were a sharp reminder of why it wasn't a good idea to give any more of my heart to Cole Walter. His warmth made me feel limitless at times, like I could do anything and be anyone I wanted. But if I wasn't careful, the spiteful side of his personality he so often wielded like a weapon had the power to cause lasting damage.

The glower on his face only deepened at my nonresponse. I had the urge to say I was sorry, that I wished things could be different, but I knew that would only make things worse.

"Everything all right guys?" Isaac hovered a few feet away, his hands stuffed in his pockets. He looked back and forth between Cole and me, immediately sensing the tension.

Cole rolled his eyes and stalked off toward the water.

"Please tell me you didn't hear that," I said quietly.

He smirked. "Trouble in paradise so soon?"

"It's none of your business."

"Oh, come on," he said as he settled back onto his towel. "What happened?"

My head tilted to the side as I contemplated his question. I could feel the sincerity in Isaac's words, but he loved to see me squirm, so I knew he might use my answer as ammo. Ultimately, I couldn't ignore the knot in my chest; the fear of sharing something real with him only to have it thrown back in my face was enough for me to keep my lips pressed together.

After a few long seconds, Isaac shrugged. "Cole is an asshole, as I'm sure you're aware, but you didn't deserve that."

I could have cried at his comment, but I kept myself under control with a few quick breaths. "Thank you, Isaac."

He nodded in acknowledgment. I thought that was the end of our conversation, but the next moment, he was speaking again, his voice soft. "Thanks for moving in with Parker. I've shared almost everything with my brother and cousins. It's nice to finally have something of my own."

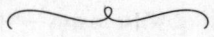

Kim cornered me the instant we returned to the Walters' to get cleaned up for dinner.

"Jackie?" she said once everyone had piled out of the truck, exhausted but content from swimming all day. "Do you have a moment?"

At her question, Alex looked up from the tailgate where he was helping Lee unload a cooler. He widened his eyes at me, gaze unwavering, and I gave him a slight head tilt in acknowledgment.

"Sure." I hitched my beach bag onto my shoulder, then nodded toward the house. The air conditioning was running at full blast when we stepped inside, and after spending hours in the sun, goose bumps spread up my arms. "Let's go upstairs," I said, fighting back a shiver. "We can change out of our suits and talk."

When I pushed open the door to my new room instead of leading her to the art studio, Kim frowned. "What are we doing in here?"

"It's a bit of a story, but I'm sharing with Parker now." I dumped my bag on my desk, then turned around to face Kim. She was standing at the edge of the braided area rug—an orange and navy eyesore that Parker refused to give up—arms pinned against her stomach. Despite being one of the tallest girl in our grade, she'd managed to make herself look small.

"I'm assuming you want to talk about Alex?" I asked.

"Yeah, I..." Her gaze dropped to her feet.

If I didn't already know that Kim was a genuine person, I'd think she was laying the guilt on a little thick—after all, she'd spent the entire day giggling and whispering with my ex—but based on the explanation our friends gave me, she'd approached the situation with Alex in a live-in-the-moment kind of way. It was something I was still aspiring to do more of, so I couldn't fault her for that.

She took a pained breath and tried again. "Everyone's already told me that you're not upset about us dating, and I appreciate that, but I feel like such an awful person. I never should have—"

I held up a hand. "Kim, I'm going to stop you right there. Like you said, I already spoke with Alex and Riley, Heather, and Skyler. They explained the whole situation to me, and to be honest, I feel bad too; if I'd known about your feelings for Alex, I never would have encouraged him," I told her. "I want the two of you to be happy, so as long as you're good with me, I'd love if we could move past this awkwardness."

Kim's head whipped up. "You really mean that?"

"Of course. I'm pretty sure Alex was yours long before I met him, but he was just too dumb to realize it." The smile I offered her was both rueful and teasing. "Besides, only one of us can put up with his *GoG* obsession, and it certainly isn't me."

There was a lingering nervousness in her responding laugh, but she sagged at my reassurance. "You're the best, Jackie."

"Wanna hug it out?" I asked, taking a step toward her as I held out my arms. "You kind of seem like you could use a hug."

"God, yes." Kim gave me a tight squeeze as if trying to convey everything left unsaid—*thank you, I'm so sorry.*

"Ugh, you're still damp from swimming." I wrinkled my nose and pulled away as she laughed for real this time. Facing my dresser, I rifled through the drawers in search of a change of clothes. "So are you taking AP English Lit this year? Nobody else signed up for it and I'd liked to have at least one friend in the class."

five

SCHOOL STARTED ON MONDAY, AND much to my surprise, the first day of junior year went off without a hitch. In addition to having a class with each of my friends and two with Alex, people no longer cared about me being the new girl. Even better, Kim stepped in when Riley and Heather attempted to grill me about how things were going with Cole; one well-placed, icy glare was all it took for the two of them to back off.

By Friday, I'd settled into a comfortable routine and decided it was finally time to pick an extracurricular. While attending Hawks, I'd been involved in multiple school organizations, from debate club to yearbook committee. Last year, however, my guidance counselor prohibited me from joining any clubs at the request of Uncle Richard so that I could adjust to my move and focus on healing. The first student council meeting of the semester was scheduled for after school, and I figured it would be a good place to start. When I arrived at the auditorium, Skylar was waiting outside the door for me.

"Well, look who it is," I said, crossing my arms. At lunch, I had asked my friends if anyone was interested in joining with me, but every single one of them laughed. "I'm surprised to see you after receiving such a thorough rejection. What was it you said? Something about not wanting to spend more time at school than necessary while being forced to work for free with a bunch of try hards?"

Skylar didn't even try to look bashful. He flashed me a wide grin. "I might have said something like that, but I'm allowed to change my mind. It would be cruel of me to let you go alone, especially when you looked so dejected and pathetic."

"Riiight…" I rolled my eyes. "Why don't I believe you?"

"After living with the Walters, I suspect you've developed an excellent bullshit detector," he said, which got a laugh out of me.

"That's true. I need it for self-preservation purpose. But for real, though. Why the change of heart?"

He stuffed his hands into his pockets. "Because I heard Chase talking about coming to today's meeting."

"Who?" I asked.

"Chase Kennedy. He's the editor for the school paper. Sometimes when the news cycle is slow, he publishes an article from my blog to fill the space."

I gasped in mock offense. "So you'll show up for some random guy when he mentions he *might* be in attendance but not for your good friend? Geez, I see how it is."

"For your information, Chase is the devastatingly handsome senior who I've secretly been obsessed with for three years," he said. "Sorry, babe, but you don't come close in comparison."

"Of course. How silly of me."

Skylar grinned and looped his arm through mine. "Glad we sorted that out. Come on. We're going to be late."

The meeting must have been about to start, because when we entered the auditorium, everyone was already seated and turned to look at us.

"What is *she* doing here?" snarked a familiar voice, which I followed to its source. Long auburn hair. Brown doe eyes. A heart-shaped face I recognized immediately. Erin was seated in front of the stage surrounded by a posse of friends who all tittered at her question. I knew I was meant to hold my chin high and pretend I didn't hear her, but before coming back for the school year, I'd made a resolution against taking shit from anyone. Not from the Walter boys or Mary and certainly not from one of Cole's old hookups.

I stared Erin down. "I'm sorry, am I in the wrong room? I thought this was student council, a *student* organization run by *students*, and I just so happen to be one of those."

Erin turned pink and averted her gaze when a surprisingly large number of people laughed. I took this for the win it was and followed Skylar over to an empty row at the back of the room.

The next hour passed in a blur of boring housekeeping information and start of term notices, the only noteworthy moment being when Erin raised her hand as one of the hopefuls running for president. When the meeting came to a close, I went to add my name to the sign-up sheet for the homecoming committee while Skylar wandered over to a guy who looked like a Disney prince come to life—perfectly coiffed ebony hair, cornflower-blue eyes, and an aggressively patrician nose. When I turned around, I nearly ran smack into Erin.

"Just so we're clear," she said in a threatening tone, "if you think you can waltz in here and sabotage my campaign for president, you've got another thing coming."

Good Lord, this girl was ridiculous. If I didn't put a stop to this one-sided beef immediately, I had a feeling she'd make every meeting from this point forward brutal. "So because a boy you liked decided he was more interested in me, I'm suddenly out to get you?"

Erin gaped at me. "What?"

"Look, I'm not here to cause a scene or sabotage you or whatever else you're thinking," I told her. If I'd known Erin was a member of student council, I might have chosen a different club to avoid the drama. "I don't have an issue with you. All I want to do is join an extracurricular to pad my college application and be left in peace."

My admission must have taken Erin by surprise, because she paused. The friend standing at her side, however, scoffed at me. "Then why don't you pick another club?"

I shrugged. "Because student council is the perfect fit for me. I have great organizational skills; I grew up helping my mom plan parties, charity events, and fashion shows; and I spent the summer interning at a top investment company. Also, I don't need your permission to join."

That shut the girl up.

"Okay," Erin said after considering me for another moment, her frosty expression melting. "Any chance you can apply those skills to running an election campaign?"

My brows shot up in surprise, but I recognized her offer for the olive branch that it was. "Yeah, I think I can manage that."

She smiled and held out her hand. "Then welcome to student council, Jackie."

By the time I went to bed that night, I had a rough plan for how to get Erin elected as student council president, subject to her approval.

Campaign Checklist
1. Brainstorm campaign slogans
2. Design a logo (maybe Katherine can help?)
3. Print, hang, and distribute posters/flyers around school
4. Create social media content
5. Network with other student organizations
6. Order T-shirts (keep as a surprise?)

7. Help Erin prep for the debate

8. Draft victory speech

The kitchen was strangely packed when I wandered in for lunch on Saturday afternoon.

Nathan, Alex, Lee, Jack, Parker, Zack, and Benny were seated at the table, Monopoly money divvied up between them. Isaac stood behind the island with a cheese grater held up to his mouth as he displayed a mostly empty box of leftover pizza.

"Going once, going twice. *Sold* to Alex for six hundred!" he announced in an exuberant voice.

"Come on," Lee groaned and banged his head against the table.

Alex hopped up. "Tough luck, coz." He exchanged the majority of his paper money for two slices of pepperoni. "Maybe you shouldn't have spent so much on a granola bar."

"How was I supposed to know it was expired?"

I slid into the empty spot at Nathan's side. "What's going on?"

"Jordan tripped and fell down the stairs," he explained. There was a Smucker's Uncrustables wrapper in front of him along with four beige hundreds and a blue fifty. "Mom had to take him to the ER, and she put Isaac in charge of making sure everyone eats lunch."

Well, that explained the loud crash I heard twenty minutes earlier. "Is he okay?"

Nathan nodded. "Broken finger, but he'll be fine."

"That's surprising, then."

"What do you mean?" he asked, his forehead creasing into a frown. "Jordan's tough. His finger was sideways, and he didn't even cry."

"I was referring to your mother, not Jordan. I figured the situation must be serious if she panicked enough to put *Isaac* in charge."

Isaac drew himself up to his full height. "I'm the oldest here."

"And yet..." I said, tilting my head to the side.

"He's the least responsible," Nathan finished with a smirk.

"Says who? Not only am I feeding everyone, but I'm making sure they have a blast while doing it."

I side-eyed Jack, who was eating out of a mixing bowl filled to the brim with ice cream. It was covered in chocolate sauce, whipped cream, and, strangely, jalapeños. "Yeah, I'm sure this is exactly what Katherine had in mind," I deadpanned. "What's with the cheese grater?"

"This is my *microphone*," Isaac said, feigning offense. "I'm an auctioneer."

"Don't you think you could've chosen something a bit more, I don't know...cylindrical?" I glanced over at the ceramic utensil holder next to the stove; it held a plethora of better options, including a whisk and a wooden mixing spoon.

Isaac's lips curved into a wicked smile. "I can give you something cylindrical."

"Gross," I said, wrinkling my nose. "Forget I said anything."

The auction continued after that. Nathan spent the rest of his money on a ham and cheese Hot Pocket, which he split with me, while Parker made the mistake of buying a mystery item. It turned out to be a container of leftovers Isaac found at the back of the fridge. Normally Parker was a black hole that would suck down anything edible within range, but even she gagged when the moldy baked beans were revealed. Only Zack and Benny had yet to purchase something as they were too afraid to spend their money and kept getting outbid.

"Next up," Isaac announced as he pulled a familiar can out from behind his back, "we have a strawberry lemonade Kickstart!"

"Hey!" Alex looked up from his pizza. "You can't auction that off. It's mine!"

I held up a finger. "Yeah, I second that."

Isaac sneered at me. "You don't need to take his side, Jackie. You're not dating anymore."

"I'm not taking anyone's side," I replied. "I don't think it's healthy to give six-year-olds that much caffeine." I'd read the back of a Kickstart before; it was basically poison in a can, and everyone would suffer if one of the terror twins turned into the Tasmanian Devil. Besides, I didn't think Katherine would consider a sixteen-ounce energy drink a proper meal.

"I doubt it's healthy for anyone to have that much caffeine," Nathan added.

"Don't worry so much," Alex told us. "I drink one of those a day, and I'm perfectly fine."

"Well, that explains why he's such a moron," Lee mumble. "All those energy drinks must have melted his brain."

Alex bristled and directed a dirty look at his cousin. "You know I can hear you, right?"

After bickering back and forth for a minute, we convinced Isaac to nix the Kickstart, which he replaced with another mystery item. Benny, who was elated to finally win something, burst into tears when Isaac revealed half an onion and a bottle of soy sauce.

Chaos quickly ensued: Alex's chair toppled over when he jumped up in outrage, Jack and Parker started booing, and Lee chucked his uneaten granola bar at his brother's face. I attempted to soothe Benny, but no matter what I said, he remained convinced that he wouldn't get to eat anything for lunch.

"I don't know how to calm him down," I said, turning to Nathan for help. Out of the corner of my eye, I noticed Cole. He was standing at the threshold of the kitchen, feet bare and hair damp from a shower. He surveyed the scene with shrewd eyes before crossing the room and squatting down in front of his little brother.

"Hey, bud." He rubbed his hands up and down Benny's arms. "What's wrong?"

"I-Isaac is running an auction," he answered, his chest hitching, "but everyone keeps winning all the good food!"

"Sounds like your cousin is being a punk," Cole said.

Isaac scoffed, but Cole didn't pay him any attention.

"You know what sounds really good right now?"

When Benny shook his head, Cole crooked a finger at him, gesturing for his brother to lean in, then held a hand up to the side of his mouth like he was about to share a secret. "McDonald's," he stage whispered.

That must have been the magic word, because Benny immediately stopped crying. "I spent all my money on the onion."

"Don't worry about that," Cole told him, his eyes soft. "This will be my treat. Just you, me, and Zack Attack. How does that sound?"

"Can I get a Happy Meal and a milkshake?"

Cole grinned and ruffled Benny's hair. "Chocolate or vanilla?"

six

I COULDN'T STOP THINKING ABOUT Cole, not after witnessing how sweet he'd been with Benny yesterday afternoon. It was
tiny moments like that that made me wish things could be different between us. I wanted to talk to someone about it, but I didn't
trust my friends not to dismiss my very legitimate concerns and push
me back into his arms for the sole reason being he was Cole Walter.
Then there was Nathan. He was usually an objective listener, but
I was convinced he was holding something back from me. Until I
knew what that was, I wasn't willing to reveal any more of my feelings
to him.

That only left Danny, and I winced. I hadn't spoken to him since
returning to Colorado, but if there was one person who knew Cole the
best, it was his twin.

There was little privacy in my new room, so I slipped out the back door and climbed the tree house ladder. Once I was ensconced in the greenery where I knew our conversation wouldn't be overheard, I pulled up Danny's contact and tapped the video call icon.

He answered on the first ring. "Hey, stranger. I was starting to wonder if I'd ever hear from you again."

It was dark wherever he was, but the sight of Danny's wry smile instantly took me home to lazy strolls in Central Park, lingering dinners at our favorite sushi bar, and lengthy discussions after each and every Broadway show we attended. It struck me as strange how I now associated one of the Walter boys with the city I grew up in.

"Sorry, things have been intense since I got back," I told him.

Danny shifted, then a light switched on. He was lying in bed in what used to be the guest room of my family's apartment. Now I thought of the room as his. "Have they? Or are you avoiding talking to me because of Cole?"

I sighed. "You heard what happened, then."

"His side of things." Danny propped himself up against the headboard. "I also spent the whole summer watching you struggle, so I know there's more to the story than what he said. And before you ask, I won't be telling you anything about our conversation."

"I'd never expect you to." When he lifted an eyebrow in that *go on* way of his I'd become accustomed to, I laughed and added, "Okay, maybe I was avoiding you a little."

"Why?" he asked. "I know we haven't known each other long, but you're family now, Jackie. You could break Cole's heart, and I'd still answer every one of your calls. Day or night, I swear. Even if I knew you needed help disposing of a body or something nefarious like that."

"Wow. There's a lot to unpack here, but most importantly—Cole said I broke his heart? Why would you be okay with that?"

"Ah, ah, ah! No questions about my conversation with Cole, remember? I said you *could* break his heart, not that you did, and I'd be okay with it because you're not a malicious person. You would never *want* to hurt him. Also, I'm insulted. Out of everything I said, is that really what you thought was most important?"

"No, actually, it was the part about helping me get rid of a body if I ever needed it," I teased. "I bet you'd be a great accomplice after watching all those crime shows."

Danny made a face. "Is that all I'm good for? How to Get Away with Murder 101?"

I pretended to think for a moment. "Well, you're also a phenomenal shoulder to cry on." And I had—many, many times. I'd have racked up a monstrous dry cleaning bill if Danny wore something other than cotton tees on the daily.

"Thanks, I guess," he said dryly.

My heart squeezed in my chest. God, I missed this—our open conversations, the easy back-and-forth, his subtle sense of humor. Now that we were more than a thousand miles apart, I selfishly wished I'd heeded Cole's plea to keep Danny from falling in love with New York. If I had, then maybe he'd be here with me right now.

"Hey, Danny?" I said in a quiet voice.

"Yeah?"

"You're my family too."

A soft smile stretched across his face. "Then I expect weekly updates."

"Phones work both ways," I said, shifting mine to my other hand. "If you were feeling neglected, why didn't you reach out?"

It was Danny's turn to look guilty. He grimaced and scratched the stubble on his chin. "I wanted to, but I was afraid you'd feel pressured considering what went down with Cole."

"Why would I feel pressured?"

"He's my *twin*," Danny replied as if that was the only explanation needed. "Wouldn't it be weird, getting a call from the brother of the guy you rejected? I didn't want you to think I was trying to change your mind."

Okay, so he had a point. But I also knew Danny wasn't like that. "Are you gonna try and change my mind?"

"No, never!"

I rolled my eyes. "Then don't be ridiculous."

"Right," he said, cheeks turning pink. "How are you holding up?"

Good freaking question. Living with Cole for the past two weeks hadn't been a walk in the park. While I understood he was upset, the cruel things that came out of his mouth when he wasn't ignoring my existence hurt. How could he say he wanted to help me through my grief in one moment, then call me stuck up and taunt me in the next? If he truly cared, wouldn't he want what was best for me?

"I'm...okay. Hanging in there."

Danny's eyes narrowed. "Cole is being a major jackass, isn't he?"

"A bit? He's mainly been giving me the silent treatment, but some of the stuff he's said to me...well, I get why he's angry—I let him kiss me, and then I did a one-eighty on him. Considering our history, it could be so much worse."

"That's no excuse." He sighed and carved a hand through his dark blond locks. "Just because he didn't get his way doesn't mean it's okay for him to throw a tantrum."

Funny, I'd had the *exact* same thought.

Thankfully, Danny was able to give me some advice on how to handle the situation. Not anything groundbreaking—be my usual self, call Cole out when he crossed the line, and eventually he'd calm down—but I appreciated it nonetheless. It gave me the courage to confess that even though he was being a jerk, a part of me still wanted to be with him. The gratitude I felt for Danny's nonreaction brought tears to my eyes.

"Of course you do," he said with a shrug, like we were talking about established facts—the sky is blue, water is wet, Jackie wants Cole. "That doesn't mean you made the wrong decision, though. If you're meant to be together, I'm sure it will all work out in the end. Until then, focus on you, but don't let him make you feel bad for putting yourself first."

"Thanks, Danny," I said, wiping away a single escaped tear, because that was exactly what I needed to hear. "Enough about Cole. How are you? How are rehearsals for *A Midsummer Night's Dream* going?"

If Cole wasn't pissed at me, he'd applaud what I was about to do with pride.

I glanced over my shoulder, but none of the teachers on cafeteria duty were paying me any attention, so I pushed open the door and stepped outside. Only seniors were allowed to leave school grounds during lunch, but so many students ignored this rule that I didn't feel bad about breaking it. The walk to LJD Custom Prints, a local screen print shop, would only take five minutes, which left me plenty of time to get back before my afternoon classes started.

While I walked, I reviewed my campaign checklist and was happy to discover I'd already tackled half of it. Yesterday morning, Erin approved the slogan I spent all weekend coming up with, along with the logo Katherine designed. The tasks I wasn't personally oversee-ing, like social media and the creation and distribution of posters and flyers, had been handed off to Erin's close friends. On top of that, I'd convinced Skylar to help me promote her candidacy to other student clubs after school, but only by agreeing to include the school newspa-per so he could flirt with Chase.

I felt confident about our chances of winning. Although Erin's opponent was the kind of guy who was friends with everyone, he was running solely on word of mouth and spent more time smoking behind the dumpsters with the likes of Isaac and Jet. But before I could turn my attention to drafting a victory speech, I wanted to get

T-shirts made for everyone helping with the campaign to wear on Friday. Strange as it sounded, I was grateful to Erin for confronting me during the first student council meeting. If she hadn't, I never would have been given the opportunity to be involved. Helping her with this showed me how much I'd missed planning and organizing and being involved in something.

As I neared the town square, a sign advertising a newly opened café caught my eye—CAFFEINATED PURSUIT. I froze in the middle of the sidewalk. What were the chances that this place was what I thought it was? Next to none, most likely, but I still crossed the street to check. When I pushed open the door and stepped inside, my breath caught in my throat.

I loved my parents, but they were routinely busy when I was growing up. Sebastian and Angeline Howard were shining examples of hard workers, which was what made the both of them so successful. The trade-off, however, was that they didn't have a lot of time to spend with Lucy and me. They made up for it by taking us to the board game café down the block from our apartment every Sunday afternoon. If their schedules got too hectic for our weekly ritual, like when Dad was away on a business trip or Mom was preparing for fashion week, Lucy and I would go by ourselves in order to feel close to them. The older we got, the more time we spent there just the two of us until, eventually, it became *our* hangout spot.

The layout of this café wasn't the same, but it reminded me so much of the Caffeinated Pursuit back home that my hands started to shake. It had the same industrial style—exposed brick and Edison pendant lights—made homey with an abundance of potted plants, handwoven rugs, and squishy armchairs, which I imagined to be just as comfy as the ones Lucy loved to camp out in. There was an entire wall dedicated to shelving all the board games customers were allowed to use, along with large wooden tables for groups to play at. The mosaic floor made up of game pieces was my favorite part—an unusual but creative amalgamation of Rummikub tiles, dominos, and colorful mandala stones.

What brought tears to my eyes, however, was when I spotted my go-to order on the menu—the Caramel Kerplunk, a dark mocha frappé doused in caramel. It was silly, crying over something as trivial as an iced coffee drink, but finding comfort in familiarity so far from home was shocking in the best way possible.

"Excuse me, miss?" The man behind the register—a silver fox type with glasses and a goatee—was watching me, his brow creased with a frown. "Are you okay? Is there anything you'd like to order?"

I laughed and wiped my eyes. "Don't worry about me. I'm being ridiculous. It's just, this café—it reminds me of another one that means a lot to me," I said, stepping up to the counter. "I'd love a grande Caramel Kerplunk. Whole milk, please."

"Oh, you're talking about our place on the Upper West Side?" He pointed to a picture on the wall of a storefront I could draw from memory. How many times had I sat on that exact orange bench while waiting for Lucy to arrive?

"Yes!" I said, bouncing on my toes. "I don't know if you've been there before, but I practically grew up in the booth next to the kitchen. I probably shouldn't admit this, but my sister carved our initials into the tabletop."

"So you know Jenny, then?" he asked as he poured ingredients into a blender.

Jennifer Clive, owner and operator of Caffeinated Pursuit, was a barista extraordinaire, game board enthusiast, and powerhouse of a woman distilled down into five energetic feet. Over the years, she'd become an important person in Lucy's and my life, a fun aunt who taught me how to play chess and always plied us with whatever pastries she had on hand.

"Since I was six," I confirmed. "She closed down the café and drove me to the hospital when my appendix burst."

The man paused, then looked up at me with wide, assessing eyes. "I'm Garrett, Jenny's cousin. I'm sorry if this is too personal, but are you Jackie?"

"You *know* who I am?"

Garrett's lips curved up. "You and your sister were Jenny's favorite regulars." The smile faded, and he added, "She was devastated when she heard of your family's passing."

Ignoring the stab of pain his comment caused, I racked my brain for memories of a handsome, older man related to Jenny but came up empty-handed. "I'm sorry if I don't remember, but have we met before?"

"No, but you know how Jenny is. She can talk anybody's ear off, so

I heard all about you." Garrett turned on the blender on, then raised his voice so I could hear him over the noise. "I was the head engineer for a NASCAR team for most of my career, so I spent my time on the road, not in the city."

That seemed like the kind of job Cole would find fascinating. Maybe I could pick Garrett's brain about it some other time, but I needed to hurry if I wanted to swing by the print shop and make it back to school before fifth period.

"Copper Valley is a long way from New York," I said once he finished blending. "How'd you end up out here, if you don't mind me asking?"

"This is where my wife grew up." Garrett poured my frappé into a to-go cup, then drenched the top with caramel and whipped cream. "She wanted to move home once I retired, and I needed something to keep me busy, so Jenny suggested a franchise. Small town life takes some getting used to, but you can't beat the scenery."

In that moment, the world had never seemed smaller.

"I understand that feeling exactly," I replied, pulling out my wallet as he slid my drink across the counter. "How much do I owe you?"

Garrett refused my outstretched card. "This one's on the house. It was nice to meet you, Jackie. You're welcome back anytime."

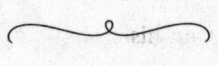

The truck was missing from the parking lot when school let out Wednesday afternoon. At first, I thought the boys left me behind, but then Alex turned up quickly, followed by Lee and Nathan. Isaac was the only no-show.

"Have you heard from your brother?" Alex asked Lee.

"No, why?"

Alex gestured as the empty spot where we parked this morning. "I thought it was obvious, but the truck is gone."

Lee frowned. "Did you give him the keys?"

Since Danny left and Cole had his own car, the keys to the truck were passed down to the next Walter in line, which was Isaac. For the past week and a half, however, Alex had been driving us to and from school because Katherine revoked Isaac's driving privileges as part of his punishment.

Alex flushed and scratched the back of his head. "Yeah, at lunch, but he said he'd be back before fifth period. I didn't think he'd dip and leave us stranded."

"Seriously, Alex?" Lee snapped. "You're such a moron."

"I'm sorry, okay? He wanted some Taco Bell. Who am I to stand between a man and his Crunchwrap Supreme?"

While Alex and Lee continued trading insults, Nathan pulled out his phone. "I'll call Cole. Tony's isn't far."

Ten minutes later, the Buick tore into the parking lot, windows rolled down and music blaring.

"Hurry up, kiddies," Cole said in way of greeting. He was wearing his work coveralls, and there was a smear of grease on his forehead. "I'm burning my break for this."

Not wanting to get stuck up front with him, I scrambled in behind

Nathan when he put down the passenger seat and climbed into the back. Once I buckled my seat belt and got comfortable, I looked up, caught Cole's gaze in the rearview mirror, and realized my mistake. While sitting in the back put distance between us, it also placed Cole at the forefront of my field of view. *As if he doesn't already live in the front of my mind rent-free.* The other boys settled into their seats as I silently cursed Isaac Walter.

Despite his demand that we be quick, Cole seemed at ease as he hummed along with the radio, his fingers drumming the rhythm of an unfamiliar song against the steering wheel. His sleeves were rolled up, and although I tried hard to resist, my gaze kept returning to his exposed forearms. He must have felt me watching, because his eyes found mine in the rearview mirror again.

My breath hitched. For the first time in over a week, Cole was regarding me with a look that could be considered something other than cold disdain. I wouldn't go as far as to call it a positive expression—guarded was a better description—but there was a smug quality to the way his lips twitched. The tension in my shoulders loosened in relief; I could handle an arrogant Cole Walter. It was his factory setting, something I'd been dealing with from day one.

The drive was quiet by Walter standards, and I couldn't tell if that was a factor in the building tension between Cole and myself as we stole glances at each other through the mirror.

From beside me, Alex cleared his throat. "Turn up the radio, will you?" he asked his older brother.

As soon as Cole complied, Alex nudged me in the side. His gaze moved from me to the driver's seat, his eyebrows raised in question.

"Everything okay?" His unspoken words were clear—*Everything okay with you two?*

I gave him a reassuring nod. While everything was definitely not okay, I couldn't talk about it now, not when Cole was trapped in the car with us. Alex looked like he wanted to push the topic further, so I pointedly avoided his gaze. Thankfully, he took the hint.

The car fell silent again save for the radio, and I spent the rest of the drive resisting the urge to look at Cole. He was watching me, I could tell. Would he be wearing that smug look, or had his expression turned sour again? I only allowed myself to glance up once the house came into view; if there was a scowl aimed in my direction, I could run away the moment we arrived. But Cole wasn't glaring. His expression wasn't smug either. I couldn't quite decipher the look behind his eyes, but it was enough to make my stomach flip.

"Jesus, let me outta here," Lee demanded before the Buick was even in park. "All this sexual tension is suffocating. Can't you two bang it out already? It's getting old."

My entire body froze as mortification washed over me. Everyone quickly vacated the car—Nathan even climbed over me in an effort to escape when I didn't move—until only Cole and I remained. After a long moment, Cole got out and pushed down his seat. Then, in a gesture I wasn't expecting, he held out his hand. Despite my embarrassment, I placed my hand in his and let him pull me from the car.

When I finally looked up to meet his gaze, he smiled at me. It was small and tight, but there was no arrogance behind it.

"Come on. I'll walk you to the door," he said, nodding toward the house as if I didn't know the way.

The gesture felt like a peace offering, so I fell into step beside him. Neither of us spoke, the silence highlighted by the crunch of gravel under our feet as we made our way up the front walk. I debated potential conversation topics in my head, but was too afraid of saying the wrong thing. In the end, I waited for Cole to speak first.

"How's being back at school?"

"Good," I said, letting out a relieved breath. This was safe subject matter, easy even. I might bore Cole to death, but I could talk about classes, homework, and studying until I was blue in the face. "I joined student council."

He snorted. "No surprise there, Little Miss Overachiever."

"Erin's running for president, and I'm her campaign manager," I shot back. *How's that for surprising?*

Cole fumbled with his car keys, which he'd been twirling around his finger. "You and *Erin*?"

I nodded. "The election is this Friday."

"Well," he said after a moment, "all I can say about that is I'm glad I graduated. You two are going to terrorize the school."

"Excuse me?" I stopped on the bottom porch step and turned to face him. Even with the added elevation, Cole was still taller than me.

"I bet there'll be a no-talking-in-the-hallway rule by the end of the month to prevent bullying and create an environment conducive to learning," Cole replied, his eyes sparkling as he held in his laughter. "Endless fundraisers, a new dress code, and heath initiatives or some other bullshit."

"Health initiatives?"

"Yeah, like mandatory Pilates or replacing soda in vending machines with vitamin water."

I wrinkled my nose. "You're ridiculous."

He pushed his bangs out of his face and grinned at me. "I have to get back to work. See you later, New York."

Momentarily dazzled by the sight of a real Cole Walter smile— eyes crinkled at the corners, singular dimple on display—I watched him walk away without offering a parting response. My brain didn't reboot until he was halfway down the walk, so I kept my mouth shut instead of calling out a dumb goodbye ten seconds too late.

The past five minutes felt like a vivid dream or a brief window into an alternate reality where Cole and I were still on speaking terms, because there was no way the two of us had a real conversation. It was hard enough to believe Cole had been a gentleman by helping me out of the car and walking me to the door, but him speaking actual English words to me? Impossible.

Hell, the two of us *bantered*.

It was wildly jarring after all his angry silence, but when I considered the past few days, I realized Cole's attitude toward me had shifted slightly. While not friendly by any means, he'd been significantly less cold when we ran into each other around the house, and he even passed me the ketchup bottle at dinner last night. The timing of Cole's change didn't go unnoticed; it lined up with the conversation I had with his twin too well to be a coincidence, but in the grand scheme of things, did it really matter if Danny was responsible? If it meant I could finally stop walking on eggshells around Cole, I was grateful.

seven

COLORADO AT NIGHT, ESPECIALLY ON the ranch, was nothing like New York City. Once daylight faded away, the near-total darkness that replaced it was all-encompassing. The lack of streetlamps, neon signs, and passing headlights used to unnerve me, but now I found it calming.

I was sitting on one of the porch chairs, knees tucked up against my chest and a blanket wrapped around my shoulders, when the front door inched open. A figure slipped out through the gap, then eased the door back into place as quietly as possible.

My eyes were adjusted to the dark, and even though I couldn't be sure, I had a pretty good idea of who was sneaking out based on their silhouette. "Lee?" I called quietly.

The figure jumped, and something heavy thunked against the floor. "Holy shit!" he hissed. "Jackie, is that you?"

"Yeah, hold on." I turned on my phone light and revealed Lee, whose skateboard was lying upside down at his feet, wheels spinning.

"Why are you sitting in the dark?" he asked, face scrunched into a scowl. "That's creepy as hell."

My mind flashed back to the night of the block party when Isaac scared me, and I had responded in a manner similar to Lee's. I was even sitting in the same chair Isaac had been. Thankfully, Lee hadn't hurled his skateboard at my head. "Just sitting. I couldn't sleep."

Today had been a strange combination of good and bad. Election results were announced during student council, and Erin won by a landslide. Everyone loved the shirts I ordered, and I was proud of our success, but I struggled to enjoy it once I remembered that today was my parents' wedding anniversary. I'd been too wrapped up in the campaign to remember, but when I got back from school and saw the date marked on my calendar, the air whooshed out of my lungs like I'd been sucker punched in the stomach. This week had been my best in ages, because for the first time since the start of summer, I was starting to feel like my old self again. That's what made grief so difficult to overcome; no matter how much effort you put in to moving on, it was always lurking below the surface, ready to pop up at any moment and leave you reeling.

The porch light flipped on before Lee could respond. He scooped up his board and disappeared around the corner in a blink. Shortly thereafter, Katherine stepped outside in her robe and slippers, looking sleep rumpled.

"Jackie?" she said through a yawn. "I heard a noise. Was that you?"

"Yeah, I dropped my phone." I held it up as evidence. "I'm sorry for waking you."

"No problem, honey. Is everything all right?"

"Just some trouble sleeping."

She frowned. When I moved in with Parker, Katherine was adamant about making sure I was comfortable with the change. Not only did she check in with me on a regular basis, but she made me promise to let her know if it ever became a problem. "It's not because of the new room arrangements, is it?" she asked for the hundredth time. "Because if—"

"No, I swear." Her frown deepened, so I offered her a watery smile and added, "It's my parents' anniversary today. I promise I'm fine. I'm thinking about them, that's all."

Katherine's expression softened. "Do you want to talk about it?"

If Lee wasn't hiding around the corner, I might have taken her up on her offer. Instead, I shook my head. Sometimes all you could do to alleviate the pain was sit with it, count your breaths through it, accept it. This felt like one of those times.

"Okay, but I'm always here to listen if you change your mind." She leaned down and pressed a gentle kiss to my forehead. "Good night, Jackie."

Once she was gone, Lee reappeared wearing a grateful look. "Thanks for covering for me."

"It was my fault you dropped your board, so it only seemed fair," I said as I fought off a yawn. Deciding it was time to head inside as well, I stood up and stretched. The blanket around my shoulders slipped off and pooled at me feet.

"Where are you sneaking off to anyway?" I asked, eyeing Lee. He was lingering by the front steps, repeatedly checking his phone for new texts.

"Skating with some friends," he answered with a rare smile.

I glanced at my own phone and was surprised by how late it was. "At one o'clock in the morning?"

His eyes glinted with a hint of mischief. "You know that new subdivision going up by the quarry? One of the houses has a giant in-ground pool that isn't filled in yet. It's the perfect skate bowl. Figured we should go at night considering the whole breaking and entering thing." Right as he finished his explanation, headlights appeared at the end of the driveway. "Well, that's my ride."

"Have fun," I said, bending over to scoop up my makeshift shawl. Goose bumps had spread down my arms in its absence.

Lee paused halfway down the steps and looked back at me. "Hey, Jackie?"

"Yeah?"

"I'm not sure if Isaac said anything already, but we're both grateful that you agreed to share a room with Parker. I want you to know that I—" He stopped and shook his head. "Never mind. I hope you get some sleep."

Parker's first rugby game was accompanied by a wave of crisp fall air—the first of the season. The leaves were beginning to show signs of changing color, spots of yellow and orange peeking through what only days before was a canopy of green. I'd originally pulled on a cozy sweater, but Cole was insistent that I wear one of his old crewnecks, the Walter name plastered over the back. I'd spent the entire drive over with my nose buried in the collar, breathing in his familiar scent.

The Walters never packed light, even for a rugby game. The two cars were stuffed full of camping chairs, a cooler of drinks, a stash of blankets, and a huge bag of sunflower seeds to snack on. We unloaded the cars, and I searched the field for any sign of Cole. As Parker's coach, he'd arrived early to run the girls through their pregame warm-ups.

I quickly located him at the edge of the field, his hands cupped around his mouth as he shouted something to his players while they went through a series of warm-up stretches. He looked over his shoulder a moment later, eyes finding mine in less than a heartbeat. My pulse stuttered in anticipation. Cole shouted one final command at the team and then jogged in our direction, the whistle around his neck swinging back and forth with the movement.

"Here, Jackie, you can use Parker's chair. It's a little small, but you should fit," said Katherine from beside me, pulling the dark blue camping chair from the back of the car.

I smiled at her in appreciation and secured the strap of its carrier over my shoulder. "What else can I grab?"

"Just a blanket in case you get cold." Katherine had barely finished her sentence before she was running after Zack and Benny, who'd spent the entire drive bickering about who would win a hot dog eating contest—Kirby or Shaggy Rogers. Now they were sprawled across the grass, struggling to pin the other to the ground.

"I can keep you warm." Cole's voice was barely a whisper in my ear, but it was enough to make me jump.

Heart racing, I turned to face him with a half-hearted glare. "You should ask Isaac what happens to people who startle me, Cole. Next time, my instincts might kick in, and I won't be held responsible for any damage done to your pretty face."

He smirked at this. "You think I'm pretty?"

I rolled my eyes. "You think you're pretty."

"I think you're pretty."

A flush crept down my neck at his words. "You should probably get back to coaching," I said, steering the conversation away from anything that would make me turn even more red.

Cole glanced back toward the field, but I could tell he was unconcerned with his coaching responsibilities. "How could I stay away when my name's on your back?" he asked, reaching over and tugging at the collar of the crewneck he'd lent to me.

I stumbled closer, which seemed to be his goal.

Leaning in, he said, "The real truth is that I'm here to congratulate you."

"For what?"

"The successful campaign you ran." He was too close in proximity for me to register anything other than the heat of his body mere inches from mine. Even with my eyes trained on his mouth, his words were a mystery to me. "Erin was lucky to have you on her side," he continued. "I bet no one stood a chance."

He released my collar just as I finally comprehended what he was saying, then sauntered off toward the field. I forced myself to breathe in slowly. Logic and reasoning had a bad habit of failing me when it came to Cole. And when he complimented me? It was like my brain turned into mush.

Huffing in annoyance at myself, both for reacting the way I did and allowing him to get that close, I turned around and rejoined the chaos of the Walter family. George and Katherine were trying to tame the youngest boys, though it was hard to keep the terror twins under control. As we got closer to the field, Benny let out a high-pitched scream loud enough to make me wince.

"Boys," Katherine scolded, struggling to pry Benny and Zack away from each other.

"I can't deal with them right now," Nathan muttered and took off farther down the field.

I made eye contact with Lee, who then glanced at Isaac. It seemed we were all in agreement with Nathan—the boys were way too obnoxious to be around, and there was plenty of chair space in the other direction. I waved goodbye to Katherine, who gave me an understanding nod, and we followed after Nathan.

The four of us claimed a sideline spot and began setting up our chairs. Lee was to the left of me, Nathan to the right, and Isaac on the other side of his brother.

"You could always join the coaches, Jackie. I'm sure Cole could make some room for you on his lap," Isaac said with an evil smirk. "Wouldn't be the first time, would it?"

I crossed my arms over my chest and let out a long sigh. "I have no idea what you're talking about."

Lee snorted in laughter. "Oh, come on. You two were practically sharing breath a minute ago."

I bit down on my lip to stop myself from snapping and turned to Nathan, hoping for some sort of support. He was staring straight ahead, his eyes fixed on the open field before us.

"Can you tell them they're being assholes? They never listen to me."

Nathan's face pinched in what looked like irritation, and the expression he sent my way was unexpected. "Tell them yourself," he snapped.

Nathan proceeded to turn away and pull out his phone. From the hard look on his face, our conversation was over. His attitude caught me off guard. Normally, Nathan was the best person to turn to for support, but over the course of the past week, he'd grown more and more tetchy. Up until this point, his ill temper had never been aimed at me. I wanted to help fix whatever was bothering him, but whenever I tried to speak to him about it, he shut me down or changed the subject.

With one Walter ignoring me and the others determined to tease me, I fixed my focus on the game. The girls were lined up for the kickoff, each team spread across the side of the field they'd be defending. Parker and Cole had told me all about rugby, and though some of it was comprehensible, the rules seemed incredibly confusing. The game began when the whistle blew. Soon after, a ball was kicked toward Parker's team, and the two sides were clashing together.

Every so often, my eyes would settle on Cole as he rushed up and down the sidelines, shouting commands at the players and cheering when they did well. It didn't help that he was glancing back at me just as much as I was watching him. I wanted to smack the satisfied look he wore off his face every time he turned around and noticed me staring.

To my right, Lee and Isaac were making commentary on the game. Both of them together created a never-ending stream of noise I'd learned to block out, at least for the most part.

Isaac let out a low whistle, finally drawing my attention away from Cole. "Dude, did you see Parker take out number seven? I think I'm a little scared of her," he admitted.

Lee agreed with his brother and mentioned something about a rule violation, but I was distracted once again by Cole. He was yelling out a play, his hands waving up and down as he tried to get the girls' attention. On the opposite side of the field, the ball went out of bounds. Cole turned around and caught my gaze yet again.

"Twenty bucks Cole gets himself kicked out for undressing Jackie with his eyes from across the field," Isaac joked. "It's a little inappropriate for a kids' game, don't you think?"

I ground my teeth together in frustration and shoved to my feet. Isaac and Lee cackled to each other as I stalked off in the other direction, more than willing to deal with the younger Walters if it meant I didn't have to listen to their unrelenting teasing.

Sunday morning came with two chore options: help George muck out the horse stalls or clean up fallen fruit from the cluster of crab apple trees that lined the side yard. Since moving to Colorado, I had learned that lots of hard work went in to running a ranch, which included tasks that were anything but pleasant. The worst, in my opinion, was stall cleanup duty, so the choice was an easy one to make.

Between me, Alex, and Nathan, we had everything picked up within an hour. Katherine was in cleaning mode, so instead of heading inside and risking being given more work, the three of us decided to hang out in the shade beneath the tree house.

"I'll be right back," Alex said when Nathan flopped onto the grass and opened his sudoku app. He jogged off in the direction of the shed.

While he was gone, I ventured up the ladder in search of reading material—Alex left his books everywhere—and found a beat-up copy of *The Count of Monte Cristo*. By the time I climbed back down, Alex had returned with a plastic T-ball bat and was trying to convince Nathan to pitch for him.

"Come on, Nate. Don't you want to spend some quality time with your favorite brother?"

Nathan snorted. "What makes you think you're even in my top three?"

"How about this?" Alex replied, ignoring the insult. "Play with me for fifteen minutes, and in return, I'll pick up my laundry and clear the dirty dishes off my desk?"

"Okay, fine," Nathan agreed, "but if this turns into a mess like last time, then I'm out."

I didn't understand what he meant until Nathan selected the least rotten apple from the wheelbarrow and pitched it to Alex. The bat connected, and I watched in amusement as the apple soared over the fence and into the field where it wouldn't ruin the lawn mower. The second hit, however, exploded on impact and showered the lawn in mushy chucks of fruit.

A screen door slammed. "What do you think you're *doing*?"

My heart stopped at the sound of Katherine's enraged voice. For a split second, I thought she was yelling at us, but then I spotted Isaac storming down the porch steps, fists clenched and eyes blazing. An old Camaro was rumbling up the driveway with Jet behind the wheel.

"Getting the hell outta here and away from you," Isaac shouted over his shoulder.

"Isaac, if you don't come back here right this second—"

"Then what?" he roared, swinging back around to glare at his aunt. "What are you going to do, *Katherine*?"

I'd never heard any of the Walter kids refer to Katherine by her first name, especially with such venom, and I sucked in a sharp breath. Genuine hurt flickered across her face before she managed to master her expression.

"Maybe I should call your father."

A single, humorless bark of laughter escaped his throat. "Go ahead. It's not like he can do anything all the way from Germany."

Without waiting for a response, he yanked open the car door, flung himself into the passenger seat, and immediately cranked up the radio. Heavy metal music blared out from the speakers, effectively cutting off the conversation. Jet threw the Camaro in reverse, and the air freshener dangling from the rearview mirror swung wildly. As they pulled out of the driveway, Isaac stuck his arm out the window and gave his aunt the finger.

Despite the huge sign of disrespect, she stayed rooted on the porch until they disappeared from view.

Once she returned to the house, Alex, Nathan, and I stared at one another in shock. None of us knew what to say.

"Maybe it's just a phase?" Alex said, breaking the silence. We all laughed at the bad joke but quickly grew quiet again.

"Do either of you know what's been up with him?" I finally asked.

Alex sighed, dropped the bat, and flopped down next to me. "I'm not positive, but I think it has something to do with his dad."

"Uncle Pete came for a visit at the start of summer," Nathan added as he took a seat on my other side. "Isaac has been like *that* ever since he left."

I frowned. "Isaac wasn't happy to see him?" I didn't know much about Isaac and Lee's parents, only that their mother was out of the picture and Peter Walter, George's younger brother, was a lieutenant colonel in the military who was stationed overseas. They rarely got to see their father, so I'd have assumed him visiting would be the highlight of their summer.

"That's the strange part," Alex answered. "He'll never admit it, but I know Isaac kept a calendar counting down the days until his dad's leave. Something must have gone down, but I didn't ask what. He and Lee get cagey about personal stuff."

We chatted about Isaac for another minute or so, trying to solve the mystery, but quickly exhausted the subject. Alex started talking to Nathan about baseball stats, so I opened the book I'd grabbed and started reading. When I checked back a few minutes later, the conversation had shifted.

"…it's a great song," Alex was saying.

"Oh!" I tossed the paperback aside and focused on Nathan with eager eyes. "Have you written something new? I'd love to hear it." If there was one thing I hated about Alex and Kim's relationship, it was that Nathan felt the need to hide away in the loft. He spent so much time out there that I never heard his music drifting through the house anymore.

Nathan picked at a loose thread on his shirt. "Sorry, no."

"Oh." I brushed my fingers against my throat and glanced at Alex, but he looked as nonplussed by his brother's answer as I felt. "Um, is that a *no*, you haven't written anything new, or a *no*, I can't hear it?"

"I'm working on something, but it's not ready yet," Nathan said as his phone buzzed with an incoming text. He read the message, picked himself up, and brushed grass off his hands and knees. "I'll see you guys later? I've got something I need to take care of."

Alex frowned as he watched him go. "Is it just me, or was that weird?"

"Definitely weird," I agreed. Concerning too. The missed morning runs, prickly attitude, and lack of new music all added up to something not being right.

"Any idea what's going on there?"

I fixed Alex with a disbelieving look. "If anyone should know, it's you. You're the one who shares a room with him." Maybe Lee was right about all those Kickstarts melting his brain.

"Right," Alex said, rubbing the back of his neck. "I suppose I've been a little distracted by Kim."

"A little?" I asked, then shook my head when he shot me a sheepish smile. If I needed further proof that Alex and I truly didn't belong together, this was it—he'd never been so wrapped up in me that the world around him went unnoticed. "Does she make you happy?"

The answer was obvious, but I wanted to hear it from him.

"The happiest."

"Good," I said with a decisive nod. "I'm glad."

"So...um...." Alex grimaced as if he didn't like what he was about to say next. "How are things with Cole?"

Nope. I was so not going there. I'd rather throw myself down a never-ending staircase than talk to Alex about my relationship with his older brother. "Do you honestly want to hear about that?"

Alex blanched. "I'd rather eat rusty nails."

Perfect. We were on similar pages, then. "That's what I thought."

eight

MY PHONE VIBRATED AGAINST THE bathroom counter just
as I turned off the shower. After wrapping a towel around myself, I
checked my messages.

SKYLAR

> Scored drinks at Starbucks.
> Be there in fifteen.

I frowned. Why would he be—oh shit!

Somehow, I completely forgot about the student council meeting
Erin scheduled for before class. Knowing that the Walters would never
willingly leave for school early, Skylar had offered to pick me up so we
could attend together, but there was no way I'd be ready in time. Still
dripping wet, I grabbed my tote and rushed up the stairs toward my
room.

Maybe I should braid my hair instead of drying it? I thought as I threw open the door. I stepped inside and—

My mind short-circuited, and I couldn't process what I was seeing: Cole lying on his back in my old bed, bare-skinned and cheeks flushed, the sheet riding dangerously low on his waist and his hand moving beneath the thin material.

Our eyes met, and his widened in shock as he scrambled to pull up the sheets. "What the—"

"Oh shit, I'm so sorry," I exclaimed, slapping a hand over my eyes.

"Morning, Jackie," Cole said, his tone shifting to light and casual, like I hadn't just walked in on him jerking off.

"This is all Erin's fault!" I blurted. "She scheduled a student council meeting before homeroom, but I forgot to change my alarm, so now I'm running behind—"

"Jackie."

"—and I still need to pick out something to wear and dry my hair and pack my bag, so I wasn't thinking, and I rushed in here on autopilot, and now—"

"*Jackie!*"

I stopped word vomiting and peeked at Cole. His lips were clamped together as he tried not to laugh.

"It's all good, okay?"

"I—what?"

"Don't give yourself a conniption. It's… not that big of a deal,"

Cole told me. "But, um, if you could close the door on the way out, that would be appreciated."

I blinked at him, his words not registering.

"Unless you'd rather stay and…" He trailed off, and his hand resumed moving underneath the sheet.

The involuntary noise that escaped the back of my throat was so embarrassing, I knew I'd agonize over it for hours to come. Cole snickered, and without another word, I shot out of the room and slammed the door behind me.

I moved through the rest of my morning in a mortified daze. Not even the latte Skylar handed me when I climbed into his Jeep helped. The agenda at the meeting revolved around homecoming, but I was too distracted to pay much attention. As I walked to homeroom, the only thing I remembered was that Chase Kennedy asked about the plan for music—apparently the DJ who performed at last year's spring fling sucked—and Erin mentioned hiring the block party battle of the bands winner. I didn't care either way. All I could think about was how I would never be able to face Cole again.

I spent my lunch period hiding in the library. My essay for AP English Lit was due at the end of the week, and I figured I could avoid thinking about the *incident* if I buried myself in work. After taking a seat at my favorite study nook, I turned on my laptop, took out my copy of *Jane*

Eyre, and opened my notes. I was finishing up my opening paragraph when I heard his name.

"Cole still works there? I thought he got into CU?"

I froze midword, fingers hovering over my keyboard.

"Yeah, on a football *scholarship*," a second person replied. "I bet he couldn't afford to go after losing it."

The reason I loved this particular nook? It was tucked behind the reference section nobody ever used, which meant hardly anyone knew it was here. As quietly as possible, I slid off my chair and crept to the end of the row. When I peeked around the shelf, I spotted two girls from my U.S. history class—a blond built like she played volleyball and a curly-haired brunette with vintage rhinestone glasses whose name I was fairly confident was Savannah. They were sitting at one of the study tables, their heads bent together as they gossiped.

"That makes sense," said Savannah as she slowly tore a piece of notebook paper into tiny pieces. "The Walters have a million kids. I bet they can't afford to send any of them to college."

"Didn't they take in that Jackie girl, though?" her friend replied. "I heard she's loaded."

Ha! As if Cole, let alone Katherine and George, would let me pay for anything. No matter how desperately they needed the money, the Walters would never take a single penny from me. They were too proud.

"I think so, but she used to date Alex, and you know how much he and Cole loathe each other."

The blond sniffed. "She probably didn't want to help him."

I clamped a hand over my mouth to muffle my snort of laughter. If the implication wasn't so ridiculous, I would have been offended.

"Is it bad that I don't really care?" Savannah asked. "Cole always thought he was better than everyone else. It's about time life brought him down a peg or two. Besides, I love having something pretty to look at when I get my oil changed."

My amusement evaporated. No doubt about it, Cole was cocky. But he wasn't the kind of person to maliciously look down on other people. Sure, he liked to tease, but it was always lighthearted. Clearly, these girls didn't know him like I did. It was a startling thing, suddenly feeling defensive of him, and I considered marching out from behind the bookshelf to give them a piece of my mind.

"Jackie, there you are!" someone said before I did something stupid.

I yelped and jerked my head back. Riley was standing beside me, a broad grin on her face.

"Don't sneak up on people like that," I said, swatting her arm. "You scared the crap out of me."

"Sorry," she replied, not looking the least bit apologetic as she bounced from foot to foot. "I've been searching everywhere for you! You'll never guess what just happened. Alex's friend Marcus asked me to go to the movies with him tonight. We're partners in physics, so I've been flirting with him all week, but I didn't think it would go anywhere."

"The guy from his *GoG* guild?" I'd only met him once before at the Walter end-of-the-school-year party, but Marcus gave me the creeps.

"What? Oh no. You're thinking of Malcolm. They're two totally different people. Marcus and Alex are on the baseball team together."

"I've never met him, but if you're happy, then so am I." Maybe if she had a boyfriend, Riley would be too distracted to bug me about Cole.

Riley gave a contented sigh. "*Beyond* happy. I'm hoping he'll ask me to homecoming if tonight goes well. Do you think I could raid your closet after school? I need to find the perfect outfit."

"Well, I have a lot of homework…"

"Pretty please?" She pouted her lips. "My mom gave me a gift card for that new café you like. If you let me come over, I can pay you in frozen caramel goodness."

"Okay, deal."

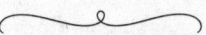

"Huh, that's strange," I said, my eyes narrowing as Riley pulled up alongside the truck and parked her car.

"What's strange?"

I pointed out the windshield to where Lee was rocking back and forth on the porch swing, a textbook in hand. "*That.*"

"Um, okay." Riley gave me a strange look before flipping down the sun visor to access the mirror. "Are you guys not allowed on the swing or something? My mom is weird about stuff like that too. There's this fancy sofa in our sitting room that we can't use because it's imported from Europe."

"No," I said, shaking my head. "He's pretending to study."

"What makes you think he's pretending?" she asked as she uncapped a tube of lip gloss, then applied a thick coat.

"Because that's a chemistry textbook."

"So?"

"Lee's a junior." I unclipped my seat belt and grabbed one of the straps on my backpack, which was tucked between my feet. "We all have physics."

"Oh," Riley said. "Maybe he's really into science?"

That was highly unlikely. From what I observed, Lee slacked off in school. Not to the same extent Alex did, but he preferred to spend his time skating over studying and doing homework. I couldn't recall a single instance where I'd seen him touch a book before today. What I did notice, however, was that Lee kept glancing up from his reading material, and of all the spots to sit on the front porch, the one he had picked had the best view of the driveway. It looked like he was waiting for something.

"Come on." I opened the car door and hefted my backpack onto my shoulder as I stepped out. "Let's go talk to him."

"Can I help you ladies with something?" Lee asked when I approached him.

"You can tell us what you're up to," I replied.

The corner of his mouth quirked. "No can do, Jackie. But if I were you, I'd use the back door."

"Is there a reason why?"

"Trust me," he said. "You'll be sorry if you don't."

Well, that was ominous. There was a point in time when I'd have scoffed at Lee's warning and done the opposite, not trusting a single word he spoke, but now I decided to take his advice. After giving him a nod of thanks, I directed Riley around the side of the house. Usually you could find at least one Walter in the backyard at this time of day—playing on the swing set, swimming in the pool, roughhousing on the lawn—but there was nobody in sight, and when I pushed open the sliding glass door and stepped into the kitchen, the room was empty.

The house was entirely too quiet.

"What do you think is going on?" Riley asked, her voice low.

"Definitely some type of shenanigans," I whispered back. "Why don't you go upstairs and start looking for an outfit while I investigate."

After reminding Riley I had a new room—left at the top of the stairs, second door on the right—I grabbed a bag of cheese puffs from the pantry and went in search of whatever mischief was afoot. As I passed by the formal dining room, which was more often used as a dumping ground and place to do homework, I spotted Jordan crouching beside the sideboard, his camera focused on the front door. A water balloon swollen to the size of a soccer ball was duct-taped directly above the transom.

I grinned, knowing I'd been right.

"Nice twist on the classic water-bucket-over-the-door trick," I said, stooping next to him so I didn't give away his hiding spot. "Who are we pranking?"

"Isaac." He spat his cousin's name as if it were a curse word. "He made Parker cry yesterday. I don't think she's done that since she was a baby. We want revenge."

For God's sake, Isaac, I thought. *Is there anyone you aren't willing to piss off?*

"What did he do this—"

A familiar crackling noise cut me off. "Lee for Parker. Come in, Parker."

"Go for Lee," Parker responded, and that was when I noticed the walkie-talkie clipped to Jordan's belt loop. It was exactly like the one Nathan kept out in the loft.

"What's your twenty?" Lee asked.

"In position. Over."

"The leather jacket jackass has landed," he told her. "I repeat, the leather jacket jackass has landed."

"Roger that."

Everything was still for a single moment, then the front door swung open. Parker, who must have been hiding around the corner, jumped out and aimed her slingshot at the bulging balloon. It broke just as Alex crossed the threshold, only it wasn't water inside. A thick, cream-colored goo hit his head and splattered across the entryway. The surprise attack made Alex freeze on the spot, and Katherine slammed into his back when she stepped in behind him.

Jordan and I didn't hang around for the fallout, both of us choosing to scramble up the stairs where we would hopefully be safe from blame, but I could hear Katherine yelling about messes and wasted money. Apparently, the mysterious substance was tapioca pudding, which was supposed to be the team snack following Parker's next rugby game.

"What the hell, Lee?" Jordan hissed into the walkie-talkie. "We told you the target was Isaac, not Alex."

Another crackle. "You didn't actually think I'd help you prank him, did you? Brother trumps cousin every time. Over and out, losers."

Swearing under his breath, Jordan dropped the device on the steps and disappeared into his room.

I scooped it up and pressed the talk button. "Lee, you still there?"

"Who's this?" he asked.

"Jackie. Thanks for the heads-up."

"No problem," he replied. "I figured I owe you for the other night."

By the time I joined Riley in my room, she'd finished going through my clothes. There were three potential outfits laid out on my bed, but once she tried them on, she decided they weren't what she was looking for. Some of my dressier tops were packed away, so with a sigh, I resigned myself to returning to the art studio, even though the prospect made me blush. Cole didn't get off work until dinnertime, so at least he wouldn't be there.

When I stepped inside the room, I kept my eyes off the bed and beelined for the closet, Riley trailing along behind me, and then quickly busied myself with searching for the right storage tub.

"Ooh, what's this?" Riley held up a garment bag.

A knot formed in the back of my throat. "My sister's prom dress," I told her. My mom designed it for Lucy herself, and I brought it back from New York on the off chance I was invited to a dance.

Riley carefully eased the zipper open and gasped. "Oh my God! Jackie, this is stunning. You have to wear it to homecoming. I won't take no for an answer."

Later that night, Cole and I got stuck on dinner cleanup duty. As everyone brought their dishes over to the sink, I lingered on the edge of the kitchen and tried not to choke on the dread working its way up my throat. I hadn't spoken to Cole since the mortifying moment I walked in on him, and I didn't think I'd find the courage to do so anytime soon.

By contrast, Cole seemed perfectly at ease, joking with Jordan as he scraped the remainder of his plate off into the trash. Once the room emptied, he surveyed the task at hand—there were dishes to wash, leftovers to put away, and counters to wipe down—before nodding to himself and cranking up the volume on the ancient stereo system mounted beneath the spice cabinet.

"You don't mind, do you?" he asked after the fact. Katherine's dinner music was notorious, but not because she had bad taste. Back in the early 2000s, she burned a CD containing all the usual suspects, like Ella Fitzgerald, Louis Armstrong, and Frank Sinatra, but at some point in the last decade, the disk drive broke. To this day, the CD was still stuck inside, making it the kitchen's one and only soundtrack.

I shook my head. My mom loved jazz, so listening to Katherine's dinner music reminded me of her.

"Cool," he said, pushing up his sleeves. "I'll wash, you dry?"

That was doable, so I offered him a nod, and we got to work. I did my best to focus on the task at hand and quickly realized that drying dishes required little concentration. That left me with plenty of room to overthink. With Cole beside me, it was impossible not to relive the humiliating moment when I interrupted his alone time. I kept my head down and eyes trained on the plate in my hands, the memory embarrassing enough to heat my cheeks. Even worse, Cole was acting completely normal. He swayed back and forth as he sang along to the music, his shoulder brushing lightly against my own. The brief contact was enough to make my thoughts spiral further, and I found myself clutching each dish in a death grip.

Cole's singing grew increasingly louder. Soon, his vocals were so theatrical, I couldn't resist glancing over at him. Soapy water slid down the spatula he was using as a makeshift microphone, and it took me several long seconds to register that Cole was serenading me with a kitchen utensil. I watched dumbfounded, unable to form an adequate response as he reached into the sink and splashed me. When the water hit my face, I let out a startled gasp, which quickly turned into an open-mouthed smile. Cole seemed pleased with this reaction, and the next moment, he was pulling me away from the sink and into a sporadic dance, his wet hands clutching mine as he swept us across the kitchen.

"You're in a good mood tonight," I said, surprised at the ease with which my words came. Somehow, he'd managed to chase away my panic with his terrible singing and a few swift moves.

Cole was looking down at me as we swayed to the music, his intense expression bathing me in warmth. My earlier feelings of embarrassment quickly faded into a different sort of uneasy, one with the power to make my insides flutter.

He pulled me closer and wrapped his arms around my waist. "I had a great day," he said into my ear.

I tried to steady my breathing as his scent washed over me. "Will you tell me about it?"

"A new customer came into the shop today looking for an engine rebuild," he explained. "He's a dirt track racer. Not famous or anything, but he competes in all the local races. I guess his mechanic quit out of the blue, so he's hired me to do it."

"I take it you're excited?"

"Yeah, I miss working on my car. Normally, all I do at Tony's is change oil or replace brake pads."

Though I couldn't see his face, I could tell Cole was smiling.

"So what exactly does an engine rebuild entail?" I asked.

I rested my head against Cole's chest as he dove into the intricacies of rebuilding an engine. Though it was nearly impossible for me to follow along, the intensity of his words told me everything I needed to know. Working on cars made him happy, and the passion in his voice continued to ease the tension in my body. It was no surprise when a fear that had been plaguing me for weeks—could we really just be friends?—flickered to awareness inside me again. My head knew I'd made the logical decision, but every other part of me wanted Cole Walter. Although I told myself it was for the best, I couldn't ignore how I felt when I was around him.

As we continued to sway around the kitchen, I imagined us in the gym, me in my sister's dress and Cole in a white dress shirt with the first few buttons undone. He looked effortlessly handsome, as usual, his hair messy and his eyes bright. Just the thought of us attending homecoming together filled me with anticipation, though I reminded myself that I'd already ensured it wouldn't happen. The realization that I'd messed up rushed over me, darkening the pretty picture of us I was painting in my head.

The sound of Alex's voice pulled me out of the daydream.

"Jackie?" he said, appearing in kitchen doorway, a book clutched in his hand. "Can you help me with the problem set for physics? I don't think I'm doing this right."

It took a moment for me to come back to my senses. Cole and I glanced at each other, and I felt an undeniable pull to move closer to him despite Alex standing only feet away. A long silence filled the room.

Eventually, Cole spoke, his voice teasing. "Don't worry, New York. I can finish the dishes on my own." He released my hand and stepped back. "Alex needs as much help as he can get."

I nodded in agreement, though the last thing I wanted to do was walk away from Cole, even if it meant getting out of our chore. Taking a deep breath, I gave him a goodbye smile and followed after Alex. I could feel Cole's gaze heavy on my back and was unable to resist glancing over my shoulder one last time. Our eyes met immediately, my heart twisting at the longing expression on his face. I allowed myself a brief moment to feel that same longing before pushing it down and turning away.

All anyone could talk about for the next week was homecoming: who asked whom, what their dress looked like or how they planned to do their hair, where dinner reservations were made, and which after-party they wanted to attend. Even the Walters were making plans for Saturday night. Alex and Kim were obviously going together, and Nathan with a group of friends. Lee, the grumpiest grump in the world, had somehow secured a date. The only person who wouldn't be there was Isaac; his grounding had been extended after flipping Katherine off.

I found the constant, single-minded focus exhausting, especially since my friends kept pestering me to come. They all had someone to go with, and I didn't want to be a third wheel. Heather offered to set me up with her cousin, but as thoughtful as her suggestion was, there was only one boy I could picture wearing Lucy's dress for. I wanted to go with Cole, but I couldn't bring myself to ask him. To do so now wouldn't be fair. Not when I'd pushed him away, again and again and again. It was a hard pill to swallow, realizing that I started running from him the moment we met. Of course, that didn't stop me from remembering how it felt to be held in his arms as he spun me around the kitchen. These indulgent recollections led to a willfully stupid idea—that I could purge the image of us together from my head if I tried on Lucy's dress.

After school, I went straight to the art studio. It was strange, knocking on what used to be my bedroom door, but I learned my lesson about entering rooms unannounced the hard way. *Twice.*

"Yeah?" came a groggy reply.

I froze, not expecting an answer. Cole always worked on Thursdays, so why the heck was he home? I'd thought I could sneak in, grab the garment bag, and slip out, leaving him none the wiser. Plan ruined, I momentarily considered retreating without a word, but the springs in the mattress suddenly groaned, and two seconds later, Cole was answering the door as he tugged a shirt over his head. It was dark inside, but light from the hall flooded the room, highlighting the tangled bedding.

"Hey," he said through a yawn. The hair at the back of his head was sticking up in different directions, and he combed his fingers through the mess, trying to smooth it down.

My stomach swooped at the sight of him looking so disheveled. In that moment, I wanted to shove Cole back on the bed and press my body against his.

"Sorry," I said, my cheeks heating. "I didn't mean to wake you, but can I grab something out of the closet?"

He held out a hand in welcome and moved aside. "Be my guest."

Not wanting him to notice the longing look on my face, I attempted to keep my gaze downcast as I shuffled inside, but my eyes kept flitting up to him. When the corner of his mouth twitched, I let my breath out in a huff. "What?"

"I appreciate your tactic, that's all."

"Tactic?" I echoed. "What are you talking about?"

"No need to play coy, Jackie." He stepped closer to me and gently tugged on the curl framing my face. I fought off a shiver when he brushed it behind my ear. "You purposely left some of your clothes behind to have a reason to visit me."

I scowled and slapped his hand away. "I don't need a reason, Cole. I literally see you every day."

"Yet here you are, making excuses," he teased, "Am I really that irresistible?"

"No, you're obnoxious."

Fed up with the conversation, I marched over to the closet and flipped on the light. Between my and Cole's belongings, the moderate-size walk-in was packed to capacity. I had to shuffle around a stack of moving boxes and step over an overflowing laundry basket to reach the back.

Cole trailed in behind me. "What's in the bag?" he asked when I extracted it from the rack where it was hanging.

"One of Lucy's dresses."

His face went blank. "For homecoming."

"I don't think I'll go to the dance, but I figured"—I swallowed the lump in my throat—"my mom made this. I should try it on at least once." I draped the garment bag over my shoulder. "I'll be back later to put it away."

He reached out to stop me. "No. I can wait outside while you change."

Before I could protest, Cole stepped into the hall and closed the door. It would take just as much time to extract myself from his insistence as it would to get dressed here, so I unzipped the garment bag, shimmied out of my clothes, and pulled the backless a-line on.

Even with the light from the closet, the bedroom was dark, so I turned on the desk lamp before moving over to the mirror. I stared at my feet for a few seconds—trying on Lucy's clothes always made me feel like a kid playing dress-up—before finally finding enough courage to look at myself.

The air froze in my lungs. Everyone always told me how much Lucy and I looked alike, but I'd never believed them until this exact moment; the girl—no, the young woman—gazing back at me was the spitting image of my sister. All I could do was stare, tears prickling in my eyes as I momentarily pretended there was no mirror and Lucy was standing here in front of me.

A knock on the door shattered the fantasy. "Jackie? Everything okay?"

My lips parted, but no sound came out. There were so many feelings coursing through me—surprise, joy, wistfulness, anguish—that I turned away from the mirror before they could overwhelm me and opened the door.

Cole was smirking like he planned on saying something teasing at my expense, but when he saw me, the mirth melted away, and his chest hitched. He was quiet for a moment before he swallowed and cleared his throat.

"You should go to the dance," he said, his voice low and gravelly. The sound made my stomach flip.

"I don't have someone to go with."

Eyes flashing, he stepped into my personal space and grasped my upper arm, but his grip was gentle. "That's *bullshit*, and you know it."

Goose bumps swept across my skin, emanating from his touch. "Is that... I mean, are you asking me?"

"That depends," he said carefully. "Are you saying yes?"

We were standing so close, I could feel the warmth of his breath on my face.

"I—yeah," I whispered. "I think I am."

"Then I'll be your someone, Jackie."

nine

I'D NEVER EXPERIENCED HIGH SCHOOL homecoming before.

Attending an all-girls boarding school made it difficult to meet guys, and even though our formals were held in conjunction with St. Clement's School, our male counterpart, I was too timid to go by myself. My confidence had grown since moving to Colorado, but this was still my first dance with a boy, and I fiddled with my mom's necklace as Cole pulled the Buick into the parking lot. He hopped out, skirted around the front of the car, and opened my door before I could even unbuckle my seat belt. When he smiled down at me, eyes warm and lips curled in that charmingly reprehensible way of his, my heart launched itself into my throat. Deep down, I knew I wasn't nervous because I was here with any old boy: it was because I was here with *him*.

"Here," he said, offering me his hand. "The pavement's uneven, and those heels look dangerous."

"What a gentleman," I replied as he helped me from the car. "Who knew?"

Teasing Cole helped me focus on something other than how my pulse was fluttering a mile a minute. He was one of those photogenic, effortlessly beautiful people, even when he wore grungy jeans and faded T-shirts. So tonight, when he styled his hair and put on a suit with a tie that matched his eyes? He was dazzling.

Cole clutched his chest, eyes wide with false affront. "Goddess, you wound me! Is my chivalry only worthy of poisoned words? A mortal dagger disguised as a compliment?"

I barely managed to keep myself from doubling over with laughter, because what in the terrible Regency romance was *that*? Maybe I wasn't the only one with nerves. "Are you feeling okay?" I asked as I tried to press the back of my hand to his forehead. "I think that's the cheesiest, most dramatic thing I've ever heard come out of your mouth."

"Damn, Jackie," he said, leaning out of reach. "When did you get so mean?"

"Not long after moving to Colorado," I quipped. "There are so many unsavory characters here that I quickly learned to toughen up. Besides, I'm pretty sure you like it."

The corners of his mouth turned up at the implication.

Even from the back of the parking lot, I could feel the *thump thump thump* of bass from inside the school gymnasium. It matched the rhythm of my racing heart as Cole studied me, his eyes flitting back and forth across my face. For a brief instant, I thought he would lean down and kiss me, but the slam of a car door from a few stalls over shattered the moment.

"Yo, Walter!" called a guy from Isaac's class I vaguely recognized. Ethan something? "Good to see you, man. Whatcha doing here?"

Cole held my gaze and smirked. "Jackie asked me to go to the dance with her," he said, then looked up to address Possibly Ethan as he tucked me into his side. My cheeks instantly flushed. "It was oh so earnest, and I couldn't possibly pass up a chance to—"

A small *oof* escaped Cole's mouth as my elbow connected with his ribs. "Dangerous footwear, remember?" I whispered. "If you don't shut up, I'll put my heel through your foot."

"Mean *and* violent? How did I get so lucky?" Cole waggled his brows at me but thankfully heeded my warning. "Hey, Evan. We're going to head inside, but let's catch up later?"

The dance had started over an hour ago, but Cole couldn't get off work on such short notice, so when we entered the lobby, it was mostly empty. With the exception of a couple having a whispered argument in the corner of the room and a bored-looking chaperone studying the trophy case, the only other person there was Erin. She sat at the ticket collection table, gaze fixed on her phone as she scrolled. The sound of my heels clicking against the floor must have caught her attention, because she looked up, a friendly smile spreading across her face as she prepared to greet a late arrival.

Then our eyes met. She glanced from me to Cole, her smile faltering. Our relationship had improved ever since she was elected president, but Cole's absence was a major part of that truce.

This was going to be *awkward*.

"Hey, Erin," I said as cordially as possible when we reached the table.

Three never-ending seconds passed before she released a deep sigh.

"Hi, Jackie. Hi, Cole." Her mouth hitched up in an approximation of the friendly expression she previously wore. "Do you have your tickets?"

Cole reached into his suit coat and then handed them over without a word, his face inscrutable. I almost elbowed him again so he'd stop being rude, but I didn't want to make things more uncomfortable than they already were. I wished I knew what was going on inside his head. Normally, he was brash in uncomfortable situations. For him to be silent now was strange.

"Do you need any help?" I asked, pushing my thoughts about Cole to the side in an effort to be polite. "I'm more than happy to give you a break." I ignored the tiny scoff that came from Cole's direction.

"That's nice of you to offer," Erin replied, "but Mateo will be here soon to relieve me. I've got things covered. Go enjoy the dance."

"Okay, see you later." I turned to go, Cole tugging me toward the gym like he couldn't get away fast enough, but then Erin called out to me.

"Oh! Jackie, hold on! I totally forgot to mention this. The lead singer of the band is looking for you. Her name is…Paula, I think?"

I frowned, unsure why someone I'd never heard of wanted to talk. "Did she say why?"

Erin shook her head. "No, but they're taking a break right now, so you can ask her. I'm pretty sure they're in the courtyard."

"What does she look like?" I asked.

"Don't worry," Erin said, a real smile returning to her face. "You can't miss her."

After dropping me off at the entrance to the courtyard, Cole promised to be back in five minutes and went to catch up with Evan. The band was standing around in a circle sharing a joint when I stepped outside. Of the four members, only one appeared to be a girl, and I instantly understood what Erin meant: her purple, chin-length bob was held back with an assemblage of butterfly clips; she had on a sleeveless, lime green trench coat covered in safety pins; and on her feet, she wore a pair of sparkly Crocs.

"Hi, are you Paula?" I asked as I sidled over to the group.

The girl's nose scrunched up at my question. "Unfortunately, it's Paulette," she answered. "My last name is Cooper, so most people call me Coop, but I'll respond to either. You must be Jackie."

"How'd you guess?"

Paulette smiled and shrugged. "Nathan's always described you as the nicest person ever, and you look wholesome."

She knows Nathan? Oh, this must be Miami Bay! I hadn't realized his friends won the block party battle of the bands.

"So..." I said, unsure how to best respond to her comment. I quickly decided to ignore it. "Erin mentioned you were looking for me?"

"Yeah but let me introduce you to everyone first. This is Kevin, Otis, and Moby," she said, pointing out each of her companions.

The first guy, Kevin, had a man bun and two full sleeves of tattoos. He nodded, but didn't say anything.

"'Sup?" said Otis, the guy standing closest to me. He looked like he worked at Hot Topic.

"Nice to meet you," I said, shaking his outstretched hand.

Moby, who was less punk rocker and more boy next door, blew out a cloud of smoke as he looked me up and down. "You're Nathan's adoptive sister?"

My eyes went wide. "No, the Walters didn't adopt me. They're just my guardians."

Otis nodded. "Makes sense. Thirteen's an unlucky number."

"Um, okay." I turned back to Paulette. "What exactly did you want to talk to me about?"

"Oh right!" Her eyebrows drew together. "I was wondering if you've seen Nathan? He's supposed to be here, and I know you two are close, so I figured if anyone knows where he is, it would be you."

"Sorry," I said, shaking my head. "I haven't. Was he supposed to be here?"

Paulette deflated. "Not necessarily, but I was really hoping he would."

"Don't get in your head about this, Coop," Moby said, slinging an arm over her shoulder and giving her a squeeze. "He probably needs more time to figure shit out. I bet it has nothing to do with you."

"Is everything okay?" I asked. Nathan's behavior had been worrying me for weeks, and now it seemed like his friends were concerned as well. Maybe they had a better idea of what was going on with him?

Unfortunately, the answer I received didn't solve any mysteries. Paulette explained that the lead guitarist for their band quit two weeks ago, and since then, she'd been aggressively—Otis's words, not hers—trying to convince Nathan to take his place. She thought he was a killer singer and songwriter, which the band desperately needed. Nathan, however, was irresolute and wouldn't give her an answer. When I pointed out that Nathan might not be interested because he preferred performing solo, I wasn't expecting everyone to burst into laughter.

"Did Nathan tell you that?" Paulette asked when she finally calmed down enough to speak.

My confused nod made her giggle again.

Moby passed the joint to Otis, who took a hit before clarifying. "Kid's lying to you."

Kevin nodded in agreement.

I blew out my cheeks in frustration, then released the breath I was holding. "I don't understand."

"Nathan gets major stage fright," Paulette explained with a crooked smile, revealing the large gap between her front teeth. "Performing in front of crowds freaks him out."

"We do gigs all the time," Otis added. "That's why he's on the fence about joining."

Paulette's smile slipped as she chewed her lip. "I figured Nathan might feel more comfortable playing for a smaller crowd of people he knows, so I convinced him to do a test run with us tonight. At least, I thought I had," she said. "Maybe I was too pushy and scared him off."

No, that doesn't sound right. Nathan wouldn't make a commitment only to be a no-show. It was out of character for him. "He hasn't responded to any of your texts?"

She pulled out her phone to check. "No."

Strange. I thought back to earlier this evening as I watched the Walter boys trickle out of the house one by one. Even though he was grounded, Isaac had slipped out the back door and taken the truck without Katherine noticing. Lee left not long after in an SUV blasting EDM. Alex had been the last to depart; Skylar picked him up, and it was weird seeing him go with all my friends.

Playing things back in my head made me realize I hadn't seen Nathan leave for the dance.

The courtyard door snicked open. "Jackie?"

Glancing over my shoulder, I spotted Cole waiting for me. "Be right there," I called to him, then turned back to Paulette. "It's weird that Nathan isn't responding and hasn't shown up, but how about this? If I hear from him, you'll be the first to know."

We exchanged goodbyes, and as I rejoined Cole, I moved Nathan to the top of my mental priority list. This was a problem I needed to solve ASAP.

"Having fun?" Cole asked, handing me a Dixie cup of lemonade from the refreshment table.

I looked over to him as one of the stage strobe lights caught his face. It was hot on the dance floor, and at some point, Cole had lost his tie and unbuttoned his collar. The brief flicker of light revealed a gleam of sweat on his brow and that his hair had started curling around his ears.

"Yeah," I shouted over the music, "but I could use a break. These heels are killing me."

His gaze dropped to my feet as I downed my drink. "I'm honestly impressed you haven't taken them off yet. Everyone else has."

He was right; most of the girls on the dance floor were barefoot or had swapped out their heels for flip-flops or flats. I felt weird about not wearing shoes in the gym, and I hadn't thought to bring a more comfortable change of footwear. Besides, a large part of me was loath to ruin my outfit by taking them off. Formal occasions were few and far between here, unlike in New York, where my family and I regularly attended charity galas or award events. On the ranch, it was jeans and sneakers the majority of the time. There was nothing wrong with that—I'd adapted and even grown to love how casual the Walters were—but I missed getting dressed up.

In the end, the pain won out over my sentimental side. "If I can't take these off in the next two minutes, you might have to amputate my pinky toe," I told him.

Cole laughed and placed his hand on the small of my back. "We can't have that. Come on. I think I saw my idiot brother and some of your friends."

We found Alex, Kim, Skylar, Chase, Riley, and Marcus sitting on the bleachers across the gym.

"Thank God," I hissed after sinking down onto the bench and kicking off my shoes. "Where's Heather?"

Riley's lips twitched in amusement as she watched me massage life back into my toes. "Still dancing. Why did you wait so long to take those off?"

"That's what I said." Cole sat down behind me and, wrapping an arm around my waist, drew me between his legs. "Apparently, she's a masochist."

"I thought we agreed that was your thing?" I said, tipping my head back to get a good look at him. Over his shoulder, I noticed the massive logo painted on the wall above the bleachers. It featured a knockoff version of the Frosted Flakes tiger surrounded by our school name. "Hey, why are we called Valley View?" I asked as I studied the design. "Aren't most high schools named for the town?"

Skylar followed my gaze, then frowned. "I think the better question is why is our mascot a tiger?"

"Because it sounds more badass than the Copper Valley Mountain

Goats?" suggested Alex, who was lying across a bleacher with his head in his girlfriend's lap.

"Sure," Kim said as she absentmindedly ran her fingers through his hair, "but tigers aren't native to Colorado. Why not pick something like a black bear or a mountain lion?"

"Babe, we played Alpine Heights tonight. *Their* mascot is a mountain lion," he said and tugged on one of her loose curls. "If everyone chose a native species, there'd only be, like, five cool animals to pick from."

"I've always been partial to the nine-banded armadillo," Chase said to no one in particular.

"Mascots don't have to be animals, though, right?" Kim continued. "Why can't we be something historical like a gold miner? There could even be a pickax in our logo."

Alex opened and closed his mouth. "Have you never heard of the Forty-Niners?"

"Oh, I know!" Riley said, her face lighting up. "How about the Valley View Golden Nuggets?"

This made Alex and Marcus groan in unison.

With a laugh, Skylar threw an arm over Riley's shoulder. "You're not much of a basketball fan, huh?"

Cole leaned down, his mouth brushing against my ear. "Wanna know the answer to your question?" he whispered as everyone continued to debate. "I can tell you, but first you have to follow me."

I nodded eagerly, then hesitated as I considered how painful it would be to put on my heels again. There was no way I could shove my poor toes back inside, so I left them on the floor and accepted Cole's proffered hand. Nobody noticed when we slipped away from the group and out of the gym.

"Where are you taking me?" I asked as we slunk down a locker-lined hall. I wasn't sure whether it was because the lights were out or the corridor was empty of students, but it felt wrong for us to be here.

"On a field trip." His tone was teasing, and I knew he enjoyed withholding information too much to give me a real answer.

Old me would have balked at the not knowing, but Cole had a habit of whisking me away on mini adventures, so I trusted him with this.

That was until he led me straight into the boys' locker room.

"Cole!" I gasped, tugging my hand out of his grip. "I'm not supposed to be in here!"

"Relax," he said, flipping the light on. "The football team went home hours ago. This is only a pit stop to pick something up, and then we'll be on our way."

The floor was slick in places, most likely from the football players showering after their game, and I kept my eyes on the ground as I trailed after Cole, not wanting to step in a puddle. Leaving my heels behind had been a major mistake. We walked past rows of lockers until we reached a small room with a wide window. Through the gaps in the aluminum blinds, I could make out a desk and some filing cabinets. Cole reached for the doorknob.

"Do you really think it—" I cut off when the handle turned effortlessly.

With a grin, Cole gave the door a little push, and it swung open. "Coach always leaves the room unlocked so his players can grab the keys and hit the weight room whenever they want. It's a poorly kept secret."

"Couldn't he get fired for that?" I asked, watching him rifle through the top desk drawer. Worse, couldn't someone get hurt? The more I thought about it, the deeper my frown grew.

Cole shrugged, clearly unconcerned. "He trusts us to—aha! Found 'em." He held up a silver ring packed with different keys, but before I could protest the theft, Cole was exiting the office, and I had no choice but to follow.

"Are you sure this is a good idea?" By my count, we were breaking at least three different school rules, and the trust I'd placed in Cole dwindled further.

He rolled his eyes. "A few months back in New York is all it takes, huh?"

"A few months is all *what* takes?"

"To forget my advice about living a little." He shook his head like he was disappointed in me.

Oh, that. I huffed in response but dropped the subject as we left the locker room.

When we climbed up to the second floor, I puzzled over where Cole was heading. There was nothing of interest up here, just the liberal arts and foreign language classrooms, but I doubted any of them were our destination. I nearly asked where we were going again, but then Cole stopped in front of a door I'd never noticed before. He unlocked it and gestured for me to go first. The temperature dropped as soon as I stepped over the threshold, but I didn't realize why until I climbed a final flight of stairs.

A gasp escaped my mouth as I stepped out onto the school roof. It was cold enough to see my breath, and once again, I cursed my decision to abandon my heels.

"Here," Cole said, shrugging off his suit coat and draping it over my shoulders. He went a step further by kicking off his shoes.

"Those look a little big for me," I said, even as I danced back and forth on my toes, trying to give the frigid concrete less exposed skin to freeze.

"Well, it's either that or I carry you." A wicked grin accompanied Cole's suggestion, and *nope*. There would be no carrying of any sort, so I stepped into his shoes before he could follow through with that option.

Cole guided me across the roof, and I clopped beside him, trying not to trip. I felt ridiculous, but my embarrassment was forgotten the moment I saw the view. From our vantage point, I could see the entire town sprawled below us, lights gleaming in the night like embers of a fire.

"See that peak over there?" Cole asked, pointing to one of the mountains Copper Valley was nestled between. "There's an abandoned ski resort about halfway up. It brought in swarms of tourists in the seventies and eighties, so the population here was much bigger back then. At some point, a second high school was built to accommodate the size of the community."

"Ah," I said with a nod. "I see where this is going."

"The original school was Copper Valley High. This one was constructed at the highest point in the valley, which consequently gave it the best view in town. Hence the name," Cole answered as he slipped a hand beneath his jacket to caress my bare back in a whisper-light touch.

"So, what happened?" I asked, trying to ignore his fingers, but each gentle brush felt like a sear against my skin, and I shuddered.

He must have thought I was cold, because Cole wrapped his arms around my waist before continuing with his explanation. "The lodge burned down, and the owners never rebuilt. That was before my time, though, so I don't know any of the details. Long story short, fewer tourists meant fewer jobs, and eventually there was no need for a second high school."

"The history's a bit sad, but the name makes sense," I said. "This really is a great view."

"Too bad it's cloudy, though. On a clear night, you can see the Milky Way from here," he replied, and I tipped my head back to look up at the sky. Not even the moon was visible behind the wall of gray, but I could see how this would be the perfect spot to stargaze from.

"Then I guess we'll have to come back when the weather's more cooperative." Next time with a blanket, snacks, and proper footwear.

"Is that your way of asking me out again?"

"Again?"

"Yes, *again*," he said, trailing a knuckle up my hip. "Don't you remember showing up in my room, trying on this sinful dress, and begging me to come with you?"

"What?" I spluttered and spun around to face him. "That is *not* what happened."

"How did it happen, then?" His breath fanned across my face, and I was suddenly aware of how close we were standing. If I pushed myself onto my toes, our lips would brush. Cole's gaze dropped to my mouth as though he could hear my thoughts, and his eyes darkened. The hand he was resting at the small of my back glided up my spine to curl around the base of my neck.

Another shiver wracked my body. "I—we..." *We asked each other concurrently* was what I wanted to say, but my brain stopped working, and the words wouldn't come.

A wolfish grin slashed across Cole's face. "We what, Jackie?"

Instead of responding, I tracked the upward curl of his lips. I didn't realize I was staring at his mouth until he grasped my chin and tilted my head back just so. His face dipped, and this time, I was sure he was going to kiss me. I closed my eyes, heart fluttering in anticipation, but before his lips found mine, a blaring siren made us jump.

"What the heck is that?" I asked, stuffing my fingers in my ears as I glanced around for the source of the noise.

Cole peered over the railing and frowned. "I think it's a fire alarm."

Sure enough, when I looked down, the entire dance was streaming out of the building into the parking lot. Nobody appeared to panic, but that didn't mean we weren't in danger.

I licked my lips. "We should leave," I said, wrapping a hand around Cole's arm. Even if there wasn't a fire, my friends were probably wondering where we were.

"Yeah," he agreed, tearing his gaze away from the scene below. "Let's go find out what happened."

ten

A PAIR OF LIPS BRUSHED against my bare shoulder.

"Cole," I said in a warning tone. Reneging on my study session with Riley had been a major mistake. Originally, we made plans to spend Sunday preparing for our physics test at Caffeinated Pursuit, but then I woke to the sound of rain battering the windowpane and quickly changed my mind. No way was I trekking into town in this weather. The problem was all the Walters were stuck inside too, and that meant the house was loud. Well, louder than usual. It didn't help that Parker had no concept of the word *quiet*. I'd been on the verge of chucking her PlayStation against the wall when Cole knocked on our door and invited me to spend the afternoon curled up in bed with him. Why I thought I'd get any work done ensconced in his room was beyond me.

Calloused fingers slid the strap of my tank off my shoulder. When he pressed his mouth to the newly revealed skin, I closed my eyes and willed myself not to snap.

"*Cole,*" I said again.

"Mm-hmm?" Another brush of his lips.

Jaw clenching, I slammed my textbook shut. "I'm going to find somewhere else to study."

"Nope, I won't let you." Cole caged me in his arms and buried his face in the side of my neck. "You're my prisoner now."

"You promised not to distract me," I whined in frustration.

He inhaled deeply. "But you smell so good."

"Physics doesn't care how good I smell," I shot back. "This test is twenty percent of my grade. If you don't cut it out right now, this prisoner is going to revolt." To prove my point, I yanked on one of his leg hairs that kept tickling me.

"Ouch!" He jerked his leg away, accidentally knocking a pillow off the bed. "Jackie, that hurt."

"There's plenty more where that came from," I told him as I pushed the strap of my tank top back into place. "I'm mean, remember?"

"Ugh, fine." Cole let go of me and collapsed against the headboard.

Half an hour passed before he started up again. At that point, I was so deeply immersed in practice questions that I didn't fully register when his knuckle grazed my thigh. It wasn't until he started fiddling with the hem of my Soffe shorts that I noticed his ministrations.

"Cole!" I squealed when his fingers slipped under the fabric and inched upward.

He took a sharp, audible breath. "Are you commando, New York?"

Before I could answer, the door to the art studio flew open.

Katherine and George didn't have many rules when it came to me and the Walter boys spending time together, but if I was alone in a bedroom with any of them, then the door was supposed to stay open. We startled apart, but thankfully, it was only Alex.

"What the hell?" Cole exclaimed, shooting a scathing look in his brother's direction. "You can't barge in here without knocking. Get out!"

Alex briefly glanced at us, his expression sheepish, before fixing his attention on the window. "Sorry, but no way am I missing this." He strode across the room in four large steps. "You've got the best view. Well, second-best view, but everyone else is already packed into Jack and Jordan's room."

"View of what?" I asked, setting aside my physics notes.

"Get over here and watch. I think they're about to come out of the house." His voice sounded odd, almost like he was horrified and fascinated at the same time.

Cole and I exchanged puzzled looks. Not wanting to miss whatever was about to go down, we both scrambled off the bed and joined Alex at the window.

The squad car parked next to the Buick made me gasp. I had a bad feeling about why the police were here or, more specifically, who they were here for. Knowing Isaac, if he were present, he'd probably place a bet on himself being the culprit as well. My hunch was confirmed less than a minute later when two officers escorted him off the porch and toward the waiting car, cuffs around his wrists.

"Holy shit," Cole said, craning forward over my shoulder to get a better look. "What do you think he did this time?"

"Lee was in the kitchen when the doorbell rang, and he caught part of the conversation before Mom kicked everyone out," Alex replied, eyes locked on his cousin as one officer opened the back door while the other put a hand on Isaac's head and steered him in. "Apparently, they were asking questions about the fire alarm incident at the dance."

"He set it off on *purpose*?" Cole asked, his mouth hanging open.

Last night, after making a quick exit from the rooftop, the two of us had rejoined what remained of the dance in the school parking lot. Most people were leaving early for after-parties, but there was still a decent-size crowd waiting around to find out what happened. We'd run into Alex and my friends right as the fire truck arrived, but they were as in the dark about the situation as we were. Cole and I hadn't lingered long after that.

I bit my lip. "If he did, then this is really bad."

The two officers momentarily stood outside the car discussing something, but the conversation didn't last long as it was still raining. They both climbed in, doors slamming.

Alex, who up until this point seemed to find the situation entertaining, finally realized Isaac might be in major trouble. His eyes widened as we watched the police car turn around, headlights sweeping across the gloom of the front yard before heading down the driveway. If I squinted, I could make out Isaac's head of messy black curls in the back seat.

"Define bad," Alex said, his gaze sliding to me.

Cole dragged a hand through his hair and sighed. "Potential misdemeanor bad."

"I'm not sure what the laws are like here, but in New York, you can be sentenced up to a year of jail time," I said as the police car finally disappeared from view. "Isaac is a minor, though. I'm assuming he's never been charged with anything before, so the most he'll probably get is some community service and a fine. Maybe probation."

My answer made Alex's brows shoot up. "You're surprisingly knowledgeable on the subject. Is there something you're not telling us, Jackie?"

"Teacher's pet by day, criminal mastermind by night," Cole teased.

"My best friend's dad is a judge," I said, probably a little too defensively, because both boys noticed and exchanged grins. It was a bizarre sight, seeing them take delight in the same situation when usually they were at odds with each other.

"You have a judge on your payroll?" Cole whistled. "That's an impressive operation you're running, New York."

"Can one of your underlings get Isaac off easy? Preferably with a bribe, but I'm not opposed to a little physical intimidation if it gets the job done," Alex added.

I shot them both a glare, even though I wasn't actually mad. "If you don't watch it, I'll send one my underlings to end you in your sleep."

Despite the gravity of the situation, Alex and Cole both laughed. Even though it was at my expense, the sound made me feel lighter. Both of these boys meant so much to me, but after everything that happened between the three of us and the lingering tension between the pair, I didn't think something as simple as enjoying one another's company was possible.

I knew it wouldn't last. Cole and Alex would go back to avoiding each other as soon as the moment passed, but for the time being, my heart was warm and full, and I let myself enjoy it.

Since I hadn't received my caramel fix yesterday, I convinced Alex to stop at Caffeinated Pursuit on the way to school Monday morning by promising to read over his *A Tale of Two Cities* essay. I was hustled into taking his, Nathan's, and Lee's coffee orders as well, but it was a small price to pay. Sleep hadn't come easy last night; I tossed and turned until nearly two o'clock, worrying about what would happen to Isaac. Slowly but surely, all the Walter kids were worming their way into my heart, even the annoying ones.

The line to order nearly reached the door, so I pulled out my physics notes to pass the time while I waited. One last review session before my test wouldn't hurt, especially after Cole's attempts to distract me yesterday. As I scanned through practice problems on Newton's third law, I couldn't help but overhear the conversation taking place ahead of me.

"—in Luke Snyder's car!"

"That's hardly surprising. Who *hasn't* ended up in his back seat? At this point, it's practically a rite of passage. No, the real bombshell is that Alex Walter and Kim Henderson got caught hooking up in the janitor's closet by Mr. Piper."

My head snapped up. The same two girls I'd caught gossiping about Cole in the library—Savannah and her blond volleyball friend—were standing directly in front of me in line.

"Wow, real classy," the nameless girl said with a snicker.

Not wanting to get caught eavesdropping, I buried my face in my notes but kept listening.

"Yeah, that whole family is a hot mess," Savannah replied, and I couldn't stop my shoulders from tensing. "Have you heard the rumor about Isaac?" she continued. "People are saying he's behind the fire alarm incident and got arrested yesterday!"

I bit my tongue to keep from snapping at the girl. How the hell did she even *know* that? None of the Walters would spread gossip about one of their own, and Katherine and George hadn't told us if Isaac was being charged with anything.

The blond giggled. "Am I a terrible person for finding that attractive? All he needs is a stint in juvie and some daddy issues, and he'll be the hottest Walter of the bunch."

"Hotter than Cole Walter?" Savannah scoffed. "Honestly, Megan. You're delusional. Did you see him Saturday night? That boy is the definition of fine."

Aha! So that was what her name was. The line shuffled forward as I added Megan to my mental catalogue of Valley View students.

"Yeah, you're right." She sighed wistfully. "His girlfriend is so lucky."

"I don't think they're dating," Savannah said, her tone conspiratorial. "I heard he's hooking up with the manager of the Gas Exchange. Apparently, he's there all the time."

Before her words could sink in and wreak havoc, Megan responded and saved me from spiraling. "Yeah, because he *works* there. I'm telling you; he's dating Jackie. Teagan heard from Heather, and those two have been friends since she moved to Colorado."

"Even if you're right, don't you think that's weird? I mean, they *live* together."

Her comment made my cheeks burn. Not wanting to hear any more of the conversation, I peeked over the top of my notebooks to gauge how close I was to the front of the line. Thankfully, there was only one person in front of the gossip twins—a little old lady with a handbag so bulky I was impressed she didn't tip over.

"Who cares?" Megan said. "They're not related."

"Sure, but the Walters took her in because she has nowhere else to go. Doesn't that seem a bit messy, dating someone who's part of your new quasi family?"

"Next!" the barista behind the cash register called.

As the girls stepped forward to order, I couldn't stop Savannah's words from echoing in my head. I wanted to dismiss the statement outright. The little I knew about the two was far from flattering, so I was disinclined to take anything they said to heart. But no matter how I rationalized, there was a part of me that wondered if she was right.

"Is this an abduction?"

It was Tuesday after school, and I was standing next to the truck, waiting for Alex to arrive and unlock the doors. Thirty seconds earlier, a familiar black car had whipped into the empty space next to me. Cole proceeded to roll down the window and tell me to get in without so much as a hello.

His response was, as usual, vague and lacking any important information. "No, it's a mission."

"Oh?" I raised an eyebrow. "And what would that involve, exactly?"

My question was met with a standard Cole smirk. "That's a secret."

Of course it was. I knew when to pick my battles, and Cole on the verge of an adventure wasn't one of those times, so I released a sigh and walked around the Buick without further inquiry.

"Hey, Jackie!" someone shouted as I opened the passenger door. "Where are you going?"

I glanced up and saw Alex crossing the parking lot with Nathan and Lee trailing behind him. Isaac was, presumably, at home. In addition to a buttload of community service and a hefty fine, he'd earned himself a weeklong school suspension for the fire alarm stunt.

"Who knows?" I said, lifting my shoulder in a half shrug. Did the answer even matter? My lips twitched with a hint of a smile when I realized that no, it didn't. I would get in the car and go with Cole no matter his explanation. "See you guys later."

"Tell Mom we'll be back in time for dinner," Cole added as I climbed in. He fiddled with a dial on the dash, and once warm air was blasting from my vents, he backed out of the spot and expertly navigated the post-school traffic.

We drove for ten minutes before pulling up to a nondescript, brick building with a cryptic sign that read simply THE RIFT.

"Well, that's not ominous at all," I said, eyeing what appeared to be a storefront as Cole put the car in park. That there were no indicators clarifying what type of store it was struck me as a poor business strategy.

Cole laughed as he drew his keys from the ignition. "I promise you'll like this."

As I followed him out of the car, more than one possibility of what the Rift could be ran through my head, each one more ridiculous than the next—an outer space–themed arcade bar; a sketchy money-laundering front; a tear in the fabric of reality that led to an alternative universe—but a thrift store wasn't one of them. A bell above the door jingled as we stepped inside, and my first impression was that we'd stumbled onto a quirky movie set instead of an actual, real-life place. The shop was poorly lit and narrow, with only three long aisles that stretched backward into the gloom. In my initial scan of the room, I spotted a bust of Shrek, an old aquarium filled with stuffed animals, and a collection of fishnet-stockinged leg lamps. Lounging beside the register was an orange tabby cat, and a second one slept peacefully on top of an old grandfather clock.

"This way," Cole said, taking me by the hand and dragging me into the depths of the clutter.

There was no rhyme or reason for the way the shelves were organized; books transitioned into household goods, then turned into electronics. Finally, we reached the end of the aisle, which opened up into a musty apparel section with racks of clothing, tables of accessories, and bins overflowing with shoes.

"Perfect," Cole said, propping his hands on his hips and surveying the room with the satisfaction of a forty-year-old dad observing his freshly mown lawn. "Nobody's here yet." He glanced over at me. "What do you think?"

"That this is the strangest kidnapping ever," I responded, still uncertain about why we were here.

"Did you happen to receive an invitation today?" he asked offhandedly.

My mouth parted in surprise. "How did you *know* that?"

At lunch, Chase had made an appearance at my friend group's established cafeteria table. This wasn't unusual—he and Skylar started dating a week before the dance—but his distribution of black envelopes closed with real wax seals was definitely different. The one he'd handed me had my name written across the front in perfect, gold calligraphy. Inside was an invitation to a costume party.

"Chase takes Halloween very seriously," Cole explained, starting toward a table display dedicated to the very holiday he'd just mentioned; a wide range of masks, wigs, and props were laid out across its surface. "His party is the only one that comes close to rivaling our end-of-the-year kegger, but that's because his parents are loaded, and they let him go all out on decorations and catering. I've only gone once, but he usually deals out invites after homecoming."

"Okay," I said slowly, even though he'd skirted around the answer to my question. Knowing Cole's history, some old hookup probably texted him today to see if he wanted to go. "Why are we here?"

He picked up a feather boa and wrapped it around his neck with a flourish. "To find our costume, obviously. I wanna get a head start before everything is picked over."

"*Our* costume?" Even though it was awfully presumptuous of Cole to assume my plus-one would go to him, my heart thumped. His assumption was one hundred percent correct, but that didn't mean I couldn't give him a hard time. "What if I want to take Nathan instead?"

"Do you?"

"No."

"Then why—"

"Because," I said, shooting him a *duh* look, "I don't remember us having a conversation about it."

With a dramatic sigh, Cole unwound the fluffy scarf, discarded it on the table, and turned to me, his eyes wide and imploring. "Jackie, can I pretty please come to Chase's party with you? I'll let you choose whatever cheesy couples costume you want."

Leaning in, I plucked a feather out of his hair. "*Anything*?"

He hesitated, then nodded.

"Well, how can I possibly say no to that?" I grinned and brushed the feather across the tip of his nose. "Thanks for asking, Cole. I'd love for you to be my plus-one."

He swatted my hand away. "You know, when I first met you, I never expected someone so prim and proper to be such a menace."

"That's because I wasn't," I said with a sniff. "It's a reflex developed from spending so much time around you and your family. I've been corrupted."

A low chuckle escaped him. "You say corrupted, but I think we've brought out the best in you," he replied as he gave my ponytail a gentle tug. "I love your sass."

I blushed. "Aren't we supposed to be looking for a costume?"

"You're right." He turned back to the Halloween display, and after a moment of consideration, he picked out a silver, foam helmet and a matching shield. "I'm sure we can find a tiara around here somewhere. What do you think about being a princess? I can go as your—"

"Knight in shining armor?" I finished for him. "Don't make me laugh. You're more the pompous prince type."

But Cole wasn't listening. He'd caught sight of something that made him perk up and toss the helmet and shield aside. "Hey! Alex had one of these when we were kids," he said, seizing a green lightsaber from a box of plastic weapons. He bent his knees into a fighting stance, then gave the sword a wave. "I think I ran over it with my bike and broke it," he added. "We should totally go as Luke and Leia. You can wear that sexy gold bikini."

Oh, *hell* no.

Cole must have clocked my reaction. Before I could open my mouth to tell him off, he beat me to it. Squaring his shoulders, he held up a finger and, in a bad mimicry of me, said, "First off, I refuse to wear an overtly sexual outfit that will result in me being objectified like a piece of meat. Second, the party is in October, Cole! Do you want me to freeze to death? And third—" He stopped ranting and frowned, but after a few seconds, he continued in his own voice. "Actually, I can't think of a third thing."

I hid a smile. "Those are both exceptional points, but what I was going to say is that it'd be weird for us to go as a brother-sister duo." Nobody knew about the conversation I overheard between Megan and Savannah. I didn't tell anyone because I didn't want to make a big deal out of nothing; Cole and I weren't stepsiblings, and there was no shared blood between us, but Savannah's comment about how weird it was that we were dating hadn't left my mind since yesterday morning.

"What are you talking about?" he asked.

"This is supposed to be a couples costume, but Luke and Leia are twins," I explained. "Her love interest is Han Solo, and he doesn't use a lightsaber."

He rolled his eyes. "Okay, nerd."

Hold on. Since when was it was a crime to remember the plot of a famous movie franchise, one *his* brother forced me to watch?

"Well, at least I don't have such kinky tastes," I said in an attempt to goad him. "Pain and incest, really?"

It worked. Cole blinked at me in bewilderment, then slowly set aside the lightsaber when he realized what I'd said. "That tongue of yours is awfully sharp." He took a step toward me. There was a wicked glint in his eyes. "You better watch it."

"Or what?" I stuck said sharp tongue out at him.

"This." Cole caught hold of my wrist, reeled me in, and crushed his mouth to mine.

It wasn't a sweet kiss. It was hot and demanding, and when he backed me up against the table, his fingers digging into my hips, something rolled off the edge and hit the floor with a thud. I responded in kind, sinking a hand into the hair at the nape of his neck and tugging. Someone cleared their throat, and if it weren't for the interruption, we probably would have gotten carried away.

I tore away from Cole, heart jolting in my chest, and noticed a guy in his late twenties wearing a Pearl Jam T-shirt and frayed jeans. He was standing in the door to the stock room, a steaming coffee cup clutched in his hand. His expression was neutral, but it was apparent from the way his lips were clamped together that he was trying hard not to laugh.

"Can I help you two find anything?" he asked.

"We're good," Cole said, sounding completely unfazed. By contrast,

I buried my face in his shirt to hide my embarrassment. "Just looking for Halloween costumes."

"Okay then," the guy replied. I stole a glance at him, and he gestured toward the front of the shop with his mug. "If you two need any help, I'll be up front at the register."

Once we were alone again, Cole tried to pull me into another kiss, but I ducked under his arm and flitted away, telling him in no uncertain terms that we wouldn't be picking up where we left off. As it stood, there was no way I'd be able to look the store employee in the eyes when we checked out. Cole laughed but thankfully suggested a return to the task at hand—finding something we could wear to Chase's party.

It turned out to be easier said than done.

"How are we going to get through all this?" I asked. After spending thirty minutes searching, we'd only gone over a quarter of the clothing section. The sheer amount of stuff was daunting.

"Divide and conquer?"

"Okay," I said, nodding at the suggestion. "You stick to the tables and bins. I'll take the racks." Starting on the far side of the room, I quickly worked my way through the men's clothes, but the only items I found with potential were a faded tie-dye shirt that looked too small to fit Cole and a red robe that gave me Hugh Hefner vibes, which was an immediate no.

Another half hour of scouring in silence passed, then Cole held up a stethoscope. "Thoughts on a doctor and nurse?"

"Overdone," I said, skipping over the selection of kids' clothes and moving on to the women's. Like the rest of the store, all the clothing lacked organization. Fur coat. Flip. Lime-green polo. Flip. Polka-dot skirt. Flip.

"What about pirates?" Cole asked ten minutes later. When I turned to look at him, he was wearing a curly, black beard—the cheap kind held in place with an elastic band—that covered the entire lower half of his face. "I found an eye patch, a hand hook, and one of those triangle-looking hats."

Under no circumstances would I be kissing him in that monstrosity. "Pass."

"An astronaut and alien?"

"Eh, I don't think I'd look good green."

Cole heaved a sigh. "Well, do you have any suggestions? I'm running out of ideas."

I pulled a pink, drop-waist skater dress out from between a swimsuit cover-up and a puffer vest. It wasn't perfect—there was a small stain near the hem—but it had potential. "What about Baby and Johnny?" I said, holding my find up for him to inspect. "All you'd have to do is wear a black shirt and slacks."

"Who?" he said, a crease appearing on his forehead.

"The couple from *Dirty Dancing*?"

He shrugged. "Never seen it before."

With a sigh, I stuffed the dress back into place.

"How about this?" When I looked up, Cole demoed a pair of shimmery pompoms using a routine I recognized from school. "I always thought I'd look slutty in a crop top," he deadpanned. "You can be the quarterback to my cheerleader."

An image of Cole wearing Erin's cheer uniform flashed before my eyes, and I instantly cracked up. When I moved on to the next rack, something caught my attention out of the corner of my eye, and I stopped laughing. Sitting on a table covered in belts and buckles was a delicate, indigo teacup decorated with a swirling, gold star pattern. My breath caught in my throat. Someone must have abandoned it here after noticing the tiny chip in the rim, but the flaw didn't bother me. All I saw was how much Lucy would love to add this to our collection. The design was unique—more often than not, teacups were decorated in pastels and flowers—and it would be the perfect gift for—

The excitement vibrating in my chest died the moment reality caught up to my thoughts. I didn't need to buy anything for Lucy's birthday this year because I would never be able to give her a present again. The sudden stab of grief was breathtaking, and the tiny cup rattled in its saucer as my hand shook.

Breathe, Jackie, I reminded myself.

Air whooshed past my lips as I released the breath I'd been holding in.

"Jackie?" Cole had to know something was wrong, because his head was tilted to the side, and he watched me with shrewd eyes. "Is everything okay?"

Despite the band of pain constricting my lungs, his concern was heartwarming. We'd been having such a good time, and I hated that all I wanted to do now was return to the ranch and curl up in bed.

Thinking back on how hard I'd laughed moments ago or the way it felt when Cole pressed me against the table, I realized how easily I'd let something as simple as a teacup ruin our afternoon together. This time, I wouldn't let my grief win.

"I found something that reminded me of Lucy, and it blindsided me a bit," I admitted, setting the cup down where I'd found it, "but I'm okay."

"You sure?"

I hitched a smile onto my face. "I will be." *I'm with you.*

"Good, because I think I found our costume." He held out a tan fedora and a wool beret. "Since you're so much trouble, I think we should go as Bonnie and Clyde."

That Friday, Cole took me to a dirt track race. I didn't know the exact details of what that meant—presumably, we'd watch some kind of motorized vehicles race around a track made of dirt—but as long as we were spending time together, I was happy to do whatever.

Everything I knew about *any* type of racing boiled down to this: although Formula 1 was the most popular racing series in the world, NASCAR had a larger following in the States; fans of the latter took offense at jokes about left-hand turns for some unknown reason; and the Indy 500 was a famous race typically held over Memorial Day weekend.

When I admitted my scant knowledge to Cole, he turned down the radio and spent the entire drive educating me. The first fifteen minutes were dedicated to the various types of motorsports, but then he started discussing different disciplines—something about circuit racing versus rallying. That was where he lost me.

It wasn't that I couldn't follow what he was saying, but I was too distracted by *him* to comprehend the words coming out of his mouth. He was talking a mile a minute, and if his hands weren't already occupied, one on the steering wheel and the other holding mine, I imagined he'd be using them to help with his explanations. Every so often, he glanced over at me, eyes sparkling, to make sure I was listening. Despite my disinterest in the subject, his passion was endearing, and I couldn't help but grin stupidly the whole way there.

The track was located a county over in the middle of nowhere, and by the time we arrived, night was falling. If it weren't for the neon ELWOOD RACEWAY sign and the line of cars waiting to turn onto a gravel road, taillights glowing, blinkers flashing, I'd have thought we were lost. There wasn't even a proper parking lot, just an endless grass field where a teen with one of those airport traffic sticks was directing all the vehicles.

The first thing I noticed when I climbed out of the Buick was that the temperature cooled off significantly during our drive. It was brisk but not uncomfortably cold—the perfect sweater weather. Before shutting the door, I reached into the back and nabbed a hoodie lying haphazardly on the seat. I'd kept the one Cole gave me at Parker's rugby game, but this one had the added bonus of still smelling like him: his cologne and a hint of musk, nearly overpowered by the scents of popcorn, gasoline, and fallen leaves that lingered in the air.

"Hey, thief!" Cole protested, but the satisfied expression on his face as he watched me pull it on was telling.

"Oh, stop," I said as I pushed up the too long sleeves. "You *obviously* love it when I wear your clothes."

"Obviously, huh?"

"Yeah, you get this feral look in your eyes."

Cole grabbed me around the waist. "If you want, we can get back in the car, and I'll show you feral." He dipped his head, and a hum of electricity surged through my blood when his lips made their way from my ear down to my collarbone.

"Oh no!" I feigned. "I have to miss some silly little race to make out with you? The horror."

He recoiled, his upper lip curling back. "Silly little... Are you *shitting* me? You did not just call it that."

"Front seat or back?" I asked, batting my lashes at him.

"Nope." He shook his head. "Not happening. We have a race to watch."

I snorted as he took my hand and marched me away from the car where we joined a stream of people heading toward the main gate. Earlier in the day, I had spent a disgusting amount of time fretting over what to wear. Eventually, I settled on a corduroy pinafore, a long-sleeve shirt to go underneath, tights, and my favorite pair of boots. When

Parker saw the outfit laid out on my bed, she laughed and told me to wear jeans. As we joined the queue to purchase tickets, I was grateful for her input. Without it, I would have been way overdressed, considering most of the crowd was wearing camo, flannel, and Carhartt.

Admission only cost ten dollars, which seemed irrationally cheap, especially considering how run-down the track looked. If the entry fee was increased, then maybe the concession stand could get a fresh coat of paint. More concerning were the old wooden bleachers that were so weather-worn, I wondered if sitting down would give me a splinter. But the shabbiness of the venue faded into the background as we took our seats; there was a spark in the air that was impossible to deny. Even though the audience was a strange mix of families with young kids and middle-aged men in NASCAR T-shirts drinking Busch Light, everyone seemed excited, and the feeling was catching.

"This first race is called a heat," Cole explained as a colorful pack of cars drove out onto the track. The actual racing surface, a banked oval made of umber clay, was smaller than I expected. "It's a qualifying round. Starting positions for the feature are determined by times in the heats."

"Who do you think will win?" I asked as Cole snaked his arm around my back.

"Number 12," he said, pointing to a red-and-gold car near the front. "He's pretty successful for a local driver. Typically places on the podium and did a regional tour a few years back."

"That's cool, but I'm rooting for number 88," I said, selecting the only car painted my favorite color.

Cole arched a brow. "Why?"

"Because it's purple."

"That," he said, his eyes sparkling with mirth, "is a *terrible* strategy."

I shrugged, unconcerned about whether my selected car won or lost. This turned out to be a good attitude to have, because 88 crashed spectacularly as soon as the race began, spinning out and plowing nose-first into the wall.

"Told you," Cole said as he laughed, but I pretended not to hear him over the roar of engines.

Watching the cars whip around the track was more fun than I expected, but my excitement quickly dulled due to the excessive amount of dirt. Whenever the cars flew around the corners, they kicked up a plume of the stuff, and by the time the first heat was over, a haze of dust lingered in the air like smoke. Squeezing my eyelids shut, I wondered how I'd get through the entire event if my eyes were already itching after one race.

"You good?" Cole asked, forehead crinkled with concern.

I frowned and tried to blink away the uncomfortable feeling. "I don't know. Was I supposed to get a face full of dirt every time the cars went around the track?"

"Here." He pulled something out from the pouch of his hoodie. My frown faded when I realized it was protective eyewear. There were two choices—safety glasses and a pair of goggles that looked a bit like the ones worn in chemistry.

"Are we doing a science experiment?" I asked but picked the second option because they had a foam seal. I'd look dorky, but that was a sacrifice I was willing to make to keep the dirt out of my eyes. As I pulled them on, my hair got tangled in the strap.

"Let me help," Cole said, gently batting my hands away. He worked my curl loose, then adjusted the goggles so they fit flush on my face.

"Well," I said, looking up at him. "How do I look?"

He bit down on his bottom lip to contain a smile. "Adorable."

I rolled my eyes. "Oh, I'm sure."

"No, seriously. The goggles really do it for me. If the next heat wasn't starting, I'd be absolutely feral."

In spite of his teasing, the goggles were a godsend, and I was able to enjoy the rest of the night without feeling like I needed to scratch my eyes out. I continued picking winners based on color schemes, and Cole continued to give me a hard time when they inevitably lost. My only deviation from this strategy was when Cole pointed out the driver he rebuilt an engine for—number 20, a mean-looking all-black car that reminded me a bit of the Batmobile—who ended up finishing fourth in his heat. Not terrible, but Cole was hopeful he'd do better in the feature.

Finally, it was time.

"That was a phenomenal race," Cole said, his voice an amusing mix of exhilaration and disappointment as the crowd swept us out through the gate toward the parking lot, "but damn! He was *so* close."

Number 20, whose name I learned was Carter, had almost clinched a win after battling from the middle of the pack up to the front. Cole and I spent the last three laps of the feature screaming at the top of our lungs, and even though the Batmobile look-alike crossed the finish line side by side with the leader, it was clear that Carter had taken second.

I grinned and swung our clasped hands back and forth. Despite the dirt, Cole's driver not winning, and the goggle lines imprinted on my forehead, it had been a night that I would think about for months to come. "Thanks for taking me. I had a blast."

"Cole!" someone shouted before he could respond. "Hey, Cole. Wait up!"

Glancing around, I spotted a heavyset man waving an arm over his head. The stranger was probably in his midforties, with a wild mop of curls and an abundance of freckles that gave him an element of youthfulness. He wore a racing suit that looked like Cole's work coveralls, with the sleeves tied around his waist.

"Do you know him?" I asked, pointing out the man.

"Yeah, that's Carter. Come on. I'll introduce you." Cole changed course, cutting across the flow of departing spectators, and I followed close behind him so we wouldn't get separated. "Sorry, excuse us."

As we approached, an unrestrained smile split Carter's face. "Cole, my man! Thanks for coming."

The two shook hands, and after a quick introduction for my benefit, they dove straight into dissecting the race. Cole wanted to know if the engine was pulling better at the end of the straightaways—was that even English?—and Carter's rapid-fire response was chock-full of terms that went over my head, so I just smiled politely and pretended to know what they were talking about. All I knew for certain was that Carter was over the moon about his performance; Cole commented on how unfortunate it was that his rebuild hadn't secured a victory, but Carter wouldn't hear of it.

"Stop being so hard on yourself," he said, slapping Cole on the back. "This was my best race ever. I've never placed on the podium before, and I couldn't have done that without you."

"You sure?" Cole asked, a seed of doubt lingering in his voice.

Carter nodded. "Absolutely. You can expect a call from me next time I need help."

I smiled to myself as Cole stood a bit taller.

"I look forward to it," he replied. His cheeks were pink with pleasure.

"Well," Carter said, glancing at his watch. "I need to go pack my trailer, but let me know next time you're here for a race. I'll see if I can get you pit passes."

"That would be amazing," Cole said as they shook hands again.

Before we parted ways, I held up my phone. "Do you guys want a picture together?"

eleven

I WAS AVOIDING THE CONVERSATION I needed to have with Nathan. After meeting Paulette and learning that he stood up the band without a word, the concern I'd felt for him since returning to Colorado bloomed into full-blown anxiety. Something was wrong, and I needed to get to the bottom of it…but Nathan had been in a foul mood since Saturday, trudging out of the house each morning for our run as if he were being punished, dodging attempts at conversation with one-word responses, and hiding in the loft whenever possible, so I decided to allow him some time to calm down.

That was a week ago, and I still hadn't said anything.

As I stepped outside for our run, I told myself that enough was enough. It didn't matter how cranky Nathan was when he showed up; I needed to confront him and figure out what was going on. Decision made, I began my stretching routine and waited for him to join me.

Five minutes passed. Then ten. By seven o'clock, I knew he wasn't coming.

A flush scalded my cheeks. I leaped to my feet and swept inside the house, screen door slamming shut in my wake. If Nathan didn't want to run with me anymore, the least he could do was tell it to my face. I was officially over letting him blow me off. Along with giving him plenty of space, I'd told him about my issues with Cole, and while he didn't owe me anything in return, our friendship was starting to feel one-sided. It made me wonder if I'd done something to piss him off.

Someone's cleats clattered down the steps as I stormed upstairs, but I didn't turn around to pick them up. I barged straight into Nathan's room, too angry to care if I woke Alex as well. Enough morning light had seeped past the curtains for me to see that Nathan was still sleeping, so I strode over to his bed and yanked the covers off.

"Time to get up," I announced. Even though I was fuming, I kept my voice calm.

He groaned and rolled over. "Jackie? What are you doing in here?"

I put my hands on my hips. "Waking you up, obviously. You're late for our run."

"I'm not going," he said, pulling his comforter back up.

"Yes, you are." I rifled through his dresser and selected a long-sleeved undershirt and running joggers, then tossed the clothes at him. "We have some things to discuss."

Nathan jerked into a sitting position and glared at me. "Can't you take a hint?"

My bravado faltered at his tone. "Come on, Nate," I pleaded. "It's me. You can tell me anything."

"Did it ever occur to you that maybe I don't want to?" He spat out each word like he'd been trying to bite them down, but they were too poisonous for him to keep inside any longer. "You're so overbearing, Jackie. Stop trying to act like my sister. I have enough older siblings who think they know best. I don't need another one."

Sharp, bone-cutting hurt cleaved through my chest, and for a split second, I couldn't breathe. Besides the ringing in my ears and Alex's soft snoring, the room was silent. I swallowed, and my throat clicked.

"Wow, okay," I said, blinking back tears. "Message received."

Alex and I were making our way to the truck when the Buick rumbled up the drive. Cole parked behind Katherine's van, cut the engine, and slowly heaved himself out. His leg must have been bothering him—sometimes it got stiff when he worked long hours—because he winced and took a moment to massage his thigh.

"You okay?"

Cole's head popped up at the sound of my voice. When he spotted me and Alex standing together on the front walk, he frowned. "I'll be fine." He paused for a beat, his gaze assessing. "Are you two going somewhere?"

I instantly felt guilty. Not because of Alex—Cole didn't get to dictate who I hung out with—but because we hadn't spent any time together since last Friday at the dirt race; the Gas Exchange was short-staffed, so Cole was working overtime, while my evenings were spent working on a project for U.S. history. Other than a quick hello in the morning and dinner with the entire Walter crew, we hadn't seen each other all week.

"O'Brady's," Alex answered, naming the local pub we were meeting my friends at.

When he didn't elaborate, I quickly added, "It's Harry Potter trivia night. Kim begged us to come."

Alex glanced at his phone and then over to me. "We should get going."

"Mind if I tag along?" Cole asked.

The question made me freeze. I was so accustomed to how Cole and Alex avoided each other, moving around the outskirts of the other's life like repelling magnets, that I hadn't thought to invite him.

"You...wanna hang out?" Alex asked. The *with me* was heavily implied.

Cole shrugged. "Why not?" His face was inscrutable, but his tone seemed sincere enough. "I've got nothing better to do. Just give me five minutes to change."

"All right," Alex said hesitantly, "but be quick about it? We're already running late."

Under normal circumstances, the amount of civility the boys were exhibiting would have left my jaw on the floor, but I was trying my best to act casual.

Sharing a ride must have been the line Cole wouldn't cross, because he grimaced. "Go ahead," he said, waving his brother off. "I'll meet you there."

Truth be told, I couldn't blame him. The last time the three of us were trapped in a car alone together was when Alex and I were still dating. We'd gotten stuck in a rainstorm after his baseball game, and Cole was forced to pick us up. I never had the guts to ask him about it, but I was pretty sure he'd seen us making out. Thinking about how awkward and tense that drive had been made me cringe.

Cole pressed a quick kiss to my forehead—he smelled like sweat and car exhaust—then disappeared inside.

"Jackie, you coming?" Alex asked.

"I think I'll ride with Cole."

"Suit yourself."

While Alex climbed into the truck, I took a seat on the porch steps to wait for Cole. He emerged five minutes later in clean clothes and a grease-free face. His mouth curled into a soft smile when he saw me.

"Thanks for waiting," he said, holding out a hand to help me up. Instead of letting go once I was on my feet, he gave my hand a squeeze and led me down the front walk.

I frowned when he let loose a humongous yawn. "Are you sure you want to come?" I asked. "It seems like you had a long day, and I doubt trivia is your thing. Besides, Kim is deadly serious about winning tonight. She might throw hands if you fall asleep at the table."

"My thing," he said, opening the car door for me, "is wanting to spend time with *you*, even if it means suffering through your dorky trivia night. If Kim has a problem with that, then she can avada kedavra me." He added the last part with a pleased little grin, like he was proud of himself for having enough Harry Potter knowledge to make the joke regardless of how terrible it was.

O'Brady's was uncomfortably packed when we arrived fifteen minutes later, and Cole snickered to himself as I squeezed past a group of thirtysomethings wearing Hogwarts robes while in search of my friends. I finally located them in the pub's prime spot—one of the oversize booths at the back of the room that could seat our entire group. Someone, probably Kim, must have arrived ages ago to secure it, and the remnants of an appetizer sampler—a single onion ring, a dip bowl nearly depleted of marinara sauce, and a few untouched sticks of celery—only reinforced my assumption.

The girls were arguing over potential team names when Cole and I slid into the two remaining spots. Heather liked Roonil Quizlib and Neville Wears Prada, but Kim was adamant about Anything for Our Moony. All the while, Riley kept throwing out inappropriate ideas that had Alex and Skylar in stitches—Dumbledeez Nuts and We're Dead Sirius to name a few—but the other two didn't bother acknowledging her.

"How about the Dumbledorks?" Cole muttered under his breath as a bartender appeared to drop off a score sheet and pencil. "Seems appropriate, considering."

Kim cut off midsentence and slowly turned her head toward

our end of the table, eyes narrowed dangerously. "I don't remember anyone asking your opinion."

"Sorry, I thought we were deciding on a *team* name." He slid the sheet of paper over to himself before anyone else could claim it and offered Kim a taunting smile as he spun the pencil around his fingers. "A team is a group of people who come together to achieve a common goal, in case you didn't know."

"I know what the definition of—" She cut herself off with a disgusted scoff. "Why are you even here?"

Cole slung an arm over my shoulder. "Boyfriend privileges," he said, and a thrill shot through me. We had yet to label our relationship, but hearing him say the word aloud made me realize how much I wanted to be Cole's girlfriend. "I have other name suggestions if you're interested. How about the Salty Squibs? You seem like the type of kid who cried when you didn't get a letter on your eleventh birthday. How come you're not playing dress-up like the geeks over there?" He gestured to the group seated at the high-top we skirted around earlier.

Sighing to myself, I slipped a hand under the table and squeezed his knee. Would it kill him to behave around my friends? Cole responded by wrapping his fingers around mine and guiding them farther up his thigh. I snatched my hand back, and his body shook with silent laughter.

Kim's face hardened. "It's called cosplaying and—wait, you know what a squib is?"

"Sure. A nonmagical person born to at least one magical parent,"

Cole's upper lip quirked as he fought the smug smile I knew was strain-ing to take over his face. "Doesn't everyone know that?"

It was comical the way her jaw slackened, but what actually made me laugh was Alex's expression—a combination of wonder and *what the hell have you done with the real Cole Walter?*

"What?" Cole said as his brother stared at him. "Danny listens to the audiobooks on rotation before bed. Every. Single. Night. Says nothing can lull him to sleep the way Jim Dale's voice does, so it was inevitable I picked up a thing or two."

"I suppose you can stay," Kim said grudgingly after regaining her composure. Then she lunged across the table and snatched the score sheet away from Cole. "Still can't name our team, though."

An amplified *thump thump* sounded through the pub. Someone at the front of the room, it was impossible to see who considering the size of the crowd, called for attention over a mic. Trivia would start in five minutes, and everyone who wanted to participate was instructed to form teams if they hadn't already done so. Heather spent every second of the downtime interviewing Cole like he was on a late-night talk show, asking inappropriate and intrusive questions. He took her brazenness in stride, and the too-honest explanations he offered her left me blushing; it wasn't until he grinned, eyes following the path of red spreading from my cheeks down to the collar of my shirt, that I realized he was doing it on purpose to fluster me. I sagged against the back of the booth when the quiz finally started, grateful for the reprieve.

Since I'd only seen the first three movies, I settled in for the show, knowing I wouldn't be able to offer any assistance. Kim performed as expected, speedily scribbling down answers as if we'd get bonus points for responding first. What little she didn't know was covered by the rest of our team. The only time Cole spoke up was to correct Kim's response to what species of dragon guarded the Gringotts high-security vaults.

He reached over and tapped a calloused finger against the score sheet. "That's wrong."

Kim's head jerked up. "Excuse me?"

"The correct answer is Ukrainian Ironbelly. The Hungarian Horntail was Harry's tournament dragon."

Alex shot Cole another *who the hell are you?* look while Kim frowned in consideration. After a brief moment, she muttered something under her breath, crossed out what she previously wrote, and jotted down the correct response.

In the end, our team lost by one point to the cosplayers because Kim mixed up fanon with official canon. This gave Alex an excuse to tease her for reading one too many stories about gay wizards from the 1970s, which made Kim launch into a dissertation-length lecture on the importance of fan fiction. By the five-minute mark, most of the table had tuned her out and broken off into smaller conversations with the exception of Alex. He continued nodding along with her rant like a dutiful boyfriend, though it was clear to anyone who spared a glance at his pained expression that he regretted his earlier comment. I took the opportunity to catch up with Riley, who'd been spending all of her time with Marcus since the dance. While we spoke, Cole sat back and listened in silence, his thumb tracing circles up and down my leg. I was so engrossed in our discussion, I nearly forgot he was there.

"Nick?" Cole said suddenly, making me jump.

Following his gaze, I located his friend standing by the secondary hostess station at the back entrance. He glanced up from his phone at the sound of his name.

"Cole, hey!" Nick strolled up to the table. He seemed unsurprised to see me as he scanned our group, but his brows rose when he spotted Alex. Which, fair. "Doesn't this look…fun," he added before returning his attention to Cole. "I wish I'd known you were in town this weekend. We could have caught the game together."

The expression on Cole's face was open and easygoing, but Nick's comment made his hand freeze on my thigh. "Well, let me know next time you're home. I'm not visiting. I decided to defer for a year."

"*What?*" Nick exclaimed, his gaze momentarily flicking to mine. "Why?"

"I need to save up money for tuition. Not all of us have surgeons for daddies." The tone Cole used was teasing, but I found the remark unnecessarily pointed. Then again, I didn't know much about their friendship, only that they'd been on the football team together. Maybe this was how they joked around with each other? There was also the possibility I'd overestimated how close they were, because why hadn't Cole shared his deferment plans?

Regardless, Nick laughed and launched into a detailed breakdown of his first month at college. My eyes glazed over as he went on about girls and partying and more girls, so I took the opportunity to use the bathroom. When I returned a few minutes later, Nick and Cole were missing.

"Where'd they disappear to?" I asked as I slid back into the booth. I scanned the pub—first the pool table section, then the bar—but even though O'Brady's had cleared out significantly since trivia finished, I couldn't locate either of them amid the thinning crowd.

"Nick was only here to pick up a to-go order," Heather said but didn't answer my question.

"Okay..." As I glanced around the table, nobody met my gaze. There was a sudden sinking feeling in my stomach, so I turned to the one person who would never make excuses for his brother. "Alex?" I prompted. "Where's Cole?"

He shifted in his seat, mouth drawn into a tight line as he dragged a finger through the puddle of condensation left behind by his empty water glass. After a tense moment where I thought he wouldn't respond, Alex reluctantly looked up at me. "I don't know, okay? After Nick left, Cole muttered something about forgetting to lock up the shop and took off."

My mind ground to a halt. Five full seconds passed before the wheels started turning again, and the gist of the situation dawned on me. "Are you saying he *left* me here?"

No, absolutely not. There was no way Cole would do that to me...right?

The awkward and sympathetic expressions on all my friends' faces told a different story.

"It's okay," Alex said, raising his hands in a placating gesture. "I can give you a ride home."

That was so far from the issue, I almost laughed. Obviously, Alex or one of my friends would make sure I got back to the ranch safely. But how could Cole abandon me without explaining where he was going or saying goodbye? Had I done something wrong? I thought back on the past hour, but nothing came to mind. Sure, I didn't participate in trivia, but Cole made it clear he didn't give a damn about the pub quiz; the only reason he came tonight was me. Whatever happened to make him leave had to have taken place while I was in the bathroom.

"Did Nick say something to him?" Thinking about it now, it occurred to me that Cole started acting strange the moment his friend showed up.

Alex hesitated, his throat flexing as he swallowed. "Not exactly."

"What does that mean?" I asked stoically. It was difficult not to snap at him, but I wouldn't take my anger out on Alex. This wasn't his fault.

"Well...Nick asked if Cole deferred school because of you."

My heart dropped. "And how did Cole respond?"

"He didn't," Alex said. "Nick's to-go order was called right after, so he excused himself. Cole left as soon as he was gone."

The door to the art studio stayed shut all Saturday long. Cole didn't even emerge at mealtimes to eat, not that I was looking for him. He knew he'd messed up. What other reason did he have to avoid me on his day off?

Now that I'd had time to process what happened, Cole's behavior didn't shock me. He had a track record of lashing out or forgetting basic human decency when something upset him. I was, however, confused. How could he proclaim himself my boyfriend one minute and ditch me without a word the next? Usually, I understood the whys of his temper tantrums even when they made me want to tear my hair out, but I couldn't for the life of me pin down his motivation in this instance. Did it have something to do with what Nick said? The mystery of it ate at me, which only fueled my anger, but I didn't get an answer until late in the evening.

Just as I was climbing into bed, a knock sounded on the door. When I yanked it open, Cole was standing on the other side wearing hiking boots and a corduroy sherpa jacket. His gaze instantly dropped to the hem of my sleep shorts.

"Nice jammies, Jackie," he teased, and my lip curled at the sight of his obnoxious smirk. If he wasn't careful, I was going to smack it straight off his face.

"What do you want?" I snapped.

"For you to change into warm clothes. We're going somewhere special, but it's cold outside."

His audacity made my blood boil. "What makes you think I'll go anywhere with you?"

Cole sighed as if I was being difficult for no reason, then moved directly into my personal space. If not for the extra foot he had on me, our noses would have brushed. He leaned down, his lips ghosting across my ear, and whispered, "Because even though you're mad at me, I still make your heart race."

I hated that he was right—despite everything, I could feel the treacherous organ slamming against my chest like a caged animal—but it didn't mean I had to put up with his crap. "Good night, Cole," I said curtly, taking a step away from him.

"C'mon, Jackie." He stuck his foot between the door and the frame to stop me from closing it. "Don't be like that."

My eyes narrowed into slits. "Don't be like what? Upset because you abandoned me? Or angry because you're acting like nothing happened?"

He deflated under my gaze. "I screwed up, okay?" All his earlier bravado dwindled, and without the nonchalant act, the bags under his eyes became obvious, but lack of sleep wouldn't earn my forgiveness. His miserable excuse for a confession didn't move the needle either.

"That's not good enough," I told him.

"I didn't plan on leaving," he said, stuffing his hands into his pockets. "It just happened."

I let out a sharp laugh. Honestly, how was *that* any better?

Parker, who up until now had been trying to sleep, exhaled loudly and pushed herself into a sitting position. "Seriously, Cole? Did you leave your brain behind at the pub too? That's the only reason I can think of for why you're being such a numbskull."

"I'm sorry, what?"

"You're digging yourself a deeper hole, dummy. Less excuses, more groveling." Parker muttered something under her breath about boys not having any brain cells as she flopped back against her pillow.

"Yeah," I said, lifting my chin. "What she said."

Cole briefly considered his sister's words before taking her advice to heart and dropping to his knees. He blinked up at me with sad, remorseful eyes, but after a moment, they lit with mischief, and I knew whatever came out of his mouth next would be ridiculous.

"Oh, benevolent goddess—"

The rest of his sentence was drowned out by Parker's groan. "Somewhere else, please?"

Sighing dejectedly, I went over to my dresser and rifled through the top drawer for a pair of thick socks. Next, I retrieved the jeans I'd worn today from my hamper. Both of Cole's sweatshirts hung on a hook near the door, but I reached for my jacket out of spite. I instructed him to wait in the hall, which he obeyed immediately, scrambling to his feet and backing out of the room so I could change. When I reemerged, there was a stupid grin on his face.

"Don't give me that look," I said before sweeping past him and moving toward the stairs, determined to get this over with so I could return to bed. I was only caving out of consideration for Parker, not because I forgave Cole. He kept up a constant stream of apologies as he trailed after me, but I ignored every one of them. They would be meaningless until I received an explanation, but Cole refused to elaborate. Apparently, he'd planned a date for us to make up for last night's debacle, and he didn't want to ruin the surprise.

I focused on appearing apathetic as I climbed into the truck. Once the engine roared to life, however, Cole pulled onto a narrow path that barely counted as a road instead of heading down the driveway, and I couldn't squash my curiosity. I glanced around in hopes of figuring out our destination, but it was too dark to see much of anything. Despite my piqued interest, I kept my mouth shut as Cole drove us clear across the ranch until we reached a forest on the edge of the Walters' property.

After parking beside the wall of towering pines and grabbing a drawstring bag from the back seat, Cole led me over to a game trail I wouldn't have found in the daylight, let alone in the middle of the night. No sooner had we stepped into the swath of trees than we were swallowed up by darkness. I took out my phone, but even with its flashlight illuminating the dirt path, I kept tripping over roots and getting caught in the underbrush. I stumbled after Cole for fifteen minutes before losing my patience.

"How much farther?" I asked through gritted teeth, then promptly pitched forward as my shoe caught on a rock.

"Whoa, careful." Cole steadied me, then shrugged off his bag. "Here, take this. We're almost there, but I think it'll be safer for both of us if I give you a piggyback ride."

By some miracle, I had yet to sprain my ankle. I wasn't willing to push my luck, so I accepted his offer without a word. As I slipped the bag over my shoulders, Cole crouched down so I could more easily climb on. Once my arms were wrapped around his neck, he hitched me up into a comfortable position before continuing onward.

It took another five minutes to reach our destination, but eventually the trees thinned, and we emerged into a grassy clearing. I slid off his back and looked around. Other than a table-size stump—the last remnant of what had once been a colossal tree—there wasn't anything worth noting to justify hiking through the forest so late at night.

"This is where we went camping as kids," Cole said. He took his bag from me, then pulled out two aluminum mugs, a thermos, and a blanket.

"Um...that's not what we're doing, right?" As thick as it looked, there was no way the single blanket he brought would keep us warm through the night.

He laughed as he spread it out on the ground. "Do you see a tent anywhere?"

His question didn't reassure me. The Walters seemed like the type of people who were outdoorsy enough to forgo one depending on the weather.

"Well, no, but—"

"We'll only be here for an hour or so. It's too cold out to stay longer than that." Cole flopped down and patted the empty space next to him. "Come sit. I brought hot cocoa."

I wasn't immune to bribery, especially the chocolatey kind, so I accepted a steaming cup and listened as Cole explained why he dragged me all the way out here. Since I didn't get to see the Milky

Way that night on the school rooftop, he wanted to take me stargazing at a time when the sky was visible. I tilted my head back and gasped. Thousands of stars sparkled above us, like some cosmic artist had thrown an ocean of glitter against the black canvas of the universe. As much as I hated to admit it, Cole's gesture was both thoughtful and romantic.

"I've never seen so many stars before," I confessed. Not long after moving to Colorado, I realized just how impossible it was to see anything in New York due to light pollution, but this was something else entirely. Out here, they were so densely packed, there seemed to be more light than sky, and I wondered how it was possible that our journey through the trees had been so poorly lit.

"That's because this is the best spot on the ranch for it," Cole told me. "If the weather was nice enough during our camping trips, we would set up our sleeping bags in the grass and sleep under the stars."

Ha! I called it.

"Do you have a favorite constellation?" I asked, still mesmerized by the shining expanse above us.

"Sure." He pointed straight up. "See that bright star right there? Now look to the left, there's another. The next one is a little farther away, but do you see how they're starting to form a hump? That's Urassus Major—

"*Cole!*" I exclaimed, nearly spitting out a sip of hot chocolate.

He snickered. "What? I said we slept under the stars, not that we studied them. I know jack all about astrology."

"You mean astronomy."

"That's what I said."

"No," I corrected him. "You said astrology." Finally tearing my gaze away from the sky, I looked at Cole, my eyes roving across his face as I tried to determine if he was joking. The easy smile he wore made it difficult to tell, so I added, "They're two different things. One is a science; the other is divination."

His face lit up in understanding. "Oh, like horoscopes? I'm a Scorpio born in Gatorade or something like that," he said with a comical amount of confidence. "It means I'm kind, mysterious, and protective."

I rolled my eyes. "Urassus Major is full of shit."

Cole made a sound of objection. "Is not!"

"You were born in May," I said, enunciating each word slowly. "That makes you a Gemini." Not to mention the bullshit traits he'd made up about himself. Kind and mysterious, my ass.

He shrugged. "I'll stick with Scorpio. It sounds cooler."

"You can't just pick whatever sign you like best!" I said in protest, very nearly slopping cocoa over the brim of my mug. I set it aside so I wouldn't spill in frustration. "That's not how it works."

"Says who?"

"I don't know," I answered wearily. "History? Everyone? It's common knowledge."

His dimple made an appearance, and it was the only warning I received before he lunged forward and wrapped an arm around my torso. I tried to squirm away from his fingers, but he held my body against his own and used his free hand to torture me. "I knew you'd be ticklish." He sounded delighted.

"Cut it out!" I gasped, tears welling up in my eyes.

He didn't listen, so I continued to flail about until my hand accidentally connected with the mug and sent it flying. Most of my drink spilled into the grass, but some of it splashed on me.

"Shit," Cole said and let go so I could twist away from the spreading puddle.

"Do you have a towel or something else I could use to clean up with?" I asked, shaking off the liquid dripping down my fingers. I considered the blanket, but the material was fluffy, and I knew it would cover me in fuzz.

"Here, let me." Cole grasped my wrist, then lifted it up with deliberation, giving me all the time in the world to pull away. I didn't, and our eyes stayed locked on each other as his mouth closed around one of my fingers.

It all happened so quickly, I didn't register the switch, but one moment, Cole was sucking hot chocolate off my skin, and in the next, he was capturing my lips in a deep, tender kiss. When his hand came up to cradle my face, I wrapped an arm around his neck and tangled my fingers in his soft hair; it was the perfect length—long enough to always look effortlessly tousled, especially if I played with it, but short enough for ease of maintenance.

Without his mouth ever leaving mine, Cole guided me down onto the blanket and covered my body with his. I let out a little, breathless gasp, and he immediately pulled away.

"Is this okay?" he asked, carefully studying my face.

"Yes." My response came out huskier than I expected, but it made Cole smile.

"Good." His eyes burned into mine. "Let me know if that changes."

Then he kissed me again, rougher and more fervent than before. Everything fell away except for the slight sting of his teeth sinking into my bottom lip, the taste of cocoa on his tongue, and the feel of his weight pinning me to the ground. Even my faculties receded as pleasure clouded my mind, which explained why I could barely remember my name when he finally pulled away from me five minutes later.

After pressing one last kiss to the tip of my nose, Cole rolled off me and collapsed against the blanket. I stared up at the sky again as my chest heaved up and down. Other than my hammering heart, the only sound that filled the small clearing was our labored breaths.

"If you guys didn't study astronomy when you were out here, then what did you do?" I asked, finally breaking our silence once my breathing returned to normal.

"Took turns giving the stars made-up names," he replied impishly. "Will always came up with the most ridiculous ones."

"Like Urassus Major?" I guessed.

A laugh rumbled in his throat. "Exactly."

The thought of Will entertaining his younger siblings as they watched the night sky reminded me of Lucy. "There's a skylight in my sister's room," I told him in a near whisper. "It's directly over her bed. Whenever I had a nightmare, I'd crawl under the covers with her, and she'd make up these wild stories as we stared out the window."

"What kind of stories?" he asked, tucking an arm behind his head.

"Space operas. Always about the same characters—Lexa, Jenny, and the Star Guards."

"Star Guards?" he repeated. "What's that?"

"A group of aliens sworn to protect the galaxy from evil." My voice wavered as all the little details my sister wove together came rushing back to me, but I continued explaining. "Lexa and Jenny were astronauts who were saved by the Star Guards after getting lost in space. Instead of returning to Earth, they decide to join them on their adventures."

"Lexa and Jenny, huh?" he said, brushing his hand against mine.

I smiled. "They were sisters."

"That's cute." He gave my arm a comforting squeeze, then shifted the subject to something less painful. "So what do you think—is there life out there, or are you a nonbeliever?"

We spent the next few minutes arguing over the existence of extraterrestrial life before moving on to Bigfoot, wendigos, and the Loch Ness Monster. That turned into a discussion about conspiracy theories—which ones we thought were real and which were our favorites, Cole's being that the reason the Louisiana Purchase was so cheap was that the land was overrun with werewolves. When we ran out of silly things to talk about, our conversation took a serious turn.

"Hey, Jackie? I'm really sorry about last night." For the first time this evening, his apology sounded sincere. "I never should have left you behind like that."

Finally. I pulled away from the warmth of Cole's body and propped myself up on an elbow to look at him. "So why did you?"

An emotion I couldn't place flickered in his eyes. "Just something Nick said. It doesn't matter."

Obviously, it did, especially since his reaction was to ditch me. We wouldn't be having this conversation otherwise. "It matters to me, though, and I think you owe me the truth. Were you...I don't know, embarrassed or something?"

He released a defeated sigh. "Yeah, kinda."

"No one made you hang out with us, Cole," I said, my heart shrinking inside my chest. Although we ran in different crowds, his more popular than mine, I never thought he cared enough about his reputation to be ashamed of being seen with my friends.

His gaze snapped to me, and he pushed himself into an upright position. "Wait, you think—Jackie, no! You've got it all wrong. I wasn't embarrassed by you or your friends. I knew exactly what I was getting myself into when I heard 'Harry Potter trivia.'"

"Then can you help me understand?" I asked. "Because it sure feels like you were."

Cole was quiet for a long time. Somewhere near the edge of the clearing, a small animal rustled in the undergrowth.

Finally, he said, "I felt like a loser, okay?"

I stared at him, sure I'd heard wrong. How could Cole Walter, the most popular guy at school even *after* he graduated, feel like a loser? Did he really not see how everyone always gravitated toward him? "But…why?"

"Because all my friends are off at school while I'm stuck here, doing nothing and going nowhere," he admitted, each and every word coated with bitter dissatisfaction.

His statement did not compute. It wasn't as if Cole's grades were so dismal he didn't get accepted anywhere. By this time next year, he'd be gone too. "Postponing your education so you can save up for tuition isn't nothing," I told him. "It's called being financially responsible. School will still be there a year from now."

"It's not just about school, though. I've got zero—I mean, I don't… *Ugh.*" Cole scraped his hair away from his face, only for his bangs to flop back into his eyes a second later. "Look, there's only two things I'm good at—cars and football. The latter is obviously off the table, so where does that leave me? Working at Tony's forever?"

"You'll figure things out," I said in what I hoped was an optimistic tone. Unsure how else to assuage him, I took his hand in mine and laced our fingers together. "Isn't that part of the whole college experience?"

"Easy for you to say," he muttered. "You already have your life planned out."

He wasn't wrong, but my stomach still churned. I hesitated, not certain if I was ready to give voice to something that had been plaguing me since this summer. "Can I tell you a secret?" I didn't wait for him to answer. "I hated interning at my father's company. Investing is *boring*."

"So...no Princeton? You could always apply to Boulder." The thought of us attending school together must have cheered him up, because a smile finally returned to his face.

"Don't be absurd," I said, giving him a playful shove. "It's Princeton or bust, but..." I trailed off, trying to organize my conflicting thoughts. "Maybe I don't want to follow in my father's footsteps after that?"

He cocked an eyebrow. "Was that a question?"

"Yes, and that's the point I've been trying to make. It's okay if you don't know what you'll do with the rest of your life, Cole. I'm unsure too. It's normal, and it definitely doesn't make you a loser."

A frown touched his face. "You might be unsure, but you still have options. I feel like I've got nothing. Well, that's not true. I have you," he told me. "You're the best thing I have going for me right now."

"I don't believe that," I said as some undefined, discomforting emotion squirmed in my gut. "What about the engine rebuild you did for Carter? Didn't he say he'd hire you again in the future? That's not nothing."

Cole gave a hum in response, and then we fell quiet, both of us talked out. The temperature dropped quickly, and when I started shivering, we decided to call it a night. Hiking out of the forest was more difficult than on the way in, and by the time we reached the truck, my muscles were aching. All I wanted to do was crank the heat and curl up on the bench seat with my head in Cole's lap.

I must have dozed off during the drive, because I woke sometime later to a gentle swaying motion and a warm, firm body pressed against mine. The first thing I saw when I opened my eyes was Cole, who was carrying me into Parker's and my room. I snuggled deeper into his arms as he approached my bed, not wanting to give up his warmth.

"What's going on?" I asked in a raspy, only half-awake voice that made him smile.

"You fell asleep on the way home." He laid me down in bed, then tugged off my shoes. "Go back to sleep, Jackie. I'll see you in the morning."

"Don't go," I replied, clutching his shirt even as my eyes fluttered shut. "You're comfy."

When Cole didn't reply, I thought he'd already left, but a moment later, the mattress dipped, and he crawled in next to me.

twelve

I WAS DRIFTING IN AND out of consciousness when a faint noise drew me from the hazy fragments of a dream.

Without opening my eyes, I knew I forgot to close the curtains last night; the room was bright, flooded with morning sunshine that warmed my face. Too comfortable to get up, I turned away from the light and nestled deeper into my pillow. The usual downy cushion was firmer than usual, but it wasn't until I noticed the slight movement—a gentle up, down, up, down—that my eyes snapped open. It took my sleep-addled brain a moment to register that Cole and I were tangled together. Not only was I using his chest as a pillow, but his arm was thrown over my side, and our legs were slotted between each other's.

The noise that woke me, a gentle rapping, repeated. "Parker, are you awake?"

Adrenaline coursed through me. That was Katherine knocking on the door! The realization washed away the final remnants of lethargy, and I jolted into a sitting position. Cole was in my *bed*, his mother was moments away from discovering us, and there was nothing I could do.

"Honey, you need to get up," she continued, the door creaking as she pushed it open. "Rugby practice starts in—" Katherine cut herself off when our eyes met.

Three agonizingly long seconds passed as she assessed the situation.

Either he had the world's worst timing or a built-in threat detection system, because Cole chose that exact moment to wake. "Don't get up yet," he said as he pulled me back into his arms, voice still rough with sleep.

I squeezed my eyes shut so I could block out Katherine's flinty glare. "Cole, let go."

"Nope." He nuzzled the back of my neck. "Not gonna."

"*Cole Anthony Walter.*"

If I wasn't currently drowning in dread, I would've laughed at Cole's reaction to hearing his mother's voice. His whole body jerked like he'd been electrocuted, and he scrambled up so quickly he almost fell out of bed.

"Mom, hi," he choked out, eyes round with panic. "This isn't what it looks like."

Katherine's lips pursed, but surprisingly, she didn't yell or raise her voice. She calmly informed us we'd be having a discussion after dinner, kicked Cole out, and then busied herself with getting Parker ready for practice.

As she moved about the room, opening dresser drawers and digging through the closet, I sat on my mattress, limbs numb and ears ringing. I'd expected a detonation when Katherine spotted us in bed together, not whatever this nonreaction was. It left me reeling long after she and Parker were gone, and that was the point, wasn't it?

The rest of my day was spent overthinking. I tried concentrating on quadratic functions and other polynomials, but my mind kept returning to the angry expression on Katherine's face. I'd seen it plenty of times before, impossible not to considering how many smart-ass kids she had, but never had that look been directed at me. Just how much trouble were Cole and I in? When he brought me home drunk this past spring, we'd been reprimanded and grounded, but this felt different. Weightier. By the time dinner rolled around, I'd entered an anxiety-induced trance where all I could do was push the food around my plate.

Once everyone was done eating, George instructed me and Cole to stay seated while the rest of the table was excused. Alex lingered behind, a curious expression on his face, but all it took was one cleared throat from his father for him to disappear. Katherine stood at the edge of the room, ears cocked and hands on her hips as she waited for multiple sets of feet to clamber up the stairs. When the sound faded, she took a seat across from us.

"Under no circumstance is it acceptable for the two of you to sleep in bed together." Her tone was calm but firm.

I hung my head, cheeks burning.

"Really?" Cole said flippantly. "Not even if—"

"Cole," George interrupted. "You better stop talking right now, or so help me, I'll—

"Okay, okay!" he replied before his dad could finish. "I'm sorry, but you guys are making a bigger deal out of this than necessary. Nothing happened."

This was definitely the wrong thing to say, and I winced as a muscle in Katherine's jaw jumped. While technically correct about nothing happening, Cole being a smart-ass would only get us in more trouble.

"I don't care what your excuse is," she snapped. "*Nothing* gives you the right to flout house rules."

"What rule did we break?" There was a challenge in Cole's question. "The only one you made when Jackie moved in is that the door has to stay open if we're alone in a bedroom with her. Technically, we weren't alone."

I sucked in a sharp breath, appalled by his insolence. A sense of self-preservation kicked in, and I inched to the side of my chair, leaning as far away from Cole as possible. Nobody spoke. It was so unnaturally quiet that I could hear the *tick tick tick* of the pendulum clock that hung on the wall in the den off the kitchen.

"You think the presence of your eleven-year-old sister makes this okay?" Katherine asked after a long, uncomfortable beat. Her voice vibrated with barely restrained anger. "I cannot begin to explain how inappropriate that is."

"Jesus, Mom," Cole groaned. "It wasn't like that."

"It. Doesn't. Matter." Katherine paused, a vein throbbing in her temple. It looked like she was trying to rein in an onslaught of violent thoughts. "Your father and I mishandled things by not explicitly stating additional rules, but that was because we thought you were mature enough to understand anything beyond that was implied. We won't be making that mistake again. The two of you are grounded until further notice."

"You can't ground me." Cole leaned back in his chair and crossed his arms with a look so defiant it made my blood pressure spike. "I'm an adult."

"Your behavior suggests otherwise," George cut in before Katherine could explode. "Regardless, you live under our roof."

Cole was going to keep arguing. I could tell by the way his brows snapped together and he drew in a breath, so I elbowed him in the ribs to prevent further stupidity. His head turned sharply to face me, but I begged him with my eyes to *please shut up*.

He must have received the message, because his shoulders slumped. "Fine, but please—don't take this out on Jackie. We were out late, and she fell asleep in the truck on the way home, so I carried her up to bed."

Or not. I sighed but refrained from banging my head against the table in frustration.

"If that was all that happened, then we wouldn't be having this conversation," Katherine replied through clenched teeth. "You seem to be forgetting the part where you climbed into bed with her."

"I didn't mean to fall asleep!" Cole exclaimed. "Don't crucify us for something that was an accident. My shoes were still on, for Christ's sake!"

My nails dug tiny crescent moons into the flesh of my palms before I forced myself to relax. I *should* have been thankful to Cole for trying to take the blame. Even though I'd been drowsy, I remembered asking him to stay with me, and that made us equally responsible. It was truly a sweet gesture, but judging by the expressions on his parents' faces, Cole was only digging us a deeper hole.

"Cole?" I said in a small voice. "Please stop talking."

This time, thankfully, he did.

George spent the next five minutes outlining our punishment, but I tuned out since his speech basically boiled down to chores, house arrest, and more chores. It wasn't until he warned that if anything like this were to happen again, drastic measures would be taken, that I snapped back in.

"What kind of drastic measures?" Cole asked warily.

Katherine massaged her temples. "Look, honey, it's the last thing I want to do, but if you and Jackie need to be separated, your brother and Haley have more than enough room."

The little amount of dinner I'd managed to eat rose in my throat at her words. If I wasn't mistaken, it sounded like she was threatening to send Cole away, and I couldn't allow that to happen.

"Katherine, George," I said, making direct eye contact with them when I spoke their names. Under the table, I wiped my clammy palms against my thighs. "I'm so sorry about what happened last night. By ignoring your rule, Cole and I stepped over a line that never should have been crossed. It was irresponsible and disrespectful, and I give you my word it will never happen again."

"Thank you, Jackie," George said with a tight smile. "We appreciate the apology and your promise."

I nodded, knowing it was one I meant to keep.

I didn't know which part of my task was worse.

The first thing that came to mind was the stench of manure. Along with permeating the air, the pungent smell always clung to my skin until I took a scalding shower where I could drench myself in soap.

That being said, drowning in my own sweat was a close second. I hated the way it trickled down my brow and back and soaked through my shirt.

Learning I wasn't as fit as I thought was irritating too. While there were many benefits to running, upper body strength wasn't one of them. As I lifted the final pitchfork of horse droppings and dumped it in a wheelbarrow, arms trembling with effort, I couldn't help but feel humbled by exhaustion.

My punishment for being caught with Cole included multiple unpleasant aspects, but this—the daily mucking out of the horse stalls—was by far the most torturous.

After spreading a new layer of pine shavings across the floor, I collapsed on the bench outside the tack room and closed my eyes. When I really thought about it, the worst part of this entire situation wasn't the lingering odor, feeling sticky, or the burning in my arms. It wasn't even being grounded and losing precious study time to chores. What bothered me the most was the pit that took up residence in my stomach Sunday night and hadn't left since.

Katherine's threat to send Cole away weighed heavily on me. What if she followed through? Imagining him being forced to pack up the art studio and leave the ranch because of my actions made me nauseous, and for the next few days, I could barely look in his direction, let alone spend time with him. It wasn't the potential separation that upset me. Most people my age didn't share a home with their significant other. As Savannah had so bluntly put it, our living situation was weird. What bothered me was that my presence had already exacerbated issues in his relationship with Alex, so the last thing I wanted was to be responsible for driving a wedge between Cole and his parents.

The barn door creaked open. It was probably Nathan escaping to the loft as usual, but I wasn't in the mood to talk to him. The wound his words inflicted was still too fresh, so I kept my eyes closed and tracked his progress across the room by listening to his footsteps. When they stopped directly in front of me, I sighed.

"I'd love to kiss you right now," said a voice that was definitely not Nathan's, "but you reek."

Opening my eyes, I found Cole leaning against the opposite wall.

His hands were tucked casually in his front pockets, and he was wearing a pair of red devil horns and a grin to match.

"Aren't you supposed to be cleaning out the basement?" I asked.

"Aren't you supposed to be mucking out the stalls?" he retorted.

I gestured at the wheelbarrow that needed to be brought out to the compost. The pitchfork had to be put away as well, but all the grueling work was done. "I'm basically finished."

"Me too," he said, but I highly doubted that.

After he was arrested, Katherine tasked her nephew with sorting through thirty-plus years of possessions that had built up in the under-croft (as Isaac had taken to calling it) over the course of raising twelve kids. With the exception of George's workroom, the Walters used the lowest level of their house like a giant storage unit. There were boxes upon boxes to go through. Everything not important enough to keep needed to be organized into different categories since it would all be donated to the community rummage sale. Cole was assigned to help Isaac when the two of us were grounded, but even with two pairs of hands, the boys had barely put a dent in what was turning out to be a massive project.

Since it wasn't my job to police him and I was too drained for our usual back-and-forth, I pretended to believe his lie. "What's up with the horns?"

Cole shrugged. "Found a box of old Halloween costumes. I think Alex was looking for something to wear to Chase's party. Isaac's got on the matching halo, but I know it'd look better on you," he said with a flirty wink. "Come hang out with us after you shower. There's a bunch of cool stuff down there. I've been going through my parents' yearbooks, and Isaac came across a chest packed with a bunch of vintage clothes I think you'll like. It must have been my grandma's."

"Didn't you say you were done?"

"I lied." He waggled his brows and pointed to his accessory. "Devil, remember?"

As if I could I forget. Although most people thought of him as the golden boy, Cole could be wicked when he wanted to. I was intimately familiar with his mean streak, and I suspected he got up to just as much trouble as his siblings. The difference was he knew how to get away with it. He also liked to push boundaries and bend rules, which was part of what drew me to him, but look where that got us this time.

"What do you say?" Cole asked when I didn't reply. "You, me, and a musty basement. I know it's not the best offer, but we'll find a way to have fun. What if we pretend Isaac isn't there? That will drive him crazy."

I wet my lips. "Um, tonight isn't good for me. I have a lot of homework to get done."

His smile sank, but he quickly hitched it back up. "Then do it in the basement." Either Cole *really* wanted to hang out or I didn't smell as bad as I thought, because he pushed away from the wall and sat down beside me. "I'll clear off the old desk and promise not to bug you. Please?" he added. "We haven't seen each other since Sunday."

Guilt speared through my chest, but I held fast to my decision and shook my head. "I don't think that's a good idea, Cole."

"Why?"

"Your parents—"

"Don't use them as an excuse," he snapped. "Be honest—are you avoiding me?"

The word *no* sat on the tip of my tongue, but that was a lie, wasn't it? For the past four days, I'd steered clear of Cole whenever he came home from work. Not because I was mad at him but because I didn't want to ruffle Katherine's feathers further than we already had. "Well, not exactly. It's just…"

"It's just *what*?" he challenged, twisting on the bench to face me.

"I don't know how to explain it, Cole," I said, dropping my gaze to my feet, "but when I'm with you, I feel…normal-ish." As the stumbling explanation left my mouth, I realized this was about so much more than the past few days. The uneasiness creeping over me went back to much bigger issues—primarily, my uncontrollable grief.

"That's a bad thing?"

"No, but…sometimes I miss my family so much, it's debilitating," I told him. "There's this razor-sharp ache in my chest that's impossible to ignore, like my heart's been wrapped in barbed wire, and no matter what I do or how much time passes, I know it'll be there for the rest of my life." Tears had gathered in my eyes, but I brushed them away before they could fall. "Then there are days when you smile at me and I just…forget. All the pain fades away, and that makes me feel so damn guilty. How can I be heartbroken in one moment and happily kissing you the next?"

"Jackie." Cole's tone was understanding but firm. "Look at me."

When I did, his features softened.

"Stop worrying about grieving wrong. It's not something you can mess up," he said, gently knocking his knee against mine. "Healing isn't a linear process. Some days will be better than others."

"That's easy for you to say." I swallowed the bitter lump in my throat. "You can't possibly imagine what it feels like, losing everyone you care about in one fell swoop."

His responding nod was so deferential it made me feel like I was being irrational. "I know I don't understand, and I mean this in the most sincere, non-jackass way possible, but—I wonder if you're using that as a reason to avoid something that scares you?" he said. "Your parents wouldn't hate you for moving on, Jackie, and no matter what, my family and I will always be here for you."

Will they, though? I'd thought the same thing about my own family.

What would happen if Cole and I continued dating, things got super serious, but then we broke up? Would the Walters be forced to take sides? Danny promised to answer my calls even if I broke his brother's heart, but was I really willing to take that chance? Why would any of the Walters choose me over their own flesh and blood?

That was when I finally understood why I'd been pulling away from Cole since Katherine caught us in bed together. What it came down to was that the Walters meant everything to me. They'd taken me into their home after I lost mine, became my new support system, and showed me how to live again. I already knew the pain of losing one family; I couldn't lose another.

The problem was, where did that leave me with Cole?

As if sensing my inner turmoil, one of the horses nickered from two stalls down.

"I'm sorry," I whispered, wrapping my arms around my waist. Until I sorted out the confusing jumble of thoughts and feelings inside my head, it would be better if we kept our distance. "I–I can't brush off last weekend like nothing happened. I need some space, okay?"

Cole's expression hardened. "What, like last time?"

I must have hesitated for a beat too long, because he scoffed and stormed off without another word.

thirteen

"JACKIE, WHAT ARE YOU *DOING*?"

I glanced up from where I lay on my stomach, one arm shoved beneath the bed. Parker stood in the doorway, rugby bag slung over one shoulder and mud smeared across her face. She was assessing the situation with a puzzled frown.

"Looking for my necklace," I said, shooting to my feet. Maybe she knew where it was? While Parker normally wrinkled her nose at my choice in wardrobe, I'd caught her inspecting my jewelry box on more than one occasion, and I knew what it was like to have a sister. I used to borrow Lucy's stuff all the time without asking her. "Have you seen it?"

"No, sorry. I'd offer to help, but..." She trailed off, eyes warily darting around our room.

Parker didn't need to elaborate for me to understand her hesitation, because where would she even start? In the past fifteen minutes,

I'd made a complete mess of our shared space. Every dresser drawer was pulled open, clothes strewn about. I'd stripped the bedding off my mattress, dumped the contents of my purse and backpack onto the carpet, and ransacked both the closet and our desks.

My shoulders slumped, and I blinked a few times to hold back tears. Until this moment, I didn't realize how much hope I had in her miraculously producing my mother's pendant.

"Have you checked the bathroom?" she asked, picking her way across the floor toward her hamper, where she plucked a shirt off the top, gave it a sniff, and then tossed it aside.

"Yes, along with the den, the kitchen, and the living room," I said, listing off the spots in the house I frequented.

Parker paused and scratched her temple. "Well, whenever I lose something, my mom tells me to retrace my steps," she said. "When was the last time you wore it?"

I mentally reviewed the past month. The most recent memory I had of wearing it was at homecoming. If I lost it at school, then I had a terrible feeling I would never see it again. The thought made my heart ache. Could it have fallen off in Cole's car? In all likelihood, probably not, but I had to check regardless.

After promising to clean up later, I rushed out to the shed where the Buick was parked. The lights were off, so I didn't notice Nathan sitting in the driver's seat until I wrenched open the passenger door.

"Oh my God!" I exclaimed, clutching a hand to my heart. "Nathan, why are you—"

The tears trailing down his cheeks stopped me in my tracks. He didn't acknowledge me. He just continued to stare out the windshield as he cried, his shoulders shaking. We hadn't said a word to each other since our fight, and even though I still felt hurt by what he said, I couldn't walk away when he was so clearly upset.

Without a word, I slid into the car and took Nathan's hand in mine. He remained unresponsive, but instead of pushing for answers, I kept him company as he wept. Eventually, he ran out of tears, wiped his eyes, and collapsed against the seat like he'd just run a marathon.

When he finally spoke, his voice was low and croaky. "I'm sorry I was such an asshole to you, Jackie. You didn't deserve that."

"It's okay," I told him. Receiving an apology was nice, but I was too preoccupied with figuring out what was wrong to care.

"No, it's not," he said, his voice cracking. "You were worried about me, but I was too angry to see that, so I lashed out and said some really shitty things that aren't true."

He glanced up at me then, and the expression on his face was so familiar to me that all the oxygen disappeared from my lungs—Nathan was *grieving*.

"Did Cole ever tell you the story about how he got this car?"

The abrupt change of subject startled me into supplying an immediate answer. "Your grandpa gave it to him, right?"

"Yeah, for his sixteenth birthday. You'd never guess it didn't run by how excited Cole was." There was a far-off look in Nathan's eyes, like he was reliving the moment. "My uncle Pete put it in a ditch right after getting his license, but Gramps was too sentimental to junk it. All the core memories I have of him are centered around restoring this car in his garage with Cole and Isaac. He gave us lessons while he worked. Of all his grandkids, we were the only ones interested enough to listen. I was too young to learn anything significant, but Cole was a natural."

"Is that why your grandpa passed the car on to him?" I asked.

Nathan ran a hand over the steering wheel. "I'm sure that's part of it, but also, Cole was the first of the three of us to turn sixteen."

"Ah," I said, as if everything suddenly made sense. It didn't, but hopefully Nathan would get to the point if I was patient enough.

"When Cole started taking shop his freshman year, he'd come home after school and teach me what he learned in class that day, just like our grandpa had. Isaac lost interest way before then, so it was just the two of us, and that became my favorite part of the day."

"Huh." Up until recently, it had been a common sight to see the hood of the Buick popped and Cole leaning over the engine. When I tried to picture Nathan in his place, the image didn't correlate because I couldn't visualize him as a mechanic. "I didn't realize you were into the whole fixing cars thing."

He gave a noncommittal shrug. "I don't mind it, but I wouldn't call it a passion either. For me, it was always about spending time with my brother."

"Really?" I said. "I never saw you in the shed with him."

"I stopped going," he replied. "Cole was so angry after he screwed up his leg, and fixing the car was the only thing that seemed to help, so I figured he could use the time to himself."

"Okay..." I expected Nathan to continue with his explanation, but he fell silent. I decided to give him a moment to gather his thoughts. As I waited, a million different questions sprang to mind, like *Why are we talking about Cole?* and *What does the car have to do with anything?* The longer the silence stretched, however, the more vacant his gaze became.

Finally, I couldn't stand it any longer. "Nathan, please—what's going on?" I pleaded. "Maybe I can help."

"You can't." Fresh tears appeared, and he swiped at his eyes in frustration. "Cole promised to pass the Buick down to me once I learned to drive."

"What happened?" I asked carefully, making an effort to keep my tone neutral. If all this angst was over a stupid car, I would lose my shit. "Did he change his mind?"

"No," he replied, shaking his head vehemently. "Cole wouldn't do that."

"Then what?" Coaxing answers out of him was like trying to get Alex to do his homework, Isaac to behave, or Cole to stop flirting— nearly impossible.

"I had another seizure at the start of summer," he finally admitted. "It was right after you and Danny left."

Understanding slammed into me like a battering ram, followed swiftly by confusion. The day Nathan ended up in the hospital was seared into my memory—it hit too close to home for me to forget—so why hadn't I considered his recent diagnosis as the root cause of his moodiness?

Nathan went on to explain that his neurologist had changed his prescription but warned him there would be an adjustment period until they found the right dose. Which meant that even though he was old enough to start driving, something he'd been anticipating, Nathan had to forgo getting his learner's permit; only once he was six months seizure-free could he legally get behind the wheel. Despite the setback, adjusting his medication did the trick—Nathan hadn't experienced a seizure since June. All he had to do now was make it one more month, and then he could start driver's ed.

He paused again, and I could tell by the way he squeezed his eyes shut that on top of everything he'd already told me, there was more to the story.

"You had a third seizure," I said, the final piece clicking into place. "When?"

"Homecoming," he whispered. "It was when I was getting ready for the dance. Luckily, I'd already gotten out of the shower, but I fell and spent a solid ten minutes smashing my head against the bathroom floor. Felt like I was hit by a bus when I finally came to."

"Does...does your mom know?"

"Yeah," he said, his jaw visibly clenching at the mention of his mother. "She's the real reason I stopped running, by the way. She wouldn't let me go alone while you were gone, and nobody wanted to get up early to go with me."

A knot of emotion formed in my throat. "I'm so sorry, Nathan."

"Don't be. It's not your fault." A single tear dripped off the end of his chin. "I know it's pathetic to cry over this, but I just feel so... What if my doctor can't find the right balance for my meds?"

I pursed my lips. "There's nothing pathetic about this." My tone dared him to challenge me, but he didn't, so I relaxed and added, "I hope you don't mind, but I did some reading on epilepsy treatment this summer. There are so many medications out there, Nathan. I'm sure your doctor will find something that works, and you'll be cruising around in the Buick in no time."

Not my best pep talk, but I didn't know how else to reassure him. Words didn't seem good enough.

"Yeah, well, I did some reading too. Did you know it's not uncommon for a regimen you've been on for years to stop working out of the blue?" He sounded so bitter, but that was to be expected.

This was about so much more than learning to drive or having the freedom to go on a run; Nathan's disorder would affect the rest of his life. He probably felt like he was losing control, and that had to be terrifying. Which made me wondered if all this—Nathan's diagnosis and its aftermath—was the reason why he wasn't playing music anymore. When I asked him, he confessed he was struggling to find inspiration and that he needed time to get over what had happened. *That* was a feeling I understood, so when he started crying again, I did too.

"Hey, Nathan?" I said once our tears dried. "I promise not to sign up for driver's ed until you can."

He cracked a smile. "Did you even have plans to get your license?"

"Nope," I replied, "but now we can take the class together. It will be fun."

This seemed to cheer Nathan up. Hoping to take his mind off things, I convinced him to come inside and watch a movie with me. As I was climbing out of the car, something silver caught my eye. I leaned over to get a better look and—

"Oh!" I gasped, scooping the familiar piece of jewelry off the floorboard.

"What's that?" Nathan asked as I inspected it for damage.

"My mother's necklace." It was no wonder I'd lost it; the jump ring connecting the clasp to the chain had broken. "It was missing, so I decided to check the car. I can't believe it was actually here." Just as I was about to slip the necklace into the safety of my pocket, an idea came to me. "Here," I said, pressing it into the palm of Nathan's hand.

"You...want me to have this?" A small furrow creased his brow "Why?"

"My mom had breast cancer when I was in grade school," I told him. "Her chemo treatment was rough, so my dad wanted to give her something special to get her through it. The lavender symbolizes healing, and she eventually went into remission, so it must have worked. Maybe it will help you too."

Nathan's chest hitched.

Then, fingers trembling, he unclasped his own necklace, added the pendant to the chain, and let it fall into place against his guitar pick.

"Keys, keys. Where are my keys?"

Looking up from my cup of coffee, I spotted Katherine mutter-ing to herself as she scoured the island, lifting Jordan's diorama of the Amazon rainforest, followed by a baseball glove, a loaf of bread, and a pile of receipts. There was a frenzied, desperate sort of energy about her, like she was running low on gas but had miles to cover before reaching her destination. Over the course of the past week, she'd been working relentlessly in preparation for the rummage sale, which started in two days' time. Her job as one of the coordinators was to organize and price all the donations, but watching her flit around the kitchen gave me cause for concern. When was the last time she took a break?

"Katherine?"

No response.

"Katherine," I said again, louder this time, waving my hand to catch her attention.

"Not now, George," she replied without looking up. She was laser focused on digging through the fruit bowl. "I don't have time. My keys are missing."

Orange juice splashed onto the table as Alex snorted into his glass. Isaac, who was seated beside him eating a bowl of cereal, smirked and set down his spoon. When he finished chewing, he folded his hands under his chin and gazed at me with a mischievous smile. His eye was swollen shut, but I didn't bother asking who gave him the shiner; considering how mean-spirited he'd been of late, any of his cousins were likely to be responsible.

"Hey, Uncle George," he said to me. "You're looking magnanimous this morning. Any chance you'll consider lifting my grounding early? There's a party tonight that I'd really love to go to."

Katherine's head snapped up, her lips pursing at the question, but the disapproval melted away when she realized that Isaac was not, in fact, talking to her husband. She blinked. "Jackie, was that you just now? I could have sworn I heard George…"

"Um, yeah," I answered, my cheeks turning pink.

Alex and Isaac both cackled, and I had a feeling they wouldn't let this go for *days*. I could already hear the endless stream of jokes about my gruff, manly voice; in all likelihood, they would think of enough content for their own stand-up routine.

"I'm sorry, honey," she told me. "Do you need something?"

"No, it's just—" I gestured to the lanyard around her neck. "You already have your keys."

She looked down. "*Oh!* You're a lifesaver, Jackie. I swear, it's always when I'm running late that I misplace them. I was supposed to be at the community center thirty minutes ago, and there's so much to do before Monday."

"If you need more help, I'd be happy to come with you," I told her, crossing my fingers under the table. Not only would the volunteer hours look good on my college applications, but I desperately wanted to get out of the house and go somewhere other than school after being on lockdown for two weeks. She hesitated, so I quickly added, "I understand I'm grounded, and I'll do my chores as soon as we get back, but I'm good at organization. Maybe I can take some of the workload off your plate?"

Those were the magic words.

"You know what? That sounds like a wonderful idea," she said, giving me a decisive nod. "Thank you, Jackie. I appreciate the offer."

"Kiss ass," Isaac muttered in a low voice so only I would hear him.

Not low enough, however.

Katherine zeroed in on him with a scowl. "Isaac, why don't you handle the horse stalls today while Jackie helps me with the rummage sale?"

He pointed at her with his spoon. "You're funny, Auntie K, but hard pass."

"That wasn't a suggestion," she said dismissively, then turned to Alex and asked him to load the boxes stacked on the dining room table into her van.

While her back was turned, I stuck my tongue out at Isaac. He flicked a Fruit Loop at me as he grumbled to himself but gave no further protest. He was in too much trouble for his usual shit.

Thirty minutes later, Katherine dropped me off at the front entrance so I wouldn't get drenched. The skies had opened up halfway through our drive, but neither of us were dressed for the weather. As I huddled under the overhang, I watched her park as close as possible, then dash across the lot with a magazine held over her head. After tossing the ruined *Country Living* in the trash and shaking off the rain, Katherine ushered me into the lobby. She waved to a burly lumberjack type sitting behind the donations table, then started down a set of stairs that led to a cavernous event space where the rummage sale would be held.

"Whoa," I said, grinding to a halt when we reached the bottom of the steps. The room had been transformed into what looked like a supersize Goodwill with banquet tables pushed together to form makeshift rows. Never in my life had I seen so much *stuff*, not even when Cole took me to the Rift. Rows of furniture, racks upon racks of clothes, stacks of books, an infinite array of knickknacks. Tupperware, toys, kitchen appliances, and decorative vases. There was even an old pinball machine tucked into one of the corners.

"Impressive, right?" Katherine said, surveying the room with a satisfied gleam in her eye.

"Very," I told her, which was true as long as you ignored how the place smelled like a cross between a cafeteria and a retirement home.

Katherine wasted no time putting me to work. "I have some paperwork that needs my immediate attention, but if you go talk to Gabby"—she pointed to a pretty redhead in a beige sweater—"she can give you something to do."

First, I helped separate and fold clothes. Boring but easy. Once that was done, I spent an hour putting price stickers on DVDs, then moved on to breaking down cardboard boxes. I had just started sorting the sizeable collection of tableware—serving platters, plastic kids plates, fancy bone china, and mason jars galore—when I felt someone staring at me. Despite his location on the opposite side of the room, my eyes immediately snapped to Cole, who was standing at the front of the room holding a storage bin.

The oatmeal I ate for breakfast turned to stone in my stomach.

His gaze was fixed on me as if he'd been waiting for me to notice him, and now that I had, he started in my direction. I tried not to panic, but the two of us hadn't spoken since our encounter in the barn, and I still didn't know how to explain myself. So far, Cole had respected my wishes and kept his distance, but it appeared his patience had run out.

Instead of watching his approach, I returned my attention to a stack of ceramic bowls, examining each one to make sure they were clean and undamaged. One had a crack extending from the rim down to its base, so I set it aside. I felt the exact moment he reached me, but I chose to finish my task rather than lift my head and meet his eyes. Cole huffed, then carelessly deposited the bin he'd been carrying onto the table, making a set of wineglasses rattle together.

"Hey, Jackie." Instead of giving me butterflies, his flirtatious drawl put me on edge. "Fancy meeting you here."

I took a second to compose myself before facing him. "What's in the box?" I asked in a toneless voice.

"More crap from the basement." He patted the lid.

A few rows over, something glass shattered against the floor, and we both jerked our heads in the direction of the noise. The burly lumberjack type from the lobby was cursing a broken lamp at his feet.

"Cole," I said after turning back to him. "What are you doing here?"

"I thought it was obvious." He gestured to the bin. It was the clear, plastic kind, packed with what appeared to be baby clothes. "I'm delivering said crap."

Yeah, uh-huh. To my knowledge, this was Cole's first time bringing a donation despite working on the basement for two weeks and Tony's being only a few blocks away from the community center.

"Well, you missed the drop-off spot." Which was in the lobby he'd walked through moments ago and marked with impossible-to-miss signage. "If you head back upstairs, I'm sure you'll find the table with a huge sign taped to the front that says 'All Donations Here.' If not, you can ask Gabby for directions," I said, pointing her out. "She's a community center employee, so she knows her way around."

"I don't see her," he said, his eyes never leaving mine. "Why don't you show me instead?"

If he was going to be difficult, then two could play that game. I set my jaw. "I'm really busy right now. I should get back to work."

Cole's gaze flicked down to the dishes, then back up to me. "I'm sure those will still be here when you get back. Plus, I don't plan on leaving until we talk."

I exhaled through my mouth, blowing the breath up into my bangs. "Okay, fine. Follow me."

After leading him back to the lobby where he delivered the bin, I headed for the front doors. Hopefully, we could slip outside before Katherine saw us. Cole removed a Tony's Auto Repair snapback cap from his back pocket and pulled it on as he stepped out beside me. The rain had stopped, but the sky was still overcast, and mist clung to the ground in swirling, wispy ribbons. Two volunteers chatted quietly as they took a smoke break. Whatever conversation we were about to have required privacy, so I gestured to a paver walkway that meandered through banal landscaping toward a grove of pine trees with a wooden gazebo at the center.

Neither of us spoke as we followed the path away from the building, and I spent those minutes arranging my thoughts. I knew I couldn't keep avoiding Cole, but how was I supposed to tell my maybe sort of boyfriend that we had to break up because I didn't want to be kicked out of his family in the event we didn't work out? The mental gymnastics was draining.

When we reached the gazebo, Cole motioned for me to step inside first. It had built-in benches, most of which were wet from the rain. I found a small section that looked dry, brushed my hand over the wood to make sure I wouldn't spend the rest of the day wearing damp jeans, and sat down.

"That was a pretty slick move you pulled this morning." Cole leaned back against the support post opposite me, tucking one foot over the other with a casual grace that was annoying and attractive at the same time. "I didn't know you had it in you."

"What move?" I asked.

"Offering my mom help with the rummage sale to get out of your chores," he replied, flashing me his dimple. "I'd watch out if I were you. Isaac is furious. He thought he was done mucking stalls for the foreseeable future, and you ruined that for him."

"First off," I said, which made Cole's smile bloom in full, "I told your mom I'd do my chores when we get home. If Isaac hadn't opened his mouth, then she never would have paid him any attention, and I'd still be responsible for the stalls. Second, how is Isaac being pissed at me news? In case you missed it, your cousin has been angry with the universe for months now."

He chuckled. "Fair. It's kinda hard to miss when he's being arrested."

"Any idea what his issue is?" I asked since we were on the topic. "Alex and Nathan said it started after your uncle visited, but they—

Cole didn't let me finish. "I didn't come here to talk about Isaac."

Down to business, then. "Okay." I calmly crossed my legs. "What would you like to talk about?"

"Don't do that," he said with a frown.

"Do what?"

"*That.*" He gestured at me vaguely. "Don't talk to me like I'm a kindergartner you need to placate while acting like everything is fine."

"I'm not acting—"

"Yes, you are." Annoyance was creeping into his voice, so he paused and slowly inhaled through his nose. "Listen, I've tried giving you space, but it's been over a week, and you won't even look at me. You know that makes me feel like shit, right? I get that you're not used to being reprimanded, and that freaked you out, but come on, Jackie. My mom won't send me away if we spend time together."

"I'm sorry," I said, wincing at his pinched expression. "You're probably right, but...I don't think we should risk it."

The notch between his brows deepened, and he straightened up. "Risk what?"

Your family.

When I didn't answer, Cole added, "Is this an excuse because you're still mad about O'Brady's? Or is it because I walked out on our conversation in the barn? I know I shouldn't have done that, but I was ticked off and didn't want to snap at you."

"I'm not making excuses, I just"—I took a deep breath—"I don't think this is working."

A taut silence stretched between us as Cole stared at me, his eyes narrowing.

"What do you mean, 'this isn't working'?" he finally asked in a carefully controlled tone. "This, as in our three-week-long relationship?"

My throat constricted. "I—yes."

"No shit, Jackie," he said through clenched teeth. Even from five feet away, I could feel the frustration pouring off him in waves. "You haven't given us enough time for it to work."

"Exactly how much time do I owe you, then?" I said as a tiny flame of resentment kindled in my chest. "A month? Three?" It was an unfair question, but there was a defiant look in Cole's eyes that said he wouldn't lie down and roll over so easily. If I had to resort to fighting fire with fire, so be it. "When I came back in August, I *warned* you that I'm not okay yet. So I'm sorry our relationship isn't at the top of my priority list, but my entire world imploded, and I'm just starting to put the pieces back together. I wish I could snap my fingers and be all healed up for you, but it doesn't work that way, Cole."

"That's what you're going with? The *you're too broken* spiel?" He shook his head. "Give me a break, Jackie. Neither of us are stupid enough to believe that."

I bristled. "So you think I'm *pretending* to be upset?"

"Of course not! Anyone with eyes can see that you're still struggling." A vein pulsed in his temple as he spoke. "Do you honestly think I haven't noticed that you struggle to breathe when something reminds you of your family? Or how you're up at the crack of dawn each day because you can't sleep?"

"What's your point?"

Cole yanked off his snapback and carved his fingers through his hair, gripping it at the roots before letting go. He jammed the hat back on. "Remember when I took you to the Rift?" he asked. "We were having a really great time, but then you found that teacup."

"I remember," I whispered as the memory coiled around my chest like a vise.

"I could tell you were on the verge of spiraling, but that didn't happen, did it?" The floor of the gazebo creaked as he walked over and crouched down in front of me. "You pushed through the pain so you could stay in the moment with me, and that means something, Jackie."

"Oh really? Like what? That being with you will *heal* me?" I scoffed and rolled my eyes even as a thread of doubt wove its way through the cracks in my psyche. What if he was right? What if being with him helped, and he was exactly what I needed?

No, stop! I couldn't start second-guessing myself.

"Well, I wouldn't put it like that, but…yeah," he admitted, his familiar cocky smile flickering to life on his face, then dying just as quickly. He reached out and put his hand on my knee. "Living in Colorado, spending time with me and my family, all that is good for you. You're doing way better than this summer, and don't try to deny it. Danny told me how bad things got. It's only been two months, but now you're running election campaigns and being a big sister to Parker and worrying about Isaac even though he's turned into a raging asshole. Don't push me away because we got into a little bit of trouble."

He said this all so easily, with his whole chest, like if he spoke with enough conviction, it would changes things. It made my heart hurt, knowing that even if he was right, my mind was already made up. He had no idea what was at stake for me, how much worse off I'd be if I lost another family.

"Cole…"

"No, listen. This is gonna sound cheesy, but being with you makes me feel right in a way I haven't felt since playing football," he told me, his voice rough with emotion. "I know you're still grieving, but let me support you through it. I don't want to lose this feeling with you."

The expression on his face was so soft, his eyes so blue.

"That's not fair," I said, shrinking away from his gaze. The tender way he was watching me was overwhelming, and I couldn't handle it anymore. "You can't put the pressure of your happiness on my shoulders."

Time paused for a single, breathless beat, but that was all it took for his mood to shift.

"Are you shitting me?" He rose out of his crouched position so he was standing over me and clenched his fists. "That's not what I'm doing at all."

"Really? Considering your whole life right now, and then you tell me I'm the only good part of it…" I lifted my shoulder in a half shrug.

"What do you mean?" he snapped. "What are you saying about my life right now?"

"You know exactly what I mean!" I exclaimed, losing my patience. "You decide to defer school, then start brooding because you feel left behind, because all you're doing is working at your jobs and have nothing going on—"

Cole reared back as if I'd struck him. "Is that how you see it?"

Crap, that came out wrong. "No, I—"

"What?" he spat. "You think I'm some loser because I don't have a bright, shiny future at Princeton lined up for myself like you do?"

I looked down at my hands in my lap. "Those are your words, not mine." This wasn't how I'd wanted our conversation to go, for Cole to believe I thought so little of him, but how could I fix things now when the final outcome would be the same either way?

"Well, you've obviously been thinking them if you feel like I'm putting the pressure of my happiness on your shoulders."

"Cole, please," I said, trying to tell him he was getting things twisted, but he was done listening, done talking, done with me.

"No!" He slashed his hand through the air to cut me off. "Just forget it, Jackie. You don't need to concern yourself with my feelings anymore. Clearly, they were never a priority for you to begin with."

Then Cole walked away just like he had that night in the barn.

The difference was this time, it felt like for good.

fourteen

"I HAVE SOME NEWS TO share," Cole told his family halfway through dinner Friday night.

I wasn't hungry, I hadn't been since our conversation at the community center last weekend, but the only remaining vestige of my appetite vanished at his words. His expression was neutral when I stole a look at him through the curtain of my hair, but that didn't stop my stomach from churning, and I immediately set down my fork as a sense of déjà vu flooded through me. The last time he made an announcement at dinner, I'd lost my bedroom as a result.

Cole paused as he waited for the table to quiet down, but that only opened the floor to his impatient siblings.

"Did you get a tattoo like Isaac?" Benny asked excitedly, which made Katherine choke and prompted a round of snickering from the rest of the group. The infamous tattoo incident had made an impression on the youngest Walter; Benny was constantly asking Isaac to see the phoenix on his back or talking about what kind of ink he wanted to get when he was older, much to his mother's distress.

"Not likely," Jordan said as he helped himself to another serving of mashed potatoes. "Even if he did, I don't think he's stupid enough to announce it at dinner."

Jack nodded in agreement. "Yeah, Mom would kill him. I bet he got another promotion or something like that."

"Are you the manager at the Gas Exchange now too?" Isaac asked, his tone mocking. "Congrats, man. At this rate, you won't need to go to college."

His comment made me flinch, but thankfully nobody noticed.

"Isaac," George said, shooting him a warning look from across the table.

"Don't be a dick," Lee added, whacking his brother upside the head.

Nathan leaned toward Jack. "This isn't about a promotion," he stage whispered, holding his hand against the side of his mouth. "I think Cole is finally going to confess that he's found his true calling as a ballet dancer."

"With *his* knee?" Alex scoffed, clearly missing the memo about Nathan's attempt to lighten the mood. "Yeah, right."

"You're all wrong," Parker said. "Obviously, he's moving to Las Vegas to become an Elvis impersonator."

"Hey!" Cole clapped once to get everyone's attention. "Are you guys done?"

"Go on, honey," Katherine said. There was a gleam of mischief in her eyes as she reached out and gave his hand an encouraging squeeze. "Tell us your news. Even if you're moving to Vegas, just know that we'll all support you no matter what. I've always loved Elvis."

The table exploded with laughter.

Cole heaved an exasperated sigh and shook his head, but the corners of his mouth turned up slightly at his mother's teasing. "Back in September, an amateur dirt track racer hired me to rebuild his engine," he said once everyone settled down. "He was impressed with my work, so he referred one of his friends to me, and this new guy is legit. He's won most of the local races, even a few regional ones. People are saying he might go pro."

"That sounds—Whoa! Careful, kiddo," George said, saving his glass of water from being knocked over as Zack reached for the bread basket. "Sorry, Cole. You were saying?"

"I've been hired by another racer," Cole told him. "One who might make a career of it."

"What does that mean for you?" Katherine asked.

"Well, in the short term, I have an engine to rebuild, but if it goes well, he said he's looking for a more permanent mechanic," he explained. "I still plan on going to school, but I think I want to start my own business, build up a client list."

"Oh, Cole!" Katherine exclaimed. "That's amazing news! I'm so proud of you."

A broad smile stretched across his face, and in a cringe-worthy impression, he said, "Thank you. Thank you very much."

As the rest of the Walters offered him congratulations, I let out a small breath of relief. For the past week, I'd been on pins and needles expecting some kind of retaliation from Cole as a result of our breakup, but so far, there had been nothing. When he cleared his throat two minutes earlier, I'd thought this was it.

The rest of dinner was a lively affair as Cole's family fed off his excitement. It had been a while since I felt like an outsider sitting at their table, but as I watched everyone share stories and laugh together, I receded into myself with a bittersweet smile. I was genuinely happy for Cole; although it was over between us, I only wanted the best for him. But at the same time, I didn't think Cole would appreciate me joining in on the celebration. This felt like a moment for family, so while everyone was listening to Jack tell a joke about aliens kidnapping Elvis Presley, I slipped away without anyone noticing.

If "Name the worst holiday to break up with someone" was a *Family Feud* question, Halloween probably wouldn't come to mind. Valentine's Day, New Year's, and Christmas would be front-runners, along with birthdays and anniversaries. But as I wandered through Chase Kennedy's party dressed as one half of Bonnie and Clyde, I realized October 31 wasn't a fun day to be recently single.

After ending things with Cole, I didn't bother finding a different costume since I wasn't allowed to attend the party. It never crossed my mind that I'd be released from my punishment after only three weeks. However, Katherine informed me this morning that I wasn't grounded anymore, which left me with zero time to come up with a new outfit.

I told myself it didn't matter, that tonight would be a blast no matter what I wore. Spending time with my friends would help me forget how miserable I'd been since Cole's and my split. There were so many emotions churning in my mind—guilt, frustration, relief, dread—that I found it difficult to focus in school. I'd even had another nightmare about losing the Walters in an accident like my family's.

Worse, Cole was acting...strange. When I told him I wanted to be friends back in September, he'd responded with spite. While the cold shoulder he gave me was annoying, at least I knew he felt something toward me. But now? Cole was being perfectly polite. He offered me smiles when we passed each other in the hall and greeted me in the morning at breakfast but otherwise couldn't be bothered. It was like I'd never been more to him than the random girl forced to move into his house. The last thing I wanted was for him to hurt, but it was startling and more than a bit painful to see how unaffected he seemed.

Chase's party was impressive—the entire Victorian-style house was decked out like a haunted mansion—but it wasn't the distraction I had hoped it would be. Even though all my friends were excited to see me, everyone was coupled up, which made me feel like a third wheel, especially when I didn't have a partner for beer pong. The constant questions were exhausting too. Those in the know wanted details about the breakup. Everyone else just wanted to know where Cole was. By the third "Hey, where's your boyfriend at?" I was done.

Returning to the ranch, taking off this stupid costume, and watching a movie would be a much better way to spend the rest of my night, but I didn't want to be a buzzkill, so I decided to wait for the party to end out in the truck. Maybe Alex had left one of his books in the back seat. If not, I could always take a nap.

When I stepped outside and found Isaac smoking on the pumpkin-lined steps of the porch, my eyebrows shot up. Although he got off easy for pulling the fire alarm at homecoming, Katherine and George were far from willing to let him off the hook. They had him on house arrest for the foreseeable future, so there was no way he was allowed to be here. He tensed when I sat beside him but didn't say anything.

"Too cool to dress up for Halloween?" I teased as I brushed a hand down my skirt, smoothing out the fabric. His entire outfit was black, from his T-shirt down to his boots. "I hate to be the bearer of bad news, but moody delinquent doesn't count as a costume."

"Who said I didn't dress up?" he replied, not bothering to look at me as he lifted the cigarette to his lips.

"What are you supposed to be, then?" I asked. "Wait, no. Let me guess... Are you a stagehand? No, that's not right. Professional mourner? How about an off-brand grim reaper who lost his scythe?"

Isaac turned and exhaled into my face. "Lung cancer."

"Charming," I said, wrinkling my nose as I waved the smoke away.

"At least I'm not missing half my costume." He eyed me up and down. "What happened to your partner in crime, Bonnie? Lose him in a shoot-out on the way over? Must be heartbreaking for you."

The smile faded from my face. "Wow, okay. You don't have to be such an asshole. I was just giving you a hard time."

"Come on, Jackie," he said, nudging me in the side with his elbow. "You should know from experience that it's a reflex for me."

It didn't used to be, I thought. Pre-summer Isaac always had an inappropriate comment at the ready, but he wasn't caustic.

"By the way, if you're looking for a replacement boyfriend, I can submit my mug shot as part of my résumé," he added. "I hear moody delinquent bad boys are all the rage."

I sighed. "Why are you here, Isaac? Katherine's going to kill you if she realizes you left the house."

His expression soured. "I don't know. Why'd you screw things up with Cole?"

"All right," I said, slapping my thighs and standing. "I'm not in the mood to deal with your shit tonight."

"Wait, don't go!" He quickly stubbed his cigarette out on the steps and lurched to his feet. "That was harsh. I'm sorry. Everyone's been at me about homecoming, and I just—look, can we not talk about the serious stuff? I'm sick of it."

Music from the party amplified as the front door opened and two drunk girls dressed as Harley Quinn and Poison Ivy stumbled out.

"Huh," I said, cocking my head as I turned back to Isaac. "I didn't realize Halloween costumes were such a serious matter for you."

"Yeah, well, I'm hungry. If you don't want me to reach peak douche-baggery, then I'm gonna need some food." He threw an arm over my shoulder and steered me toward the sidewalk. "There's a diner up the block. I'll pay."

"Thanks," I said, shrugging off his arm, "but I ate before the party."

"Of course you did. You're the responsible type," he replied. "But something tells me you're not in a festive mood, so let's get outta here. This place makes the best French silk pie, and pie fixes everything."

Well, he had me there, so I sighed and gestured for him to lead the way.

The Neon Grill was everything I expected from a small town diner. There was a prominent counter with round stools, direct service, a window into the kitchen, red vinyl booths cracked with age, and a checkered floor. Eclectic signage and newspaper clippings about hometown success stories covered the walls. The place was even decorated for the holiday—paper bats hung from the ceiling, plastic jack-o'-lanterns sat on the edge of each table, and fake spiderwebs covered the windows.

It was late, so there weren't many customers, and we were able to snag a booth away from the door. After looking over the menu, Isaac ordered a full breakfast—coffee, two scrambled eggs, pancakes, bacon, hash browns, and a slice of pie—while I opted for a side of fries and a Dr Pepper. We played hangman on the paper placemats using crayons while we waited for our food, and I beat Isaac every time because he only picked inappropriate words, like expletives and body parts.

Once our food arrived, I waited until Isaac had polished off his stack of pancakes before easing into a real conversation. "I promise this isn't me trying to interrogate you, but I have to make sure. Are you okay? I know things have been rough lately."

He had already made it clear that he wasn't interested in talking, but I wanted Isaac to know I was willing to listen if he ever changed his mind. I'd been in a similar place over the summer—drowning in guilt and grief but unwilling to discuss it. Danny checked in with me weekly despite my silence on the subject. If he'd given up, I never would have eventually unburdened myself to him, and although it had been painful, the experience was cathartic.

Isaac stopped chewing. For a split second, he looked like a deer caught in headlights, but then a smirk overtook his face. "I've basically been on lockdown for two months, so I could be better. Wanna know what would help?"

"I swear to God," I said, pointing a fry at him, "if the next comment that comes out of your mouth is pervy, I'll dump my soda on you."

He batted the crinkle cut out of my hand. "Stop making it so easy, then. Do you know how many dirty things I can say using the words *come* and *mouth*?"

"Isaac…" I said, grabbing my glass and raising it threateningly.

"Whoa!" He held up his hands in surrender. "Chill, Jackie. I definitely won't be okay if I'm drenched in Dr Pepper. What happened to comforting your friend in his time of need?"

"I don't remember making any offers of comfort, but all right. In what *PG* way can I make you feel better?" I asked, making sure to stress the PG part.

"Well, I've been so down lately." He sighed dramatically, his shoulders slumping like a cartoon character. "I could really use a distraction."

I rolled my eyes at his theatrics. "Like what?"

Isaac slathered his toast in grape jelly before answering. "Why don't you tell me all about what happened with you and Cole?" he said after setting down the butter knife. "He's been frustratingly tight-lipped on the subject."

Why the request caught me off guard was anyone's guess. Isaac was such a gossip. He'd fit right in with Megan and Savannah, so it was only natural that he wanted all the details, but I was unwilling to share them for his entertainment. "What happened to not wanting to talk about serious stuff?" I deflected.

"I meant *my* serious stuff." He piled some scrambled eggs and a strip of bacon onto the piece of toast. "I'm all for hearing about yours," he added, then took an enormous bite of his concoction.

"That's not going to happen," I told him with a laugh.

It was quiet for a moment as he chewed his food. "That's fine," he said once he finally swallowed. "I'm more than happy to go back to discussing your mouth and me coming."

"*Isaac!*" I glared and chucked a fry at him. "You can't say stuff like that. I know you're winding me up, but one of these days, someone won't find it funny, and you'll get reported for sexual harassment."

His smirk instantly vanished. "Right, sorry." I'd never seen him look embarrassed before, so it was fascinating watching a flush spread across his cheeks. "I...um—I think I use it as a defense mechanism," he said, rubbing the back of his neck, "but that's no excuse."

I sighed. No, it wasn't, but I was glad he realized it. "How about instead of trying to make me feel uncomfortable so you don't have to, we take turns opening up to each other?"

"And how would that work?" he asked cautiously.

"You get one question, and I promise to answer it truthfully," I explained. "In exchange, I can ask one as well, and you have to be honest. I'll even go first if you want."

Isaac hesitated, then slowly nodded his head. "Yeah, okay."

"I'm assuming you want to know about me and Cole?"

He leaned into the table, his eyes practically glowing with excitement. "Yeah, the breakup. Was it because he ditched you at O'Brady's? That's what Alex said."

As annoyed as I was that Alex made assumptions based on what happened that night and then gossiped about it, maybe I could use the rumor to my advantage and dodge a painful bullet. I wouldn't lie, but just because I promised Isaac the truth didn't mean I wanted to give it. Thinking about Cole made my whole chest hurt.

Keeping my expression as neutral as possible, I said, "Is that your question?"

"Wait, no." Isaac tapped his finger against the table a few times, then reworded. "Why *exactly* did you break up?"

Oh well, it had been worth a shot. "Because I'm afraid of losing your family."

A deep crease formed on his forehead. He'd more than likely expected to hear some scandalous story, not a confession about what had become my biggest fear, but I'd promised honesty. "I'm not following."

"It's kind of hard to explain," I said, rubbing a hand down my face, "but I *really* like your cousin." I couldn't—no, wouldn't—use the other L word. "I know he feels the same way, so if we gave dating a real go, then I think it would lead to something serious."

He gave me a *no shit* look. "Yeah, that's kinda the whole point of dating someone…"

"That doesn't mean we're going to end up together," I replied. "We're both so young, and I just… What if things end badly? I don't want your family to have to choose sides."

Isaac threw back his head and laughed. "That's the stupidest shit I've ever heard."

My head jerked back. "Why? Most relationships end in—"

"You do realize that things have already ended badly, right?" he said over me. "My aunt and uncle would never kick you to the curb over something as stupid as a breakup, and even if people did start picking sides, I'd bet everything on you winning that contest. Cole's a cocky jackass. You're much more likable. This is also the moment where I'd usually say something inappropriate, but I'm gonna bite my tongue."

I shook my head. "But… I'm not a Walter."

"Jesus, you're ridiculous," Isaac muttered, then reached across the table and, to my utter surprise, took my hand in his. It was the sort of comforting gesture I never would have expected from him. "Jackie, we might not have the same last name, but you should know by now you're one of us."

An impossibly large lump formed in my throat. "Thanks, Isaac. I appreciate the sentiment."

"Hey, if you wanna give up what you have with Cole because you're afraid something bad *might* happen, then do you," Isaac said, letting go of my hand and giving it a patronizing little pat. "Just know that I think you're being a massive idiot."

"Noted," I said, lowering my gaze to the half-eaten plate of fries in front of me, "but you got your answer, and I don't want to talk about Cole anymore. It's my turn."

He blew out a breath in a *let's get this over with* way, then nodded.

My fries had gone cold a while ago, but I popped one into my mouth as I contemplated the perfect question. Isaac probably expected me to inquire about homecoming, but asking why he set off the fire alarm didn't guarantee an explanation for the rest of his angry, destructive behavior. While I wasn't a hundred percent certain, I was willing to bet Isaac's issues stemmed from his father. When he started pushing the rest of his eggs around his plate instead of eating them, I realized I was taking too long.

After washing down another fry with a sip of soda, I asked, "What happened between you and your dad when he came to visit this summer?"

Isaac's jaw unhinged, and his fork clattered against the table, sending a chunk of scrambled egg flying. "How the *hell* do you know about that?" he exclaimed. "You weren't even here."

As if he needed to ask. "Family of gossips, remember?"

"I'm not sure I like this opening up to each other bullshit," he grumbled.

With a little smirk, I yanked Isaac's pie across the table in case he was thinking of backing out of our exchange. I'd already given him an answer. Now he owed me one. "I'm holding this hostage until you start talking."

"Keep it," he said, waving me off. "I'll just order another."

"*Isaac!*"

"My dad's a selfish piece of shit, okay?" he snapped. "That's what happened. That's always what happens with him." The muscles in his neck were corded, but when I looked into his eyes, the anger I expected to find there was missing. Instead, they were hollow. It was a startling expression to see on his face, and I—

Oh crap. This was Nathan all over again, wasn't it? All I wanted to do was be helpful and supportive, but somehow I'd made things worse by being pushy.

"I'm sorry," I said, sliding the piece of pie back over. "We don't have to talk about this." It was obvious that I hadn't simply asked an uncomfortable question or poked a bruise; I'd struck a nerve that went down to Isaac's core.

"No, fair's fair," he said in a clipped tone. "You just surprised me."

He scraped his fingers through his hair in such a rough manner that my own scalp ached, but before I could make a second attempt at letting him off the hook, Isaac dove into his story. Some of it I already knew. His mom left after Lee was born, and they stayed with Katherine and George because their dad had been stationed overseas since they were little. But most of what he shared was new information. Peter Walter's MSO—military service obligation—was up this year, and he'd promised to request resignation and move home so they could be together as a family. What Isaac thought would be a permanent reunion turned into another too-short visit when his dad announced that he'd been promoted from lieutenant colonel to colonel. That meant he'd be stationed in Germany for the next six years, and while it wasn't dangerous like some of his previous posts, Isaac's dad didn't want to uproot his kids from their lives.

Translation: just because George Walter was an outstanding father didn't mean that good parenting ran in the family; evidently, his brother wasn't up to the task.

"Isaac, I don't know what to say." *Your dad sucks* didn't quite do the situation justice.

A laugh broke free from his throat, but there was no humor to it. "Did you know I used to play soccer when I was younger?" he asked, paying no notice to my previous statement. Words kept spilling from his mouth, almost like he couldn't stop talking now that he was finally letting out the poison. "I got into it because it's my dad's favorite sport but quit once I realized even *that* wouldn't get him to come to one of my games. I was good too. Probably could've made varsity."

I scrunched up my face. "I'm trying to picture you with a letter jacket instead of a leather one, and I just don't see it."

His lips twisted into a false smile. "You'll get a kick out of this, then. Freshman year, I was on the AcaDeca team, and we won state. Of course, dear old dad didn't even congratulate me, but that's par for the course."

My mouth fell open. "Hold on—*you* did Academic Decathlon?"

"This might come as a shock to you," he said matter-of-factly, "but I have the highest GPA out of all my cousins."

"How is that even possible?" I asked, my voice pitching higher than usual. "You skip class all the time!"

He shrugged. "I don't have to try. School's always been easy for me. Besides, why should I waste my time when, no matter how well I do, my dad doesn't give a shit?"

"So this summer when he told you he wasn't coming home, you what? Decided to flip an asshole switch?" I said, ignoring the tinge of jealousy curling in my gut. My report cards were always flawless, but I worked hard for my grades, and it was annoying when others didn't have to put in the same effort. "What were you trying to do? Get his attention some other way?"

Isaac flushed. "I wanted him to feel as pissed and disappointed as I did," he admitted. "You don't have to tell me. I already know it was stupid. Katherine contacted him after I was arrested, and guess what? He couldn't even bother to be annoyed with me. Just promised to send me away to a military academy for my final semester if I get in trouble again."

"He didn't care at all?" I asked quietly. I couldn't imagine how that felt.

"Nope," Isaac said. "You're lucky. Your parents might be gone, but at least they loved you."

I sucked my cheeks in and counted to five. Nothing about my parents being gone was lucky, but I also understood that Isaac was too wrapped up in his own issues to realize how insensitive his words sounded. Reaching across the table, I whacked him over the head. "I've listened to a lot of stupid stuff come out of your mouth before," I replied as calmly as I could, "but that was the most privileged, ignorant bullshit I've ever heard. My parents are *dead*. Don't tell me I'm lucky."

"Oh shit." His face drained of color. "Jackie, I'm so sorry. I didn't mean—"

"I know you didn't, Isaac," I said, pinching the bridge of my nose, "but you're so bitter about your dad that you're forgetting the most important thing—Katherine and George love you. They're your parents in all the ways that matter. You have this amazing, wonderful family that some people would kill to have, but if you keep hurting them, they won't be there for you when you need them the most."

He pressed his lips into a tight line. "You sound like my brother."

Huh. That was interesting…

"Oh my God," I gasped after a second. "Is *he* the one who gave you that black eye?"

"Maybe," he mumbled in a disgruntled tone that made me giggle. "It was a cheap shot."

"I'm honestly shocked," I told him. "Lee's done nothing but defend you, so whatever you did must've been spectacularly crappy. He even went so far as to sabotage a prank Jordan and Parker targeted you with."

"Well, you're not wrong." Isaac dipped his chin, unable to meet my gaze. "He, um, didn't like that…that I…"

"You don't have to tell me if you're not ready to. I think you've been open enough for one night. Just remember I'm willing to trade a truth for a truth next time you're pissed off or want to get something off your chest, okay?"

"Yeah." He nodded. "I can handle that."

"Good." I took one last sip of my soda, then set it aside. "Let's pay and get you home before Katherine notices you're missing."

fifteen

OPERATION SNEAK ISAAC BACK INTO the house went smoother than I expected.

After paying for our food and walking back to Chase's, I found Alex and Kim making out on the patio. Interrupting them was uncomfortable—nothing says awkward like witnessing your friend shoving her tongue so far down your ex's throat that you wonder about potential choking hazards—but ultimately worked out in our favor. Alex didn't bat an eye at the sight of Isaac standing next to me. In fact, he enthusiastically handed over the truck keys when we mentioned wanting to leave. None of the other Walters had been invited to the party, so Alex could stay over at Kim's if he didn't have to drive me home.

When we got back to the ranch, I made no effort to soften the sounds of my arrival. While Isaac was busy scaling the tree outside his bedroom window, I walked straight through the front door, letting the screen door slam shut behind me, and kicked off my heels by the shoe cubby. Trick-or-treating must have been successful, because when I stepped into the kitchen, my attention was immediately drawn to the den where the youngest Walters were gathered, costumes still on, candy hauls dumped on the floor in front of them, and *Hocus Pocus* playing softly in the background. A fierce negotiation was taking place between Parker and Jack, but eventually she pushed five Almond Joys over to him and he handed her a Tootsie Pop in return. It was almost ten o'clock, so I was more than a little shocked to find them still up but recognized an excessive amount of sugar was probably the culprit when Benny let out a high-pitched scream and tackled his twin to the floor.

I heard a heavy sigh, then what sounded like the page of a book turning. "Back so soon?"

How I'd missed Katherine when I first entered the kitchen was anyone's guess, but she was sitting at the table, a paperback in one hand and a glass of wine in the other. A few pieces of fun-size chocolate bars were arranged in front of her.

"Wasn't really up for a party," I told her.

Katherine frowned slightly but let my comment go. "Is Alex with you?"

"No, he wanted to stay. One of my friends gave me a ride." Isaac had parked the truck behind the shed where it wouldn't be visible from the house, left the keys on the front seat, and texted Alex to move it back to its usual spot once Kim dropped him off in the morning. I hated lying to Katherine, but it was a necessary evil to make sure Isaac wasn't sent away to a military academy, so I appeased my guilt by offering my help. "I'm not tired, so if you want, I can stay up with the kids and get them to bed once the movie is over."

The speed at which Katherine downed the rest of her wine and jumped up made me grin. "You," she said, grasping my head with both hands and pressing a kiss to my forehead, "are an angel."

She gave me a few instructions—mainly don't let anyone trick me into putting on another movie and make sure everyone brushed their teeth—then retreated to her room. The sugar crash happened not long after. By the time the closing credits rolled, the kids could barely keep their eyes open, and it didn't take much effort for me to corral them upstairs. Teeth were brushed, pajamas were donned, and then I was standing in the middle of the upstairs hall, not sure what to do with myself.

Despite the late hour, I was wide awake.

I'd spent most of the movie fixated on what Isaac told me at the diner. I desperately wanted to believe him—that I was one of the Walters now. On nights like tonight, when I was treated like an older sister, it wasn't so difficult a notion to accept. But there were other times, like dinner yesterday, when I wondered if a small part of me would always feel like an outsider. At that moment, what I wanted the most was to talk to Danny. He'd learned over the summer how to distract me from overthinking, but I didn't want to chance waking him, because dress rehearsals for the play started tomorrow, and he needed to get a good night's sleep.

Nathan was a good listener, and things were better between us now that he'd told me about his continued seizures, but he typically kept to a sleep schedule. I glanced out the window even though there was no way he was awake at this hour, then did a double take when I noticed the light still on in the barn.

That decided things, then.

I was almost to the stairs when I heard whispered voices. The door to Katherine and George's room was ajar, a soft golden light pouring through the crack.

"...think we were too hard on them?" Katherine asked as I passed by.

Not wanting to invade their privacy, I kept going, but then George spoke, and it brought me to a standstill. "Not at all. They had to learn that we have expectations for their behavior, especially if they're dating."

Oh hell. Nerves churned in my stomach as I realized Katherine and George were talking about me and Cole. Eavesdropping on their conversation made my skin prickle in discomfort, but at the same time, I'd been worrying nonstop since Katherine caught the two of us together. I bit my lip as I considered what to do. If this was my chance to know how she really felt...

"I'm not sure if they are dating anymore." A surprising amount of disappointment laced Katherine's tone.

George chuckled softly. "Well, that was quick."

"Don't laugh," she hissed at him. "I'm worried it's our fault. Jackie's been withdrawn since our discussion, I haven't seen them spend any time together since, and now *this*?"

I had no clue what she meant by "this," but the way she emphasized the word made it seem bad, and an unsettling chill skated down my spine.

"Love, it's going to be okay," he replied, and I could hear the smile on his face. "They're teenagers. Breakups happen."

"I know, I know. But seeing them together? It put a ridiculous thought in my head that I can't stop picturing."

"What's that?" George asked.

Katherine paused for so long, I thought I'd missed her response. "That she'd be our daughter one day," she finally said. "Officially."

"It's a nice thought," George replied with another soft laugh, "but Jackie will always be a part of our family regardless of her relationship with Cole. You know that, right?"

His declaration made me sway slightly on the spot.

"Yes, but..." Katherine's voice cracked. "What if she goes off to Princeton and never comes back?"

I leaned in closer, desperate to hear George's answer, but the floorboard creaked below me. Heart slamming against my rib cage, I scrambled away as quietly as possible and fled to the safety of my room. Once I was inside, I stood with my back pressed against the door as my chest rose and fell in quick succession. My mind was racing with everything I'd overheard.

For starters, what the hell was Katherine thinking, picturing me and Cole married? I was only sixteen, for crying out loud! Marriage wasn't even included in my ten-year plan. And George! Was I losing it, or had he really said I'd always be a part of the Walters family? If he truly meant that, did that mean... Was Isaac *right*? I really was one of them now?

Pulling out my phone, I slid down the door and opened my photo gallery. Before leaving for New York, I'd taken a picture of the mural Katherine had painted on the side of the barn. I'd been so touched by her gesture to include me. At the time, I'd thought she added me because she felt bad that I didn't have anyone else, but it still warmed my heart to know someone was thinking of me. Once I got home, however, all the pain and guilt I'd been avoiding came flooding back, and I hadn't been able to stomach looking at it. How could I when my real family was gone?

Now, though? I couldn't look away.

There I was, right between Cole and Alex. Danny was beside us, and I—

Oh no.

My eyes snapped back to Cole. He had his arm wrapped around my shoulders, his hair tousled just so. With the exception of his letterman jacket, which probably felt like a sore subject for him now, Katherine had captured her second oldest perfectly. She'd even gotten his smirk down right.

God, I loved that smirk. He sure knew how to use it to irritate me, but that was half the fun of things, wasn't it? The back-and-forth, testing each other until we knew all the right buttons to push. What we had was so much more than the banter and flirting, though. It had taken Danny an entire summer to learn the ins and outs of who I was: what my tells were, what made me laugh, when to back off versus when to dig deeper, how to comfort me. Those were all things that his twin knew intrinsically. Cole had me pegged from the moment I arrived in Colorado, and he'd used that understanding to help me get by, even if I didn't realize it at the time.

Cole was right; I had been afraid. In fact, I'd been so afraid of what I might lose that I forgot the very first thing he taught me when I moved to Colorado—that it was okay to live a little. And because of that fear, I'd thrown everything I had with him away.

But maybe I could get it back.

By now, it was nearly one fifteen in the morning, but I knew Cole had picked up an extra shift at the Gas Exchange instead of going to the party; I'd seen the Buick parked in the lot when we drove through town on the way to Chase's. When Cole worked second shift, he typically got home between one and two, so if he was home, maybe he was still up?

I jumped to my feet and stepped back into the hall. There were no more whispers coming from Katherine and George's room, but when I reached the art studio, I was relieved to see the door partly open and a light on.

As soon as I stepped inside, I immediately knew something was wrong. Cole was a bit of a slob, but the space was tidier than normal—bed made, no clothes on the floor. The real sign that something was amiss were the packing boxes. Only three, but they were all filled to the brim with Cole's belongings. The light I'd seen from the hall was coming from the lamp on the computer desk, and when I walked over to turn it off, I noticed the letter. It was addressed to me.

Jackie,

I have a confession to make, but I'm not much of a wordsmith so bear with me.

For as long as I can remember, my mom has always told me that the sky's the limit. I could be whoever I wanted to be, do whatever I set my mind to, and all that was required of me was to put in the work. Sometime around my sixth birthday, I decided that my dream was to be a professional football player (lofty and cliché, I know). I started doing drills with my dad in the backyard to improve my abilities, and not to brag, but I was a natural. I went from being the MVP of my flag football league to making varsity freshman year.

Back then, being a wide receiver meant everything to me. It gave me purpose, and there was no better feeling than burning a DB and catching a deep ball over the top for a touchdown. And the pressure I felt when it was the last play of the game and I knew I had to make something happen to win? Pure bliss. Maybe you're right about me being a masochist, because I didn't mind taking a hard hit every now and then. Getting the wind knocked out of me was a good reminder that I was alive.

But my mom was wrong. Limits exist, and not all dreams come true.

When I was forced to quit because of my injury, it was like a piece of my very identity had been carved away. Without football, I felt empty and broken. I went through the motions day after day, and the only thing that made life feel less monotonous was working on the Buick.

Then something happened that changed everything. You came along. Suddenly, that hollow feeling inside my chest started to fill up whenever we spent time together. Don't ask me why, because I'm still confused by how much you affect me. Maybe it's because you never knew me as Cole Walter, the best receiver in the state. Or maybe like recognized like? You were so broken when you first came here, not in the same way I was, but we'd both lost a major part of who we were. Whatever the reason, I quickly realized you were the antidote to everything wrong with me.

I think that's a contributing factor to why that empty feeling crept back in while you were away this summer.

All my friends were leaving for college, and I knew I couldn't afford to go. And even if it were possible, I didn't know what to study. Football had always been my plan. So where did that leave me? No scholarship, no school to look forward to, and no concept of what I should do with my life. I was being left behind to work my ass off at multiple dead-end jobs. That's why you felt like the only good thing in my life.

Before you get angry, I'm not saying all this to guilt-trip you or wrangle an apology. The truth is I'm the one who owes you an apology. I'm so sorry, Jackie. You were right (you usually are). Instead of figuring out my shit, I turned to you as my main source of happiness. I was so focused on me and us that I didn't listen when you told me what you needed. It was selfish of me, especially since I knew you were trying your hardest to heal.

If I'm being honest, I think that scared me a bit. Because if you put yourself back together, would that leave me alone in my brokenness? It's not that I don't want you to reconcile with your grief, because I do. I wish you all the happiness in the world. You deserve it more than anyone I know. What it comes down to is that (as previously mentioned) I'm selfish.

But I can't be selfish with you anymore. It's not fair, and if you can overcome the worst sort of tragedy, then

I can damn well move on from something as trivial as football. To do that, though, I need to get out of this house. If I don't, I'm afraid of backsliding into depending on you. Will and Haley offered me the apartment above their garage, and I've decided to accept. It's drafty and cramped, but at least it's a place of my own. Even after you moved in with Parker, the art studio always felt like yours, so it's only right that the space is returned to you.

Please don't worry about me. I'm going to focus on fixing myself and figuring out my future, whatever that looks like. Maybe when I do, the timing will finally be perfect.

All my love,
Cole

"Today, we need to decide on this year's holiday fundraiser," Erin said after taking roll call. She flipped through her notes until she found whatever she was looking for. "Last week, we brainstormed a few good ideas: we could run a toy drive, host a hot cider stand, sell candy cane grams, or plan a winter carnival. I'm partial to the candy canes. It's cheap and easy to set up, and they sell well."

I tuned her out as the student council meeting continued.

Three days had passed since Cole moved in to Will and Haley's, and I'd spent every waking moment agonizing over the best way to apologize. I knew I'd be miserable until I found a way to resolve the situation, even if the outcome meant we didn't end up together. Reading his letter made me realize that neither of us were without blame. We'd both made stupid, selfish decisions driven by fear, and I felt particularly awful for throwing his insecurities in his face. Especially since I was just as responsible if not more so than he was. Had it been intentional? No, but that didn't make my comment about how he had nothing going on in his life any less cruel.

That wasn't how I saw him at all.

Cole oozed confidence like he had extra to spare, so it never occurred to me that he might feel lost. What I needed to do was show him that he was so much more than the sport he played in high school, and in my mind, having a conversation wouldn't cut it. Not after he'd put pen to paper and poured his heart out to me.

An idea finally popped into my head yesterday at lunch when Chase joined our table to eat with Skylar. He'd given his boyfriend a reminder; if he wanted his latest blog post ("How to Build a Capsule Wardrobe: A Guide for Beginners") to be in next week's edition of the school paper, then the final copy had to be in Chase's inbox by the end of the day. That was when I remembered what Skylar told me during the first week of school. *Sometimes when the news cycle is slow, he publishes an article from my blog to fill the space.*

If Chase needed content, I was more than willing to provide him with some, and by the end of seventh period, I had a working outline. After that, the rough draft of the article basically wrote itself. Now all I needed to do was convince Chase to publish it.

"By a show of hands, who's in favor of the candy cane grams?" Erin asked in a tone that implied she expected people to vote her way.

I raised mine in agreement, not really caring what fundraiser we went with. All I wanted was for her to wrap things up so I could talk to Chase, but whenever I glanced at the clock, time seemed to be moving backward. I didn't even notice I was fidgeting until Skylar frowned at me and plucked the pen from my hand, which I'd been clicking incessantly.

"Chase, do you have a minute?" I asked the instant Erin released everyone. "There's something I'd like to discuss."

"*Ooh.*" Skylar bounced his eyebrows a few times as the three of us stood and collected our backpacks. "Sounds like someone is in trouble."

"Sure," Chase said to me, paying zero attention to Skylar's ribbing. "What's up?"

"I have a proposition for you." As I spoke, we filed down the row at the back of the auditorium. It had become Skylar's and my spot after sitting there during the start of semester meeting. "It's about the school paper."

Chase glanced over his shoulder at me with a raised a brow. "Planning to oust me from my position so you can run it like you did

Erin's campaign?" he asked. "People are already talking about how you're most likely to be elected president next year."

Were they really? I'd be lying if I said I hadn't considered running.

"No," I replied as my cheeks warmed, though it wouldn't be a bad idea to shadow him. Chase was graduating in the spring, and if I learned the ropes directly from him, maybe I could take over as editor when I was a senior. It wouldn't hurt to add another extracurricular to my college résumé. "Skylar mentioned that sometimes you need extra material?"

When he reached the main aisle, Chase let us step past him before perching on the armrest of the end seat and crossing his arms. I'd envisioned us finding an empty bench in the lobby, but I suppose we were having the rest of our conversation here.

"That's true," he said, an almost smile playing on his lips.

Well, here goes nothing… "I have an idea," I told him. "I think you should start running a monthly alumni column. It would feature notable former students, giving a window into their lives postgraduation. The article can highlight their accomplishments both from when they attended Valley View and after. Not only would it be beneficial for current students to—"

"Okay, I get it," Chase said, raising a hand before I could finish my pitch. He rubbed his chin, considering. "Do you have a suggestion for who our first feature should be?"

Skylar pressed a fist to his mouth to cover a cough, but it sounded suspiciously like "Cole."

I looked daggers at him, then turned back to Chase. "Yes, and I have a rough draft for you as well." I handed over the pages I'd printed out this morning in preparation.

As he read over what I wrote, Chase's eyebrows rose. "This...this is really good, Jackie. I'm impressed." When he met my gaze again, I could tell he was on the verge of saying yes. "Do you have any images we can use?"

The question threw me off for a single heartbeat, but then I remembered the picture I took of Cole and Carter at the race track. "I have something that should work."

"All right."

"All right, meaning?"

"I'll run the article," he said with a nod.

"Yes!" I squealed, rising onto my tiptoes and clapping my hands together. "Thank you so much. I promise you won't regret—"

Chase held up a finger. "On one condition," he added, and I went still. "You have to join the school paper and continue writing this column."

As if that was some great hardship? "Fair enough," I said as I bit back a smile, "but I have a counter condition."

sixteen

SILENCE.

I stopped pacing across the worn-out rug and turned to face Nathan. "Well, what do you think?"

Not much, if the expression on his face was anything to go by. He was sitting in the same position I'd found him in when I showed up at the loft looking for reassurance that tomorrow would go smoothly—cross-legged on the single couch cushion that wasn't sunken in, sudoku booklet clutched in his hands, and a walkie-talkie at his side. The only difference now was that he was staring at me with raised brows, not unlike Parker had when I told her I didn't know how to throw a spiral or what that even was.

"It's certainly well thought out," he said, though his tone suggested otherwise.

My shoulders sagged as I released the breath I'd been holding. "What's that supposed to mean?"

"Nothing," he replied, but his gaze darted to the puzzle in his lap so he wouldn't have to look me in the eyes.

Yeah, I wasn't buying that. Nathan had never been a very good liar.

I circled around the coffee table, plopped down beside him, and gently nudged his side. "What is it? I promise I can handle the truth."

He sighed, stuck his pencil between the pages to mark his place, and let the booklet fall closed. "Don't you think that's a little...I don't know, much?"

My condition for becoming Chase's new columnist was that he had to release this month's edition of the school paper three days early. It meant a ton of extra work on his end, but once I explained my reason, he reluctantly agreed. Instead of this upcoming Monday, it would come out tomorrow, which just so happened to be the same day as the next dirt track race. Cole's current client would be competing with the engine he rebuilt, and the entire Walter crew was attending to support him. Hopefully the driver did well, because my plan was to find Cole after the feature, present the debut alumni column to him, and apologize for making him feel less than. When I told Nathan my plan, I never expected him to be skeptical. Amused or disinterested, maybe, but still supportive.

"To be honest, I'm worried it won't be enough." I tried to shake off the negative voice inside my head that was whispering all the things that could go wrong, how I'd fail and that Cole would never forgive me, but the more I ignored it, the louder it grew. "I really screwed up, Nathan. This has to be perfect."

"I get that, but…why do you need all the extra stuff?" He shifted sideways, rearranging himself so we could look at each other as we spoke. "The article, the timed arrival after the race—it's a bit over the top. Can't you just tell him you're sorry? I think he'd appreciate you being straightforward instead of setting all this up behind his back. What if he doesn't want something written about him in the paper?"

Oh shit. Despite overanalyzing my plan to death, I hadn't considered that Cole might not want his business published for everyone to read about, because he was never one to shy away from attention. But it was too late now to change things. "You might be right, but Cole bared his soul to me in a novel-length letter. A casual apology doesn't feel like enough to make up for how I treated him." I chewed my lip as I thought things over for the thousandth time. "What if he doesn't believe me? I have to—"

The barn door slammed open, cutting me off. "Where the *hell* are you, New York?" shouted a familiar voice that never failed to give me butterflies, both the good kind and the bad. "We need to talk."

My eyes widened. What was Cole doing here? More importantly, why did he sound so angry? The last time I saw him was the day after Halloween when he cleared his remaining belongings out of the art studio. He didn't say a word to me then, and I hadn't seen him since.

When I didn't answer, Nathan cupped his hands around his mouth. "We're up here!"

"Traitor," I hissed, shooting him a furious glare and scrambling off the couch. Not to hide—that would be childish—but if I had to face Cole now, then I wanted to do it standing. I heard the exact moment he started scaling the ladder, and the sound made my pulse race. Pressing a hand to my chest, I wondered if it was healthy for my heart to beat so fast.

It felt like ages before he reached the top, but once he was standing in the loft, the air between us hummed in anticipation like it was a living, breathing thing. We stared at each other for a full minute, neither of us speaking. There was a weird look in his eyes, like he wanted to pull me into his arms and punch the wall at the same time. The moment broke when he stepped forward and tossed something onto the coffee table. It hit the wood with a smack.

"What is this?" he demanded, and even without looking, I knew what it would be.

Sure enough, when I glanced down, a copy of tomorrow's school paper was staring up at me.

COLE WALTER'S WINNING STRATEGY
He Was Fast on the Field. Now His Expertise Is Building Racing Engines for Speed

Two years after his football dreams ended in injury, Cole Walter, once considered the best wide receiver in the state, has caught a new dream career for himself. Losing his CU

Boulder football scholarship meant he had to rethink his future even before college...

"How did you get that?" I asked, my voice wavering. I needed to buy myself time to think, because this wasn't how things were meant to go. I was supposed to have the night to form a carefully worded apology, one I planned to rehearse over and over after dinner. I should have known better; things never went according to plan for me when a Walter was involved, especially this one.

"Chase sent it," he replied, shoving a hand into his hair. It was messier than normal, his blond locks sticking up at odd angles and curling around his ears like he'd been running his fingers through it incessantly. "He thought I should have an advance copy seeing as how I'm the subject matter of one of the articles."

"You're mad," I guessed.

"Yes!" he exclaimed. "No. I mean, I don't know." He threw a hand into the air, then collapsed on the couch where Nathan had been sitting only moments ago. The little sneak must have slipped away when Cole and I were sizing each other up. "What you said...it was great, Jackie. Probably the nicest thing anyone has ever said about me, but I don't understand why you wrote it."

"Because I wanted—well, what I mean is..." I was floundering, unable to get any words out. I wanted to tell him how I felt, that he'd been right about me being scared, and that I was sorry about how things went down when we broke up. That he thought I saw him as a loser when, in actuality, he was the most special person in my life felt like a knife to the heart.

Nathan had been right, hadn't he? The article was the wrong move. Whenever Cole wanted to communicate something to me, he *showed* me. Instead of telling him how I felt with words, maybe I needed to tell him with action.

Deciding to change tactics, I glanced around until my eyes landed on the rope hanging from the ceiling; I hadn't touched it since Cole forced me to try it out all those months ago.

"Could you drive us into town?" I asked, removing the scrunchie from my wrist and pulling my hair back into a ponytail. "There's something I need to show you."

He crossed his arms. "No offense, but I'm not exactly in the mood for an excursion."

"I understand," I said as I moved toward the side of the loft, "but I promise to explain things when we get there."

"Or you could just tell me now."

"Remember in the spring, when you brought me up here for the first time?" Reaching the edge, I leaned against the railing and stretched out until my fingers brushed the rope. Once I had it in hand, I put my foot on the bottom rail and stepped up. "I was having a terrible day, and for some ridiculous reason, you thought it would cheer me up to jump into the hay, but I wasn't having it."

Cole's eyes widened as I swung my leg over the top and climbed over. "Jackie, what are you doing?"

"You promised me it was safe, that you did it all the time as a kid," I said, giving the rope a firm tug as a precaution. Blood was pounding in my ears, so I inhaled slowly to calm myself. "You wanted me to trust you even though I was scared of getting hurt. I know I don't deserve it right now, but please. I need you to trust me on this like I did you."

I flashed him a wistful smile, and then I jumped.

"This is where you're taking me?" Cole asked, glancing over at Caffeinated Pursuit as he maneuvered the Buick into the only open parking spot on the street. "A café? It doesn't even look open."

"It's not just a café," I said, but he was right about one thing—despite it being a Thursday afternoon, the open-closed sign was currently flipped to display the SORRY WE'RE CLOSED message. The lights were on, though, so I undid my seat belt and grabbed my purse. "Come on. I know the owner."

If this surprised Cole, he didn't let it show.

I slid out of the car and onto the sidewalk without giving him a chance to respond, hoping he would follow. The driver's side door slammed behind me, and I allowed myself a small smile as I headed toward the entrance. Thankfully, when I peered through the window, I spotted Garrett just as he stepped out of the kitchen carrying a box. He noticed me straightaway, set down his load, and came over to open the door.

"Jackie, it's good to see you!" he said, ushering us inside. We'd built a rapport in the past month and a half, nothing like I had with his cousin, but Garrett went out of his way to talk to me whenever I came in.

Cole's eyebrows rose as he gave Garrett a once-over, but he didn't say anything.

"Guess who I spoke to last week?" Garrett continued, but he was too excited to wait for my answer. "Jenny! She was thrilled to hear you found me and said it was fate, although she also insisted that I had to tell you her Caramel Kerplunk making skills are better than mine."

I laughed. "Next time the two of you talk, let her know she's still my favorite barista and that I'll make sure to visit when I'm back in New York." I should have stopped by when I was home for the summer, but it was hard enough living in my family apartment. I hadn't been brave enough to visit another place swimming in memories, but after discovering this café and experiencing nostalgia, I knew that was a mistake.

"I can do that," Garrett replied with a smile. He glanced at the clock, then back to me. "Did you want to order something? I had to close early, but if it means dethroning Jenny as your favorite barista, I'm willing to whip up your usual."

"Oh, no! You don't have to do that. I was going to show my—I mean, this is Cole," I said, gesturing awkwardly to him. "I wanted him to see your place, but you look busy. We can come back another time."

Garrett appeared to be in the middle of setting up for some kind of event. A buffet had been assembled opposite the café counter, its silver chafing dishes waiting to be filled with food, and two of the oversize gaming tables were missing. In their place stood several covered high-tops. On the one closest to us was an assortment of tea lights, glass candle holders, and a utility lighter.

"We're rented out for an engagement party, but it doesn't start for another hour," Garrett explained. "I don't mind if you hang around for a bit. In fact, why don't you grab a table at the back? I've got a surplus of apps. You can taste test them to make sure they're worthy of serving."

Cole watched him disappear into the kitchen, then turned to me, his lips pinched tight with displeasure. "You two seem close."

"Really, Cole?" I grinned at him. "I'll admit the man's handsome, but he's older than your father. What are you implying?"

"Nothing! I didn't—that's *not* what I meant," he spluttered. "It's strange, that's all. How do you two even know each other?"

"He's related to a friend of mine, but we only met last month. I stopped in here because it had the same name as a café in New York where Lucy and I spent a lot of time as kids," I said, watching Cole turn in a slow circle as he checked things out. "Turns out this place is modeled after the one back home. Here, I can show you." I walked over to the register and pointed to the photograph of the original Caffeinated Pursuit that hung behind it on the wall.

"What's with the picture of Stuart Calhoun Junior?" he asked.

I had no clue who that was, but Cole was studying an image of Garrett next to a man in a racing suit holding the checkered flag, and I assumed he was a famous driver. "Garrett used to be the head engineer for a NASCAR team," I said, and the frown Cole was wearing faded as I spoke. "You should talk to him about it sometime. I think you two might have some things in common."

The kitchen door swung open, and Garrett reappeared holding a plate piled high with food. He placed it on a table tucked into the corner at the back of the room, then wiped his hands on the server apron tied around his waist. "Let me know what you think," he told us, then returned to setting up.

The last trace of Cole's disapproval vanished the moment he spotted the fried mac and cheese balls, stuffed mushrooms, and gyoza. "This looks amazing," he whispered as we sat down, "but who has an engagement party at a board game café?"

A smile tugged on my lips as I glanced over at the colorful wall of games. "Probably someone like your brother and Kim."

He snickered. "Alex wishes he could be this classy."

"He doesn't need to," I replied. Under the pretense of scooting up to the table, I shuffled my chair closer to Cole. He'd surprised me by taking the spot to my left instead of across from me, but it gave us both a view of the room. "Kim has enough sophistication for the both of them combined."

"Not sure if that's true since she's dating him," Cole muttered as he split a gyoza down the middle. Steam poured out from inside.

Lifting a single eyebrow, I almost pointed out that *I* had dated Alex but caught myself at the last second. Reminding Cole of his brother's and my relationship wouldn't go over well on a good day, let alone now.

When he offered me half of the dumpling, I shook my head, too anxious to eat. He must have come to a similar conclusion, because he stared at the food for a moment before setting down his fork.

"Right," he said, pushing the plate away. "Why did you bring me here, Jackie?"

My stomach fluttered with nerves, but I forced myself to take a steadying breath and plow on. "When I first moved here and you gave me a tour of the ranch, you took me to all your favorite spots—the loft, the stables, the waterfall. I wasn't exactly thrilled about going horseback riding, but we watched the sunset together, and it was amazing," I said. "You're always doing things like that for me, and I wanted to reciprocate."

Cole was quiet for a second. Then he said, "What things?"

"Pulling me along on adventures and pushing me out of my comfort zone."

"Such as?"

"Well, last semester, you convinced me to cut school," I told him. "You took me to that kinda cool but also creepy warehouse with your friends to take my mind off something terrible Mary said, remember? That was the first time I'd ever ditched class, got drunk, or played spin the bottle."

He frowned. "And that's a good thing?"

"Okay," I said, wincing, "maybe that wasn't a great example, but the only reason I found this café is that I left school grounds during my lunch period. Before meeting you, I never would have broken a rule like that."

His gaze cut to me as I explained, his eyes shrewd and serious, and I couldn't tell if I'd said the wrong thing again or if he didn't believe me.

After what felt like an endless minute, he snorted. "So you're saying I'm a bad influence."

"No. My point is that you've been sharing aspects of your life with me from the moment I arrived. In the past two months, you showed me around the block party, snuck me onto the school roof, and took me stargazing." I hesitated, then covered his hand with mine. "We're here because I wanted you to see a small part of my world. I know it's not the same as actually being in New York and that the game board stuff is a little gimmicky, but this is the only place in Colorado where I can feel close to my family."

But sitting here with Cole made me realize something. From the moment I walked through the door, I'd felt a sense of belonging. This place was a much-needed home away from home, somewhere in Colorado that had more relevance to me than it did the Walters. It wasn't perfect, though. Something undefinable was missing; possibly the soundtrack of the city—sirens blaring, horns honking, buses rattling by. There was a collective noise to New York City that seeped through the walls no matter where you were, and it made Colorado feel like a library in comparison. Also, Lucy had never set foot in here. A minor detail to get hung up on, but her absence felt like a constellation missing its brightest star, unnatural and incomplete.

As I looked at Cole, I felt that missing something now—it was him.

"I…appreciate that, Jackie, but this and the article?" He pulled his hand away. "I don't know. It feels—well, you're the one who broke up with me, remember?"

"That was a mistake, one I regret with my whole heart." I paused for a second to get my head on straight, not wanting to butcher my words. " I'm so sorry, Cole. You were right all along. When your mom threatened to kick you out, I panicked because it reminded me that our relationship didn't exist in a vacuum. Us dating affects the rest of your family, and—"

"Hold on," he said. Confusion rearranged his features. "What does our relationship have to do with my family?"

"At the time?" I replied as warmth crept up my neck. "*Everything.* I pushed you away so I wouldn't lose them." Even after it sunk in that I had a permanent place with the Walters, just thinking about life without them made me choke up.

"Lose them?" Cole repeated. His brows were drawn tight, and I could see the gears turning in his head as he digested my confession. "How would that even happen? I already told you—all of us will always be here for you."

"Yes, thank you. I figured that out," I said in a huff. Out of the corner of my eye, I noticed Garrett starting to light the candles, but I kept my attention fixed on Cole. "It didn't matter what you promised, because they were your family first, and it scared me to think about what might happen if we didn't work out. I know that sounds ridiculous, Isaac already told me so, but besides my uncle Richard, you guys are all I have left."

Cole didn't say anything as he studied my face. The silence that filled the space between us was so taut, it felt almost tangible, like I could reach out and shatter it with a single touch. His granite expression was unreadable and should have been concerning, but in that moment, my nerves drained away. Even if he decided he didn't want to be my someone anymore, I could weather the storm; it was like he said—the Walters would always be there for me.

Finally, he spoke. "Okay, just so we're clear—are you saying that we broke up because you like my family more than me?" The playful note in his voice sent a jolt of hope through my body. "I've been through my fair share of breakups, but I've never heard *that* excuse before."

"Sorry," I choked out, half sobbing and half laughing, "but can you blame me?"

"No, I get it. Benny is a stud." He flashed me his trademark smirk but it disappeared in an instant. "I suppose there are a lot of worse reasons to be dumped."

After reading his letter, I could see it now—the blink-and-you-miss-it moments when Cole's insecurities reared their head. I rubbed at my chest as I remembered exactly how I'd prodded that self-doubt to drive him away. "You know you're amazing, right?" I asked softly. My fingers twitched in my lap. I had the urge to reach out and brush his bangs out of his eyes, but he'd pulled away the last time I touched him, so I pinned my hands under my thighs and tried to reassure him with words. "I don't care that you're still figuring out who you are post-football, that was never who you are to me."

"Feel free to keep going," he drawled in a cocky tone that I would have rolled my eyes at under normal circumstances. "I won't stop you."

"Well, you're a supportive older brother, an incredibly hard worker, sweet when you want to be, and, according to your zodiac sign, incredibly mysterious." I said the last bit jokingly, and his mouth quirked. "But in all seriousness, I do really miss being with you, Cole. I never should have shut you out, but I didn't realize how terrified I was until it was too late and I'd messed everything up. But I need you to know that I'm not afraid anymore."

"Jackie," he said, his pupils so dilated that they nearly swallowed the beautiful blue of his irises, "you're forgetting my best trait."

"Oh?" I tried to sound nonchalant, but it was no use—the frantic drumbeat emanating from my chest was so loud, I didn't doubt that he could hear it. "What's that?" Cole leaned over, curled his hand around the back of my neck, and claimed my lips in a bruising kiss. I melted into him, every nerve ending in my body lighting up as I looped my arms around his neck. My heart expanded, so full of joy and affection that it was subject to burst, and made the grief still lingering inside me recede into the background. Not gone, but bearable. That was what true healing was, wasn't it? Acknowledging your pain but choosing happiness—and I was ready to choose Cole, over and over again.

When we pulled apart and I opened my eyes again, I could sense the atmosphere in the room was different—the lights had been dimmed, and all around us, the candles were flickering. They cast a golden warmth over the room, transforming the space into something more romantic than a board game café had any right to be.

"Weren't you going to tell me what your best trait is?" I asked once I'd regained my composure. His ability to kiss me breathless was a strong contender.

"Obviously, it's my minnow-racing prowess," he said with faux haughtiness that made me laugh, but his eyes turned serious a second later. "Jackie, I want this, I want us, but you should know that I'm not moving back to the ranch. If I want to make a change, then I need to do this for myself. Plus, I've got my own bathroom at Will and Haley's, and they don't have any rules. Is that...will you be okay with that?"

His leg was bouncing underneath the table as if he were worried our new living arrangements would be a deal-breaker for me, so I nudged his foot with mine.

"No rules, huh?" I said, wiggling my brow suggestively. "I think I can get behind that."

The bell above the café door rang, and both our heads turned toward the sound. A woman in a cocktail dress walked in followed by an older couple who looked like her parents. Garrett glanced over at us, and I nodded my head in understanding.

It was time for us to leave. We gathered our things—my purse and jacket, his phone and keys—and as the two of us made our way toward the exit, Cole glanced over at me. "Thanks for sharing this place with me, Jackie. I appreciate getting a glimpse into your life back home. I'd love to go to New York with you at some point." He slung an arm over my shoulder and tucked me into his side. "If you're ever interested in showing me around, I'd love to see more of it. We should visit Danny sometime."

Something about his comment felt off, but I couldn't put my finger on how.

"Since you've always been my tour guide, it seems only fair that I take a turn," I told him. "There's a lot more to New York than the Caffeinated Pursuit."

As I thought about all the fun spots I could take him, it dawned on me why Cole's words stuck out. New York would always be my home; it was the place of my birth, the backdrop of my childhood, and the city of my heart.

But home was also where your family was, and the Walters were here.

That made Colorado my home now too.

DON'T MISS

The Heartbreak Chronicles

THE SWOON-WORTHY SERIES FROM ALI NOVAK!

BOOK 1: THE HEARTBREAKERS

Stella just had a moment at the coffee shop with a cute guy named Oliver. She has no idea he's lead singer of the world's hottest band…

BOOK 2: PAPER HEARTS

Felicity's always been the "good girl." But now she's setting out on a rebellious road trip with Alec, the bass player for the Heartbreakers!

READ ON FOR A SNEAK PEEK OF

Heartstrings

THE LONG-AWAITED THIRD BOOK IN THE HEARTBREAK CHRONICLES!

Indie's long been in the shadow of her famous sister. When she meets sweet, boyish guitarist Xander, he understands how that feels. Maybe together they can make their dreams happen…

one

I COULDN'T REMEMBER THE LAST time my dad graced me with his presence, so when he strode into the kitchen Sunday morning, his ever-present Bluetooth headset clipped to his ear, I nearly choked on my bagel.

"No, the contract is already signed. Has been for weeks now," he said, talking in sweeping arm gestures. "I'm sorry, King, but it's my job to do what's best for Violet, end of story." Dad was so dialed into his conversation he didn't notice me sitting in the breakfast nook.

The fact that this was my first *Pater Absentem* sighting in weeks—even though we lived in the same house—spoke to his status as an expert level workaholic. We'd made plans to hang out today, but it was still jarring to see him standing in the kitchen as if this were his natural habitat. I was used to having my sister's beachfront property all to myself.

"Absolutely not! We've been over this a million times and I'm done arguing about it," Dad exclaimed. "Call my lawyers if you have a problem." He hit End without so much as a goodbye and jammed a fresh K-Cup into the Keurig.

"What'd the coffee maker ever do to you?"

Dad spun around at the sound of my voice. "Indie, I didn't see you there."

"And that makes it okay to manhandle the most important appliance in the kitchen?" I teased.

"Sorry, it's been a rough morning."

I brushed a few stray crumbs off my shirt and slid to the end of the bench. "Everything okay?"

"You know how King Williams is." He rubbed his forehead. "The man's an overbearing control freak who throws temper tantrums when things don't go his way. But don't worry. It's nothing your old man can't handle."

As I carried my dirty plate over to the dishwasher, I tried to imagine the CEO of Mongo Records having a toddler-esque hissy fit, but couldn't conjure the image. Then again, I hardly knew the man. The Williams were family friends, but King was too busy expanding his music empire to have time for potluck dinners or camping trips with us. I was totally okay with that: there was something about his icy demeanor that gave me the creeps.

"Well, good thing you get to spend all day with yours truly." In one not-so-graceful hop, I planted my butt on the island countertop, heels banging against the lower cabinets. "When are we leaving?"

To celebrate the start of October, our local theater was hosting a Halloween marathon, starting at noon with *The Exorcist*. I'd inherited my love of scary movies from Dad, so the following fifteen hours of monsters, gore, and jump-out-of-your-skin scares would be the perfect father-daughter bonding time.

All the essentials were piled on the counter next to me: gift cards to buy popcorn and soda, five different boxes of candy I planned to smuggle in inside my purse, a bottle of caffeine pills to keep us awake, and oversized sweatshirts in case the theater was chilly. My excitement level was so far off the charts, I hadn't been able to sleep last night.

"Leaving?"

My stomach dropped at the question. "For the horror marathon at Cinépolis, remember?" I forced myself to sound upbeat, but it was never a good sign when I had to remind Dad of our plans.

"Sweetie," he started, and I knew I wouldn't like what he said next. Dad only used that particular endearment when he felt guilty. "You know I can't take the day off. What with Violet's promotional work for the final season of *Immortal Nights* and her new career direction, I'm swamped."

Surprise, surprise.

Dad was picking her over me again.

I should've known better. Violet's priorities always eclipsed everything else. It hadn't always been this way, although it was getting harder to remember our lives before my sister was famous. We used to be a happy family—Mom, Dad, Violet, and me—but then my sister decided she wanted to be an actress. On my thirteenth birthday, she was cast as vampire princess Lilliana LaCroix in the MTV series adaption of *These Immortal Nights,* the wildly popular young adult trilogy.

That was five years ago, but it felt like a lifetime.

Pressing my lips tight, I counted to ten. I would *not* lose my shit. "Dad, you promised."

"Are you sure?" His eyebrows gathered together as he studied his phone. "I don't see you on my calendar."

I gripped the edge of the counter as my entire body tensed. Ever since he quit his job as a bank director to be Violet's manager, Dad had become increasingly unavailable, but this was beyond ridiculous. "My bad," I snapped. "Didn't realize I had to schedule an appointment to hang out with you. Should I email your assistant so he can pencil in my birthday?"

Welp, so much for not losing my shit.

"Indie, don't be a brat," he said, shooting me a disapproving look over the rims of his glasses.

"Hey, just calling it as I see it." Dad was right, of course. It was a bratty thing for me to say, but I couldn't help it. This was the third time he'd bailed on me for Violet since the start of the school year.

"*Indigo Josephine Mitchell-Jamiolkowski.*"

Oh crap. The full name. I only heard that pretentious mouthful when I landed myself in dangerous waters. Letting out a frustrated sigh, I pushed back my bangs. "I'm sorry, Dad, but this sucks. I've been looking forward to spending time with you."

The scowl on Dad's face softened. "I know, Indie. I'm sorry. Violet's schedule will get less hectic soon and then we can do something together just you and me, I promise." The Keurig let out a long beep, and he turned to collect his mug as steam rose in lazy tendrils from the freshly brewed coffee.

"Yeah, sure," I replied, swallowing back my disappointment. There was no point in arguing with him, not when it involved Violet's career. Work always came first.

Dad beamed. "That's my girl." His phone buzzed less than a second later, and he punched the talk button. "Hi, this is Edward Jamiolkowski…. Ah, Courtney! So good to hear from you. I've been meaning to call so we could discuss the lineup for…"

I heaved a sigh as Dad swept out of the room. A small part of me thought he'd change his mind, but when his office door slammed shut, the hope flickering inside me petered out. For a moment I considered calling Julie, but even watching action movies freaked her out. There was no way she'd make it through a horror long haul. I could always text some friends from orchestra, but I doubted anyone would be up for a fifteen-hour commitment on such short notice.

Guess that meant I'd be attending the movies solo.

Whatever, more popcorn for me.

Waking up Monday morning after the marathon was brutal.

That being said, Freddy, Jason, and Michael were well worth the lost shuteye, and somehow I made it through the day without falling asleep in class. By the time I got home, all I wanted to do was pass out, so when I reached my bedroom, I ignored my violin case resting in the corner and collapsed face first onto my mattress.

You should practice right now, the voice inside my head chastised me. Because that was my routine: three hours of violin every day after school. I only had two months left to select and perfect my repertoire before my college application was due.

A knock interrupted my guilt trip. "Indie, you in here?"

"No," I muttered into my pillow, because I didn't currently have the mental capacity to deal with my sister. Maybe if I ignored her she'd go away.

No such luck.

When I lifted my head a few seconds later to see if Violet was gone, I found her standing in the doorway.

"You need something?" I asked. Aside from acknowledging one another's presence around the house, she and I rarely spoke. What could Violet possibly have to say to me?

She took a hesitant step into my room. "Yeah, do you have a minute? There's something I want to run by you."

"Nope," I replied, flopping back down and locking my hands behind my head. "Kinda in the middle of something right now."

Violet gave my post-school sprawl a once-over before crossing her arms. "Really? You don't look busy."

"That's because I'm not."

"Oookay—you seem irritated. Did I do something to piss you off?"

Ding! Ding! Ding! We have a winner.

"Dad was supposed to go to the movies with me yesterday," I said, glaring up at the ceiling. Something that looked like fluffy gray carpet lined the top of the fan blades, and I tried to remember the last time I'd dusted.

"But... he didn't?"

That she had the audacity to sound confused pissed me off even more. "Of course not! He was too busy doing stuff for *you*."

Sighing, Violet ran a hand over her ponytail. "Haven't we gone over this before? I don't set Dad's hours."

"Yeah, whatever." I turned away and curled onto my side, hugging the duvet against my chest.

"Indie, I'm sorry. I had no clue he canceled on you. I'll talk to him about it, okay?" she said, but I didn't bother responding. Why should I when I was never considered a priority in this family?

A tense silence stretched between us. It lasted so long I momentarily thought Violet had walked away, but then the mattress dipped as she sat down beside me. "Aren't you sick of always being mad at me?" Her question sounded weary, so I flipped over to face her.

"Vi," I said, not unkindly, "what do you need?"

"Well, about that... I know this isn't the best time to ask for a favor, but I have a major crisis on my hands. Jenny called last night. Poor thing broke her leg, so she can't come to New York with me this weekend. Obviously I feel terrible, but her timing is awful."

I rolled my eyes. Jenny was Violet's personal assistant. Heaven forbid she went one day without someone to fetch her nonfat, unsweetened *café au lait*. Always the drama queen, my sister.

"Gabe will be there and he promised his assistant Sadie could help me out," Violet continued. Gabe was her *Immortal Nights* co-star, who did a lot of promotional appearances with her. "But I know she'll be too busy on Saturday to lend a hand."

My brow inched up in speculation. Despite the absurdity of its direction, I had a feeling where this conversation was heading. "And what does any of this have to do with me?"

"Well, I was hoping you could fill in for Jenny."

Ha! Over my dead body.

On Thursday, the doors to the East Coast's largest and most kickass gathering of geeks, fangirls, and pop culture aficionados would open—New York Comic Con. The cast of *Immortal Nights* would have a busy schedule packed with autograph signings, press interviews, and of course, a panel. No doubt my sister would run me ragged if I took Jenny's place.

"Not going to happen." If I wanted a good dose of torture, I'd stick my hand down the garbage disposal.

"Just hear me out before you say no." The alarm in her voice made me pause, and she seized the opportunity to keep talking. "I only need your help on Saturday. I'll pay you five hundred bucks for the entire day, and you'll get to skip school on Thursday and Friday. You can do whatever you want with your free time—sightsee, check out the convention, maybe take a tour of Juilliard? Please say yes. I'm desperate here."

I had to give it to Violet, she made an enticing offer. I'd been dreaming of Juilliard since picking up my first violin. Throw in a Get Out of School Free card, cash to spend, and a weekend trip to New York, and any normal teen would jump at the opportunity.

Then again, most kids my age didn't have a celebrity for a sister. If I did this, I was in good conscience agreeing to participate in the *Violet James Show,* which meant screaming fans, paparazzi, and watching everyone and their mother kiss my sister's ass. The thought made me cringe.

"I don't think so, Violet. I have a test in Calculus on Friday and—"

"That makeup artist you like," she interrupted. "What's her name?"

"Melody Nguyen?"

"Yeah, her. She's on a panel called Behind the Prosthetics. It features a bunch of Hollywood's top special effects makeup artists. If you help me out on Saturday, I'll give you a break to go see her panel."

I pursed my lips. Violet must have saved Melody as a trump card in case I refused her offer. Because we both knew there was no way I'd pass up a chance to meet one of my idols, even if it meant spending time with my sister. The question was, how much did Violet need an assistant?

Studying my nails, I tried to appear as uninterested as possible. "Make it a grand and you've got yourself an assistant."

Violet's lips curled in a triumphant smile. "Done."

acknowledgments

Returning to the world of the Walter Boys eleven years after the first book was published has been the wildest roller-coaster ride I have experienced as an author. I always wanted to continue Jackie's story, but life kept getting in the way. Most recently, assisting my mother as she battled stage IV cancer. I'll never forget the extreme paradox of emotions I felt when I first watched the trailer for the Netflix adaptation of *My Life with the Walter Boys*. I was sitting in the ICU with her, not knowing whether she would be with us when it premiered, and bawling my eyes out as I witnessed a story I wrote as a kid being brought to life on-screen.

Fortunately, my mother is still with us today. With her health improved and the outpouring of support from the release of the show, I knew it was the right time to continue Jackie's story. As I started writing this sequel, I felt a heavy sense of pressure to live up to the hype of the first book, but there are many amazing people who helped me along the way.

First, thank you so much to my editor, Wendy McClure, for keeping me and this story on track. Your guidance has been invaluable to this novel. Without your patience and assistance when I was second-guessing myself and struggling with writer's block, I'd still probably be fiddling with various scenes. I appreciate you dragging me across the finish line more than words can express.

Thank you to my sister, Flynn Novak, for helping me finish the scenes that were not working; to Kelly Anne Blount for being my sounding board while I was plotting the book; and to Cass and Vicki Kalnins for beta reading the novel and providing feedback. Z. W. Taylor, thank you for helping with the title of the book. It perfectly encompasses not only Jackie returning to the Walter boys but the readers and myself returning to the world as well. I owe you a bag of fresh Wisconsin cheese curds the next time I see you.

I'd also like to thank my incredible agent, Alex Slater, for everything he's done for me.

Thank you to everyone at Sourcebooks for your help with this story, in particular Jenne Abramowitz, Jenny Lopez, Olivia Haase, Thea Voutiritsas, Sabrina Baskey, Brittany Vibbert, Jessica Thelander, Deve McLemore, Karen Masnica, Lia Ferrone, and Delaney Heisterkamp.

To all the readers who have been with me since the Wattpad days or the initial published release, thank you for sticking with me and this world. I know it's been a really long wait, but I hope you enjoyed the sequel just as much as the original. To those who found my work through the Netflix adaptation, thanks for purchasing a copy of the book. Each and every one of you mean the world to me.

Finally and most importantly, thank you to my husband, Jared. You are the only reason I got through this past year, and this book would not exist without your support. Not only are you my best friend, but you're my rock, my favorite semiprofessional race car driver, and the love of my life.

about the author

Ali Novak was born and raised in Wisconsin and is a *New York Times* and internationally bestselling author of contemporary young adult novels. She started writing her debut book, *My Life with the Walter Boys*, when she was only fifteen. Since then, her work has received more than 150 million reads online. When she isn't writing, Novak enjoys traveling with her husband, Jared; binding fan fiction; and reading any type of fantasy novel she can get her hands on. You can follow her on Wattpad, Facebook, Twitter, Instagram, and TikTok @authoralinovak.

sourcebooks
fire

Home of the hottest trends in YA!

Visit us online and
sign up for our newsletter at
FIREreads.com

....

Follow
@sourcebooksfire
online